Character Illustrations by Adam Riong
Map Illustrations by Alec McKinley

Printed in the United States of America

First Printing, Jan 2025

ISBN 9798992188837

Niall of Nine Ventures
PO Box 431064
Minneapolis, MN 55443

LIST OF PLATES

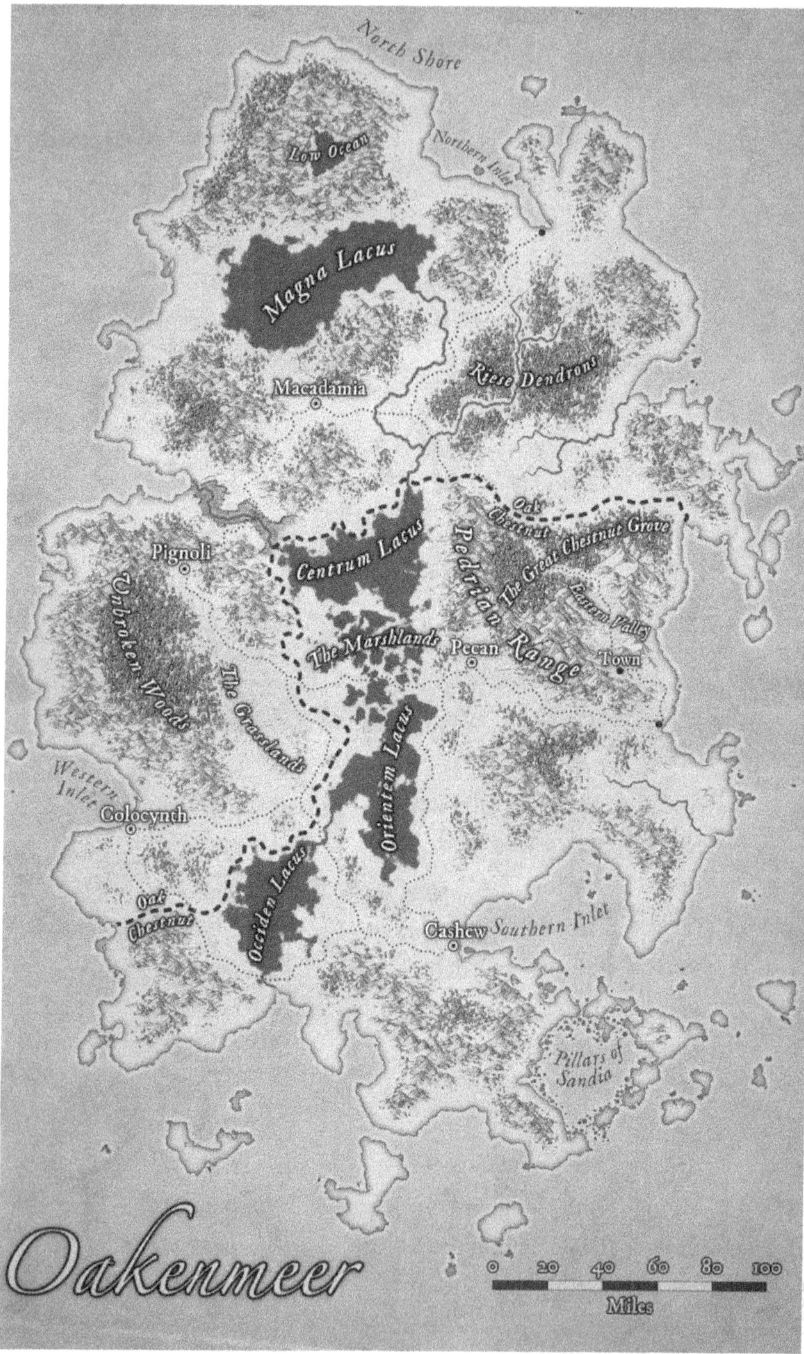

North Shore
Low Ocean
Northern Inlet
Magna Lacus
Macadamia
Riese Dendrons
Pignoli
Centrum Lacus
Oak
Chestnut
Pedrian Range
The Great Chestnut Grove
Eastern Valley
Unbroken Woods
The Marshlands
Pecan
Town
The Grasslands
Orientem Lacus
Western Inlet
Colocynth
Occiden Lacus
Oak
Chestnut
Cashew
Southern Inlet
Pillars of Sandia
Oakenmeer
0   20   40   60   80   100
Miles

Oakenmeer

Johnny O'Shea

For Pepino

IN THE LAND OF OAKENMEER, every living thing has an ancient origin within a tree, and every creature has a bark of skin over the sapwood of their growth. Drawn to the trees by an inherited force of nature, they cannot help but want to live in harmony with the forests around them. Even their smallest wooden fibers contain the power of the largest tree. It is a power that would not be studied for many generations to come, and as such, the true value of these wooden people has yet to be defined.

Each of the five Surviving Kingdoms has both an Open Forest and a Closed Forest. The Closed Forest is the capital city of any kingdom, and on most days, any person of good report can enter freely. The Open Forest is all the surrounding territory beyond. This vast landscape is the origin of all that sustains life. While imaginary borders to claim parts of the Open Forest have been drawn throughout the history of Oakenmeer, none of it can truly be controlled any more than the fate of one person or another.

People of royal sap will frequently quarrel over the dimensions of their kingdoms, and if such politics extend into a war, it should rightfully be conducted amidst the trees. The sap of all who die should always be returned to the trees, for in a world where royals have so much power, a return to the trees is often the best any humble person can hope for.

The Kingdom of Macadamia is the largest and northernmost territory within the Surviving Kingdoms. They export an abundant variety of goods for nourishment and industry, and while healthy trade can keep a royal from desiring more land, not all kings and queens hold ownership of that wisdom.

Chapter 1

AT A QUIET CLEARING in the Open Forest, the afternoon sun shines through colorful leaves and innumerable tree trunks. On a mossy area of this clearing rests a fabric rucksack full of nuts, slumped over by its own weight and some of its contents spilled out. It has been neglected by the person who gathered this bounty, though the inherent value of it is too important to be ignored for very long.

Overhead, the trees of this forest are as enormous and full of girth as any sublime force. A dense canopy of multi-colored leaves stretches upward for hundreds of feet. The variety of this scheme gives the sunlight a kaleidoscope effect, which cascades down the rugged bark of these monoliths. Only occasionally does a strong and focused beam of light escape to the ground below, and when it does, it gives a warmth that is cherished by everything that truly lives.

It is said by many that the trees of the Open Forest in Macadamia are so grand that other trees grow upon them. Larger and more bountiful trees do exist, but others would say those are just a myth. Reality or myth, the vision of colors in the Open Forest is like some impression of the world only available in a child's imagination. It is precisely this which suddenly appears here.

Like a rugged hero swinging onto an enemy's frigate, an adolescent wooden farm girl swings through the varied colors of the forest on a well-positioned rope. Being a hundred feet up does not deter her, and with a yelp of joy, Fortia laughs at the excitement of this moment. Executing a well-practiced maneuver, she uses her feet to bounce off a tree trunk then skillfully lands on a nearby branch. There is a brief second of panic as she struggles to keep her balance, but she is lean and very capable. Using the leverage of the rope, she regains a foothold, and an expression of joy covers her face.

"Did you see that, Arty!" she yells down to the ground.

Far below, on a thatch of dirt and moss, a little wooden dog dances around. He's a stocky pup, chunky like a wooden pig, and energetic in the way that only a young dog can be. Arty yelps up to her with glee, clearly feeling the happiness of the moment.

Fortia glances around with smiling eyes. Her face beams with an intense desire to feel the next rush of adrenaline in her sap. Where to play at next? These trees have been her playground for all the years of her young life, and her pup Arty has been her only friend since the age of ten.

Being young, she has the trunk of a child, thinner than an older person's trunk would be, displaying a light green bark that is soft like suede. She has led a very active youth, and her light, flexible habitus has prepared her for moments of play such as this.

Fortia's look intensifies. Having spotted her next branch, she uses a thin rope lashing from her pocket to pull back her leaf-like hair, or it might obscure her vision. There is a thick limb some distance of fifteen feet away and ten feet below her current perch. Leaving the rope to dangle nearby, she readies herself for a good jump. She has spent her youth in rugged outdoor play in this forest, and as a result, her young feet and hands are slightly larger for her age. Her bare wooden toes dig into the thin moss covering the branch, and her knees bend slightly. Boldly, she prepares for this treacherous leap.

"Ready, Arty?" She is fearless, but Arty lets out a whimper of concern, not quite bold enough to undertake such a risk. Fortia's flexible wooden arms relax in preparation, and she sets her eyes on the target branch with a strong desire as she leaps.

Arty hides his eyes as his master flies through the air. She stretches herself out to reach for the branch. Her strong hands grab and make friction on the limb, and her body swings momentarily as the momentum settles. Once again, her face lights up. She made it.

Fortia dangles there for a moment and enjoys the success taken from this risky jump. She skillfully moves her right hand forward and re-grips the other side of the branch, then twists her body. Having turned herself around, she is now facing the rope again.

There is a sharp cracking noise. Fortia glares with intensity across the base of the limb. It appears unstable under the new weight, and the branch is giving way.

Arty barks, alerting her to this threat, but she is already on the move. Suppressing a moment of panic, she shimmies herself closer to the trunk of the monolith and swings her weight forward.

The limb gives out, and Fortia falls forward toward the rope. She grabs at it, pleading with her fingers until she snags the rope, and her grip tightens.

Her freefall stops roughly forty feet from the ground. Holding tight, she rests for a thankful moment. Her eyes widen in realization as she glances downward with concern.

"Watch it, Arty!" The massive branch plummets toward her best friend.

The little dog snaps to his master's voice and sees the branch coming. He dodges away with a skill that no pet confined to the home could display. The limb crashes down with a thundering weight. Twigs and leaves are thrown upward and slowly settle all around. Fortia dangles above it with an expression of fear as she watches for any sign of life below. Arty barks out, declaring that he is safe. He emerges intact from a cloud of dust and leaves all around him.

Fortia breathes out in relief. She shimmies herself lower and lower on the rope, then jumps down the last stretch of ten feet. The excitement of the moment is still with her.

"That was close, huh, boy!?" Arty rushes to her. He now feels some sense of excitement from the event as well.

Her brow wrinkles with confusion. "Strange…That branch seemed so strong."

Arty leaps into her arms, and she carries him over to inspect the felled limb. It is easily four feet around at its previous joining point. Under normal circumstances a limb of this girth should never have fallen from the minimal weight of this girl. Low and behold, a family of sappy beetles have made a home inside it. They crawl and shuffle around inside the base of the fallen limb. Fortia and Arty watch them with curiosity. They are roughly two dozen in numbers, chunky-looking wooden insects with wings that fold over their grainy exoskeletons. Each of them has two white antennae, and when their delicate wings lift up, they reveal a spiraling shell pattern that is distinct from their scarab-like species.

"Hungry little suckers. They must have been eating that branch for a while now." Arty huffs at them, still a bit sour over nearly getting squashed. Fortia moves off in the opposite direction, and holding her pup with one arm, his frustrations soon melt away in her embrace.

"Now where did I put that bag?" She struggles to recall where she last saw the rucksack. Arty cocks his head, not much help to her now. "Don't worry, boy…We'll find it."

"Fortia, what is this mess?" a strong, deep voice from behind stops her in mid-step. Fortia turns slowly to see her father, Constans, who offers her a rather judgmental look.

He has a strong trunk of age around his body and a broad, sturdy head on his shoulders. His rugged face is highlighted by a thick beard of bark and long, flexible branches of hair that are trimmed well enough to not need a binding. As he approaches her from the edge of the clearing, there is a hollow jingling noise of raw nuts, which emanates from a massive rucksack on his back. It could easily weigh as much as he does, and these are clearly part of the extensive work he has been engaged in today.

Constans is a frontiersman of sorts, a farmer and a nut oil miller who has spent his whole life in these woods. Like Fortia, his clothing is relatively simple canvas garments. Particularly while out gathering nuts, there is not much room for ornament. While he may be a humble-looking man, his very intonations command respect from his child. Fortia does her best to appear innocent, but Constans has a sincere gaze. He can see right through her.

"Papa, I was…" Fortia struggles to find the right words. "I mean, the tree was—"

"Stop fooling around, Fortia. We need to head home soon. Where is your bag?"

Fortia points behind, fairly certain it is over there, but Arty is glancing to his left. Constans shakes his head in frustration…

"I'm assuming your cart is full of nuts now, or you would not have been playing?"

Fortia thinks about the best response, but Constans already knows the answer. He rolls his eyes with a tolerant frustration.

"Find your bag, empty it into your cart, and fill it once more before heading home. Be back in time for dinner, or there may be none to have."

"Yes, Papa…" she grumbles, and her neck bends with a reluctant obedience. She remains still as her father marches away. With each step, the noisy rucksack on his back jingles out a hollow clattering of nuts. It grows more distant soon enough.

Fortia turns and trudges toward the presumed location of her bag. She steps heavily and plods over tangled roots below her, shuffles around the soft remains of smaller limbs.

"We're not allowed to have any fun, huh, boy?" Arty huffs in response. "When I grow up, I won't do a single bit of farming! Not even a little…I don't know how Papa didn't die of boredom growing up."

Arty's ears perk up. He stares into the distance and soon jumps to the ground, where he runs ahead of her.

"You found the bag! Good boy!" Together, they gleefully run off between the trees.

~ ~ ~

The angle of the sun has greatly diminished, now lending itself to the formation of a beautiful multicolored sunset. It casts a brilliant silhouette around everything in its path. At the same time, though, it is nearly blinding Fortia as she struggles to push a wooden wheelbarrow full of nuts down a thin dirt road.

Arty lounges comfortably over a pile of nuts in the cart. He has stretched himself out in the laziest manner possible, as though no work is being done. The little pup slobbers out a yawn of boredom.

"Easy for you to say." Fortia drops the cart handles to rest and huffs out the exhaustion. She takes a welcome sip of water from her wooden canteen, positioned well to hang from an arm of the cart. "I guess we're almost home. Hope we didn't miss dinner." Arty perks up at the thought of food. "Yeah, yeah…We'll get there eventually."

Fortia reluctantly grabs the handles of the cart and lifts it again. With a breath of frustration, she drives the cart forward. Arty's ears perk up as he glances behind them. He sees something further down the road. Fortia takes notice of him, and her curiosity soon builds when a distant rumble of noise begins to grow closer.

A large six-person carriage moves at high speed with a furious cloud of dirt kicking up behind it. Four wooden horses huff and snort as they pull the load. They are massive and powerful beasts, and their wide hooves pop with a hollow acoustic blast each time they strike the compacted gravel road. The carriage is colored with a royal green pigment, and it is well ornamented. For such a regal conveyance it is certainly moving very fast.

Almost startled by this, Fortia pushes her cart to the side of the road. She knows that the road is scarcely wide enough for two horses, let alone her cart and the approaching carriage. Standing aside, she watches the large regal conveyance. It approaches at a speed that is almost threatening, though it will clear her position well. Arty is perched on the edge of the cart rail now and he appears somewhat suspicious of this rapidly moving vehicle.

As it grows nearer, the emblem over its door becomes apparent to her. Fortia's eyes widen with realization.

The standard carved into the door depicts a blocky wooden relief of the sun and a ray of light reaching down to a tree with five limbs. Fortia knows this symbol; it is the family crest of King Serenus, the King of Macadamia. She has scarcely had the chance to even see the king in her lifetime, so seeing this carriage is something very momentous for her.

"Watch yourself, child!" a rugged driver yells to her as he speeds past them. A cloud of dirt is kicked up everywhere and she coughs on it. Arty barks at the offensive noises, but as they recover from the dust, Fortia has a very bright smile on her face.

"Did you see whose carriage it was, Arty!? It's the king's carriage! I wonder where he's going so fast?" Fortia grabs the handles of her cart, now eager to shove off. "Let's get home and see what Mama and Papa know!"

She has found new energy and digging her toes into the gravel below. She pushes the cart with the same youthful enthusiasm she had while playing up in the trees.

~ ~ ~

Positioned within the Open Forest is Fortia's family home. It is like many farmer's homes, though perhaps somewhat larger, as the oil trade can sometimes be lucrative. The residence has two levels, with a steep roofline to address the burden of any snow, and it has an abundant but not overly impressive footprint.

Near the center of the roofline is a bold chimney with two caps, suggesting a large hearth underneath, which would service at least three spaces. The home is mostly built of wood timbers, though a bead of stone from the foundation is revealed out of ground level. The timber rafter tails under the eaves provide some decoration as they terminate with a scooping design, and the windows nearby them are a thick leaded glass. These provide just enough light for function, but for practicality's sake, they do not give a very clear view in either direction.

Without question it is a humble home that was built by those who have lived there, and it displays the particularities of their own charm. The sculpted image of an oil carafe is cut into the front door, which is situated within a somewhat ornate entry event. This carafe marks the home as the dwelling place of a nut oil miller. Being the home of farmers as well and relatively isolated, it is also the home to many animals large and small. A stone fence surrounds much of the property and restrains a clunky gathering of wooden fowl and steer. Covered by rugged bark-like feathers and grassy fur, they root around the property while minding their own business. The steer make short work of trimming the grass. The fowl are busy with attempts to fly but will occasionally stop to peck at morsels of grain scattered all around.

Inside the home, a scattering of distorted sunlight shines through windows and across a timber dining table into a generous kitchen space. Fortia's mother, Sedo, casually shells nuts at a countertop not far from the kitchen's hearth. She enjoys her life in this place, and as she works, she quietly hums a gentle tune to herself.

Sedo is nearly the same age as her husband and has an equally stern posture, though all of this is enhanced with a touch of grace to be appreciated. Like the rest of her humble family, there is a quietness to her choice of attire, which is made more ornate by her own charms.

The kitchen is adorned with everything one might imagine necessary to cook for a family, and the aesthetic is beautiful in a way that only a woman of experience and detail could arrange.

Sedo walks over to a grand hearth and tends to a large pot of stew. Stirring it with a long wooden spoon, she needs both hands to get the thickness of the meal moving in a circle.

The pot is hanging on an iron crane assembly, which is itself mounted to the stone of the hearth. This firebox is but one side of the huge hearth that makes up the centerpiece of this home. An array of shelves and counter space is to the left of this, and a wide threshold to the right leads directly into the living room. Her complacent humming is interrupted by the sound of a cart outside, and she smiles at the familiar noise.

Out in front of the home, the chickens flutter about as Fortia rumbles by the stone fence line with her cart. Still moving at an excited sprint, she struggles to slow the cart now, only to turn and then speed through an open metal gateway. Her cart creaks and bounces to a halt in the sideyard, where it spills a scattering of its cargo. Fortia is determined, though, and she does not stop to gather the spillage. She immediately sprints to the side door with Arty following close behind her.

In the kitchen, Sedo smiles as the footfalls of her daughter rapidly approach. Fortia bursts through the side door with enthusiasm as Arty gleefully barks after her.

"Mom! Did you see it!? The king's carriage rode by! Did you see it!?"

"The king's carriage?" Sedo chuckles at the excitement, still working to stir the grand pot of stew. "I must have missed it. How big was it?"

"It was huge! Four horses! Easily three times the size of our carriage. It was so loud and dusty and—"

"So that's why you're covered in dirt. Child, you are just like your father was as a boy, a mess of wood and dirt. Clean yourself up for dinner."

"But Mom…? What about the carriage and the horses and the king and—?"

"Go upstairs and get yourself ready for dinner, Fortia. Maybe your father knows something when he gets home." She resumes humming her favorite tune as she stirs the pot. Fortia slouches off, not convinced on the merits of this plan.

"Dad never tells me anything about the kingdom…" Her feet clomp heavily on the hardwood floors, and it feels like her joy for the moment has been crushed.

"Don't worry, Fortia. I'm sure he will know why the king was in such a hurry."

Fortia and her pup mope into the living room and move adjacent to the main hearth, almost dragging themselves across this comfortable living space.

The rear stones of the firebox here are a common wall to those in the kitchen. This relatively grand hearth structure is the heart of the home. It is the only source of heat on both floors. All rooms in the house are situated near it to some degree, and in the winter, the fire will always be kept alive on both levels.

Just opposite the fireplace, here is the cozy setting of the living room. Numerous comfortable chairs are positioned around side tables, all of which are framed by a large immaculate rug composed of multiple trimmed deer hides. A shelf with a handful of ornaments and leather-bound books is adjacent to this space. As in many homes of this type, the front door is rarely used. It is the expected entry event of the home, though, which immediately signals to a visitor what the layout of the living space beyond will be.

The pair of adventurers drag their feet through a threshold at the opposite end of the room, which leads directly to a stairwell. Each footfall on these old wooden stairs creates a heavy crackle and screech. It is hard to move quietly on the timbers of an old home.

~ ~ ~

The kitchen windows have lost their sunlight, but there is still a quaint atmosphere in the room. Semi-transparent stone lenses are propped in front of candles and work to amplify what light is available. They produce a very pleasing illumination for the dining area.

Dinner is underway, and Fortia tries her best to sit up straight as her mother serves a ladle of stew into her bowl. Down on the floor, Arty's head is buried in a small bowl of his own food, busy replacing the energy he lost earlier. Strangely, Constans is still missing from the table when Sedo finally sits beside her daughter. She tastes the stew, and her eyes light up with an appreciation for what she has created. Fortia does not hesitate to enjoy dinner now that her mother has started.

"So, Fortia, how many bags of nuts did you collect today?"

"Only twelve," she says, with a disgruntled tone.

"Twelve! Well, that's a good amount…More would have been very impressive."

"I got bored. Dad caught me playing in the trees."

"If I had a gold piece for every time your father and I got caught playing in the trees as kids, well, we would be as rich as the king."

They both chuckle a bit, and a flash of excitement comes over Fortia's face.

"You should have seen me, Mom! I was on this tree limb, it cracked, and I barely grabbed the rope in time!"

"Fortia! You could have cracked a leg." Sedo looks at her with an eye of concern. Fortia sheepishly turns back to her stew, tries not to get into any more trouble.

"How big was the branch?" Sedo has an inquisitive smile on her face. Fortia sees this, and her excitement returns.

"It was big, Mom! Four! Feet! Wide! But it had a family of sappy beetles living in it."

"Did I ever tell you that sappy beetles are good luck? I used to catch them as a little girl and keep them in a spice box in my father's shed. That way, I would always feel lucky."

Fortia thinks for a moment. What a grand idea that is…She soon returns to eating her dinner.

The creeping noise of the side door moves through the kitchen, and Sedo smiles at the sight of her husband returning home. With slow and sullen movements, he closes the door and removes his boots, but rather awkwardly, he stays silent. Sedo regards him with concern. She can see that something is off here. Standing to greet him with an embrace, a silent hug is shared between them. He begins whispering something into her ear, and his words have a swift impact on Sedo's mood. She listens as he recounts a story, and her endearing look begins to melt away.

Fortia pays little attention to this. Using her spoon, she cheerfully drops a softened nut from the stew past the table's edge. Arty snags it in the air, and Fortia chuckles, tries not to make much noise, though. Soon, Sedo and Constans join her at the table, but Fortia is too eager to wait any longer.

"Papa, did you see the king's cart today? It was sprinting down the forest road."

"Certainly. The horses are beautiful, aren't they?"

"I guess so…" She hadn't really thought about that. "Why was the king in such a hurry?"

Sedo serves her husband a ladle of stew. He smiles to thank her before turning his attention back to his daughter's question.

"Fortia, it appears that today, the king has died." Even the thought of it brings a frown to his face again.

Fortia stops midway through chewing and glances at her mother to confirm this story. Sedo gives a sad smile to her, and Fortia can now feel the calm morbidity that is suddenly defining this room.

"Does…" Fortia stammers, "does this mean they'll have a ceremony for the prince tonight? A coronation?"

"I suspect so," and he eats a spoonful of stew.

"Can we go see it?" she sheepishly asks.

Constans ponders this for a moment, then glances to Sedo for her thoughts. He's not sure it's a good idea, and this is only confirmed as Sedo gives a frown of disapproval.

"No, Fortia," Constans responds, "we need rest. We have to finish the latest batch of oil tomorrow morning."

"But DAD—"

Sedo stops her with a gesture just before the whining gets going. "Fortia. Your father said no." She sternly looks her in the eyes.

Fortia stares sourly into her bowl of stew and plays with it for a moment. There's no point in arguing, or she'll just get spanked with a nut cake turner then sent to bed without dinner. Seeing Fortia's quiet demeanor, Arty lies beside her in silence. He is ever the faithful friend.

"Sedo, my love," Constans smiles to her, "the stew is a masterwork."

They exchange the gentle and comfortable type of look that defines two people who appreciate one another. It is only after some quiet time passes during dinner that Fortia realizes her mother and father are holding hands. They appear at peace in this place. They have a life worth living here, and it seems that a life in the Open Forest is all they may ever need.

Chapter 2

LATER THAT NIGHT, Fortia and Arty are asleep in a thick and cozy bed. Even in the dark, her room appears to have some dimension to it and is clearly meant for her to grow up in. Wooden toys for both children and dogs are scattered around, but that is the extent of the disorder.

The headboard of Fortia's bed displays a fascinating engraving. An oak tree nut with a single eye inside of it. The rays of the sun extend from it and continue the whole width of the headboard.

Fortia stirs in her sleep, apparently still at the entry to the dream world. The door of the bedroom creaks open briefly as Sedo cautiously checks on her daughter. She is pleased to see Fortia at rest. Regardless of the sudden changes in this kingdom today, their child can sleep in peace.

The candlelight in the hall is dim. Constans approaches quietly from behind and Sedo can see his brow is still furrowed with tension. Sedo leaves the bedroom door cracked as she turns her attention to her husband.

"Fast asleep," she whispers as she embraces her husband once more.

"I must go, my beauty." Constans gives her a subtle kiss. "The others are waiting."

It is a long and comforting hug, but something must definitely be out of place in the Kingdom of Macadamia to keep this man from going to bed with his wife at night.

In Fortia's room, the sound of Constans descending the staircase is clearly audible. Arty's ears perk up with interest. His eyes open slowly to scan the room as he listens and waits.

Noises in the adjacent bedroom start to grow as Sedo readies herself for sleep. Subtle movements are made, closets opening and closing, a noisy bed receives a person's weight. Then silence fills the air. The quiet of night is abundant.

Arty patiently waits. There is nothing but a soft wind outside. Somewhere below, a doorway to the home opens and closes. Constans can be heard just outside greeting someone, and muffled noises of talking follow this. Little time passes until the sound of snoring can be heard from the adjacent bedroom.

Arty recognizes this noise, and his eyes light up. He hops up from rest and hurriedly spins around. With the power of a twelve-pound dog, he grabs the blanket on Fortia's bed and yanks it down the length of the mattress. Fortia stirs in her sleep, and Arty eagerly nudges her leg with his chunky wooden nose. Fortia is still asleep, though.

Determined, Arty jumps on her chest, and she startles awake. Quickly, she realizes the situation and they both freeze for a moment. They cautiously listen for noises. Fortia hears the snoring of her mother in the adjacent room and her eyes light up. She pets him with a smothering of hands.

"Good boy!" she whispers to him as she grabs Arty and gently places him on the floor, careful not to let his wooden paws clatter around. Fortia cautiously steps out of bed, and the weight of her body makes brief creaky noises on the old floorboards. She sneaks over to a dresser, where she quickly throws some clothing over her pajamas, then gestures to Arty for silence with her forefinger.

In the hallway there is only moonlight from an end window to light the way. Fortia's door slowly opens as it avoids every creep and scrape of the hinges. The girl and her dog tip-toe into the hall. Arty works twice as hard to stay silent.

As they pass Sedo's bedroom, the sound of snoring becomes very abrupt, all the better to conceal the noises of the staircase just ahead. Fortia tiptoes up to the edge of the top stair and sits down, her feet resting two steps below. She perches Arty onto her shoulder, and he lays as flat as he can. A well-practiced maneuver for these two deviants.

One riser at a time, Fortia shuffles her body weight down the stairs. The width of her rear end distributes the weight across each noisy surface below her, which minimizes the screeching of dry old wooden risers. Regardless of the occasional creeping noise, the rhythmic snoring of her mother is still prominent.

Nearing the bottom of the staircase, Fortia lifts Arty off her shoulder and places him quietly onto the floor. They sneak across the floor of the living room but soon halt.

Men talking outside with a strong tone can be heard, blunted by the wall separating them, but still louder than is expected at this time of night. They can hear the scraping sound of horse hooves languishing nearby. The rhythmic snoring from upstairs stops.

The child and dog freeze, and their eyes widen with fear. Her mother is moving around upstairs, and the foot falls on the floorboards above are like explosions in Fortia's ears. Arty is almost shivering, and Fortia closes her eyes, as if saying a silent prayer to not be discovered. A window slides open upstairs, and the muffled sound of Sedo's voice follows.

"You men hurry along now. There's a child sleeping…"

"Yes, ma'am," Constans and his companions respond as a group, and moments later, the muffled sound of hoof beats shrinks into the distance. It is silent again. The window slides shut. Sedo's footsteps are brief but remain concerning. A sense of relief only arrives when Fortia hears her mother return to the noisy bed. Some moments pass as they remain frozen, and soon after, Sedo returns to the dreamworld, sawing up every log in the house.

In the sideyard, the kitchen door of the home is dimly lit by a small oil lamp beside the entry stoop. The door slowly and silently opens, but only wide enough to allow the small wooden dog to step out. Arty runs down the stoop and over to the stone fence. He jumps up onto the flat of the fence, and with a look of vigilance, he scans the area.

He returns to the door and uses his front paw to scratch it. The door opens slightly, and Fortia carefully slips her thin wooden body through the gap.

"Good boy, Arty!" she whispers as the pup slobbers an acknowledgment.

Fortia shimmies the door shut. A minimal bump is made as the door panel strikes the jam. She smiles brightly.

They are home-free now as they run through the sideyard. The gate of the property is closed, but they expertly hop over the knee-height stone wall.

"Let's go meet the new king, Arty!" Arty eagerly bounces around as they both run down the dirt road. Events like this in Fortia's life have been few and far between. To see a new king receive his crown would have been only a distant dream for her, and it feels wrong to let this opportunity pass.

The moon gives just enough light to let the path be visible but not so much to keep a thick bed of stars from being brilliant. Perhaps it is written in those stars above, but it seems that tonight will be a good night for a coronation.

~ ~ ~

While Macadamia is now a peaceful kingdom, there was a time when war was waged on a regular basis, and the girth of that history is still present. The walls of the Closed Forest are dynamic in their design. Every section of wall is fifty feet tall, composed of neatly stacked stones leaning backward at an angle of twelve degrees off vertical. These stones are supported by compacted dirt and gravel at a depth of thirty feet, which terminate on the city side with an equally well-constructed surface of stone.

Beyond the walls are abundant trees that fill up the city to some degree. Many of these trees are easily eight or ten times as high as the walls themselves, and from a distance, they appear to be scarcely any different from the trees resting outside the walls.

The tree line of the Open Forest is set back from the wall at a distance of a hundred feet, and its perimeter is essentially parallel to the wall itself. This open space reveals strategically located embattlements that extend from the plane of the walls at regular intervals. Having a wide triangular shape that blooms outward from the longer stretch of wall, their value to the defending army cannot be overstated. When positioned inside them, a heavy crossbow would have the advantage of a flanking angle in two directions to defend against any siege weapon or surge of militants nearby.

The entire assembly of these walls was the greatest expenditure undertaken by King Serenus's grandfather. The constant vigilance that they provide has assisted in giving peace to Macadamia for many generations. These walls have never been breached by a frontal attack, and thus far, no person has designed a weapon that could truly challenge their mass.

Thousands of people live and work within the Closed Forest. They share the same protection of these walls, just as the king's residence does. While they do protect the life and freedom of Macadamia's citizens, they also protect the oil reserves that are needed by many other kingdoms.

Nut oil has a value per ounce that, while not equal to gold, is far higher than many precious metals or gems. While food is abundant in the Open Forest, those who live in a city or who are not accustomed to foraging for themselves often struggle to find a reasonable source of protein or fat for their diet. Nut oil is stable on the shelf and serves as a valuable export for Macadamia. Oil millers invariably live in the Open Forest, but the storage and aging of oil is done within the protection of the Closed Forest.

All of Oakenmeer relies on the products that the forest provides, and the labor required to modify the fruit of the forest gives those products great monetary value. Most forms of labor give operative value to the trees, and the act of labor gives man a speculative value in relation to this. When asked about this topic many years ago, King Serenus once said, "God resides in the trees. To manipulate or enjoy the fruit of the trees is to consider the nature of God."

~ ~ ~

Tonight, even from outside of the city, there is an obvious air of festivity within the Closed Forest. A haze of light emanates above the walls, and music is prominent in the night.

Fortia and Arty run along the gravel road in the moonlight. Their energy for this event has not diminished even as they are approaching what appears to be an end to this path. This road terminates at the city wall, but beside every embattlement is a smaller gate that would normally be guarded by soldiers. Tonight, all are welcome to enter and see the crowning of the new king.

People are collecting at the gate to gain entry as Fortia and Arty run past them. They rapidly sneak around a few stragglers who slowly funnel into this portal. This small gate is just wide enough for horses or a small carriage, and it leads immediately to a tunnel beneath the wall. For an attacking marauder, this narrow passage would spell certain death as there would be no form of cover to hide in. For Fortia, though, passing through the tunnel is something of a novelty as the approaching exit reveals the city.

She and Arty have had numerous chances to enter the Closed Forest, but each time they are still amazed by the complex fabric of the city. For them, their house is singular and stands alone in a mesh of woods. As beautiful as it is, living in the Open Forest can become lonely. So many people here in the city, their homes and shops constructed closely together. It all has a manmade density that she and Arty may never become accustomed to. Most residential or commercial buildings here are built between, around, and even through the enormous trees that populate this place. Like those in the Open Forest, these tree trunks are behemoth in size. The trees often have passages of their own, to and from one street and the next. Bridges between the trees have been built at frequent intervals, connecting many of the trunks at various angles and often on multiple levels. All these structures have the strongest columns that this land can conceive of. The trees themselves. It is not uncommon for there to be as many as ten levels of bridgeways and homes built between two trees.

As the trees are in a constant process of growth, the structures that are built around them must occasionally be rebuilt in order to accommodate their motion. While this may not seem ideal, Macadamia is a relatively wealthy kingdom, and many of its citizens are dedicated to the arts and crafts. The rebuilding of structures to accommodate the trees is something of a joy for these people. The framework of each structure, sometimes only half completed, displays that they are built to last regardless of an inevitable need to be reshaped.

Fortia and Arty move through the city in a steady but reluctant manner. She does know her way around certain areas, but only the path to the city center, where the market and oil storage depot are located. The pace of things is also different tonight. The people who live and work here have a different energy right now, hustling from place to place. All their shops and storefront windows are open at night when they would otherwise be closed. As a result, Fortia is feeling somewhat cautious as she turns the corner onto a nearby road.

She ducks through a large portal in a tree and next down a short stretch of road, then under a bridge between two adjacent trees. There are people everywhere, resting in front of their homes, milling about in conversation, peddling fabrics, nuts, meats, and other goods from their shop windows. Fortia scampers through the open passage of a flower shop and makes a fast left turn down a thin alleyway into another narrow passage that is littered with merchants.

A chunky and elderly wooden man perched on a rugged donkey clogs up most of this alley. They are moving much too slow. Fortia is stuck behind him, and she sighs out with impatience. Arty knows what to do, though. A single loud and distinct bark stirs the donkey as Arty comes up on the animal's heels.

Filled with fear, the donkey speeds up. Arty yaps at it again, keeping it motivated even as the rider pulls on the reins. Fortia chuckles as she follows close behind her pup. The donkey charges past the end of the alley and recklessly enters the street. An approaching carriage is forced to halt, narrowly avoiding a crash.

Fortia and Arty gather new energy as they hear the noises of a crowd nearby. They make a sharp right turn and rush down the street. The courtyard is ahead, where the festivities of the evening are taking place.

A crowd of eager attendees has gathered around the raised platform of a wooden stage, and festive music flows from a band of instrumentalists at the edge of the square. She and the pup gleefully sneak between people packed into the crowd. They maneuver their smaller bodies up to the front, gaining the best possible view of the event.

There is an acrobatic performance already in process as two jugglers toss around swords and axes. They quickly and deftly pass these weapons to and from each other as the performance unfolds at breathtaking speed. Fortia is stunned by their skill and the precision of each movement.

"Look at this, Arty!" She grabs the little dog and holds him up close to the stage, where his eyes light up to match hers. Together, they watch in amazement. It is almost a struggle to follow the path of an ax as the performer tosses it high up in the air. It falls effortlessly back into his skilled hands.

The show is coming to a crescendo, though, and the jugglers toss their axes and swords up as high as they can. They dance around on stage for a moment, inevitably standing underneath the weapons as the blades begin a terrifying descent. The jugglers pause and strike a practiced pose when the falling blades clunk into the stage top. They land perfectly on the stage at a measured distance between the performers.

The crowd goes wild. Clapping and cheering all around. Fortia laughs at the fun of the moment, and Arty barks out his excitement. The jugglers gather their props and clear away the mess of the performance. A regal and well-dressed man with a distinguished and elegant walk approaches center stage. The crowd seems to know him, and they rapidly quiet down.

"I greet you!" he says with his arms wide and his chest broad. Cheers from the crowd rapidly follow, and he waits for them to settle down before continuing.

"Citizens of Macadamia, and welcome visitors! In the time-honored tradition of our five Surviving Kingdoms, here is the moment you have all been waiting for!"

More cheers follow as the crowd appears to be in anticipation of this event.

"If we may take a moment to settle ourselves…" He quiets his gestures, and with this, he quiets the crowd until just a murmur of noise remains.

"We all know the importance of this moment. The passing of our great King Serenus's power from father to son." He gives a skilled pause, and the anticipation gathers.

"I am pleased to present…" Another pregnant pause. The hush of the crowd is all around.

"The Golden Nugget…"

It is nearly silent. Only brief whispers of pleading and expectation come forth from the crowd. Even Fortia, at her young age, knows the importance of this tradition. They all gaze to the right of the stage as another regal-looking assistant steps forward. In his hands, he carefully balances a lush purple pillow with an ornate wooden covering. He cautiously maneuvers himself, careful not to stumble with this prize.

A guard nearby has handed the orator a small decorative table. He positions it at center stage, and the approaching assistant eases the pillow onto the table. The orator reaches forward and swiftly removes the lid. The crowd can suddenly see it, the Golden Nugget…

Fortia has only heard stories about this object. It has been vaguely mentioned by guests at her home and rarely ever spoken about by her parents. To her, it was essentially just a myth, but one that is now redefined in the darkness of this night. It sparkles there, the light of a dozen torches reflecting off of it and into the sappy viscera of her young eyes as they instinctively widen to gather up even more of this object.

It is a large nut, bigger by a stretch than the largest walnut, but not so large that it cannot fit into a person's mouth. The shiny golden hue to it is clearly the source of its name, but there is so much more to the nature of this nut, more than anyone here could possibly know. The shell of it displays an intricate latticework of squares, which seems to betray it as an object of art, but this is the uniqueness of this nugget. The beauty of it alone should make a person question the thought of crushing it, and perhaps that is its power. Only those who can look past its beauty alone know well enough how to lead.

The orator continues his presentation, though.

"As tradition demands, Prince Tonitro will now take the Golden Nugget into his jaws, and if he is successful in breaking its mystical form, all of the Kingdom of Macadamia will see that he is worthy of the crown."

The orator bows slightly and steps aside. As he retreats to the side of the stage, he kneels, now respectfully waiting for the event to unfold before him. Only the silence of the crowd remains, and like many people gathered here, Fortia and Arty are enamored with this moment.

Prince Tonitro steps swiftly onto the stage. Even with a thick plating of tooled black leather armor as his vestments he is able to move quickly and with intent. His gestures are bold and confident. His trunk is taller, and his bark seems thicker than his young age would suggest. Regardless of moving with purpose, every step he takes is nearly silent, as though he has made a practice of walking softly.

He approaches the nugget, and without hesitation, he takes it into one hand and inspects it. Something on this nut seems to puzzle him...

As beautiful as the nut is, he does not appear to be in awe of it. Perhaps he is looking for something on it that other men do not normally see. For all the boldness of his posture, his mannerisms have a degree of elegance. He rotates the nugget in his hand to inspect each side of it, and his fingers seem to move with an unexpected slight.

Fortia and Arty take in this moment with admiration. They had scarce opportunities to see King Serenus before his death, let alone to be so close to the future king now.

At last, Prince Tonitro smiles. It seems that he has found what he wants. Placing the mystical nut into his mouth, he tenses his arms and straightens his back. With his jaw wide, he begins to apply pressure to the meaty little orb. He bends slightly, as if to engage the strength in his chest, but the nugget does not give way. Not even a little.

He relaxes for a second, and a murmur develops in the crowd. Some question of this moment is clearly developing. Tonitro will not give up, though. Nothing about his mannerisms would suggest he ever has. Bracing himself, another attempt is made. His face tenses tight. His jaw summons up even more strength. A great huff of breath is pushed from his lungs.

The Golden Nugget cracks and shatters. A dozen pieces of it fragment all around and the crowd explodes with cheering. Fortia laughs at the excitement, and Arty barks out with joy. It's an incredible moment as a new king is seconds away from taking the crown. The cheering continues as Tonitro gazes over his people and smiles bright. He chews up the nugget with a posture of pride and confidence, boldly establishing his place in the kingdom.

The crowd quiets down. Not far away, an exquisite and regal-appearing older woman steps up to the stage. Queen Julianna approaches her son. She has a thickened trunk that is typical of people in older age, but this is partially obscured by her ornate and delicately woven clothing. In her hands, she respectfully carries the crown of the King of Macadamia. She is a proud queen today, approaching her son with a unique smile that only a mother and queen could likely understand. Tonitro knows instinctively to kneel, and with humility in his spine, he bows to her. Without a word, she places the crown on his head.

Tonitro stands, turns to face the crowd with even more energy now as he lifts his hands triumphantly. The crowd roars out for him as they clap and yell in rejoice. The new king walks off stage with his mother, and much of the bustling crowd attempts to follow them.

"Let's head home before Dad gets back." Fortia seems satisfied by having seen this incredible event tonight. Arty yaps an agreement.

She lays him on the ground as she turns away to move through the sea of people. Arty barks out, though, and Fortia stops, turns to see him focused on something. There is a small object on the ground just in front of the little dog. The sea of people surrounding them slowly shuffle past as Fortia moves closer, wanting to see what this curious object is.

"Whatcha found, boy?" There is a small sparkling shard of the Golden Nugget only inches away from Arty's nose. Fortia grabs it and inspects it. Studying it inquisitively, she smells it. For a brief moment, she seems puzzled; the scent is almost familiar, but she quickly shakes this off. Dropping the shard of nut into her pocket, she turns and pushes her way through the crowd.

"We'll look at it later, Arty. Need to get home."

The festivities of the evening have not yet ended, but for these two adventurers, the fun must come to an end.

~ ~ ~

The moonlight is still making itself known through the windows of Fortia's bedroom. She and Arty have settled into sleep while the sound of the snoring matriarch is heard in the distance.

The door of Fortia's room creeps open as Constans checks on his slumbering child. As glad as he is to see her safe and sound, he does not smile or feel any true sense of joy. Clearly something is still weighing heavy on his mind as he looks over his daughter with a somberness.

Constans steps backward, quietly closing the door. He stops, though…Something has caught his attention. Something in the distance near Fortia's bed. On the night table.

Now disregarding the noises of his movement, he pushes past the creaking door and swiftly makes his way over to the night table. Constans's eyes widen as he singles in on the shard of the Golden Nugget, still sparkling somewhat, even while the light here is pale.

He picks it up and inspects it. He sniffs it, and his eyes grow wider still. Pondering this object for a moment, his thoughts are racing. It is difficult for him to stand still. After a moment, his curious face transitions into a drooping despair. A tear begins to gather…

Constans gently caresses his daughter's shoulder, quietly waking her from sleep. He is careful to let Arty stay at rest.

Fortia rubs the sleep out of her eyes and looks at her father with a questioning gaze. Constans, still holding the shard of nugget in his hand, shows it to her. Seeing that he has found her souvenir, she quickly grows concerned about his reaction, but he gently smiles to her.

"Please tell me, Fortia," his tone is disarming, "where did you get this?"

"Dad, I…" she stammers, still frightened of how her father will react.

"Fortia, I'm not mad at you. Just please tell me, where did this come from?"

She is still suspicious and unsure what to make of this. Her father's calm demeanor is very obvious, though, and she realizes it is okay to come clean.

"Arty and I snuck out of the house while Mom was sleeping." Her head falls in shame as she admits this misdeed. "We went to the city and saw King Tonitro crush the Golden Nugget. Arty found this piece of it, and we took it home for a souvenir."

Constans turns away from her. His mind is stuck on a thought as he looks out the window adjacent to her bed and contemplates a decision. He can tell she is not lying, and he begins to pace the room, still pondering what steps are needed.

"Dad, we didn't—" Constans raises his hand for silence, and Fortia heeds the warning. She watches in confusion as her father thinks through some kind of unspoken dilemma. Soon enough, though, he frowns, finally accepting the thought that is stuck in his head. He turns with purpose and moves over to the bureau, where he grabs some clothing for her.

"Get dressed, Fortia. We need to take a little trip."

~ ~ ~

Fortia and Constans ride on his horse at a steady pace through the moonlight of the Open Forest. Tired from a long day, she begins dozing off against her father's back. Constans is riding with intention, though, his brows furrowed with sincerity as he nudges the horse to speed up. Regardless of the events that have unfolded in Macadamia, the troubles of the day have yet to be confronted.

They arrive at the Cowan's Eaves, a small tavern and inn that is isolated from the main road by a long gravel drive. The structure appears to be more of a rustic private home, which was expanded and made into an inn. Many of the outward accouterments of this humble establishment are similar to Fortia's home. Good moonlight is available here due to the open space surrounding the front of this structure, and a handful of blazing torches announce that they are open for business.

Numerous horses are hitched to the outside posts, and the noise from inside reveals the ongoing cheer. As far as the people inside are concerned, there's something to celebrate. Even at this late hour of the night, the festivities will continue.

When they arrive at the hitching area, Fortia sluggishly dismounts with her father. Constans whips the lashing to a post beside a half dozen other horses, and with a gesture, he encourages her to follow.

She looks over this quaint building with hesitation and curiosity. Having never been in a tavern before and being late at night, even the cheerful noises within do not fully assuage her concerns. At times like this Arty would be her reliable force of confidence, and it doesn't take long for her to want him at her side.

Inside the rustic-looking pub, the atmosphere is jolly and somewhat active. A small string band is playing somewhere in the distance, and their music keeps the energy fresh in the room. This is met well by a group of half-drunk men and women standing near the high-top tables. They play a knife-throwing game where two people take turns tossing knives at wooden targets that are decorated as animals. A knife strikes the carved form of a bull hanging from the wall, and the crowd goes wild.

Fortia and Constans enter from the side door. The cheer of this place has an immediate impact on her mood, and it quickly sets her at ease.

Together, they push past the group and move toward the counter, where another handful of people are in lively talks. Constans lifts Fortia and sets her down on a sturdy barstool. The bartender knows him, and together they smile. They greet each other with an awkward handshake followed by a strange sort of hug. Fortia notices these unique motions, but she takes little interest. She is too intrigued by the knife-throwing game.

"Fortia, this man is Tiler." Constans gestures to the bartender, who smiles at her with acknowledgment. He is a svelte and slightly taller middle-aged man, not at all appearing complicated in his choice of attire. If you didn't look right at him, you might not even notice his quiet mannerisms, though his pale birch-like bark is slightly distinct. Fortia smirks at him cautiously, she is pleased to meet him but still very uncertain of this place. Her father confidently puts his hand on Tiler's shoulder.

"Tiler is my very good friend, and I trust him with my life. He will watch over you for a while. Sit here and wait for me. I will come to get you soon, but until then, you must wait here, Fortia."

She recognizes the sincerity in her father's face and nods an agreement. A moment of fear develops, though, when Constans quickly turns and walks with purpose through a doorway to the right of the bar. He swiftly closes it behind him. Soon enough, though, Tiler serves her a cup of warm, fragrant nut tea. Fortia sheepishly smiles to thank him.

She settles into the worn wood of the barstool. Intrigued, she turns to watch the men tossing knives and the temptation to have a go at it is hard to resist. Remembering what her father said, she turns back to the bar and has a relaxing sip of tea. Her elbows rest on the waxed wood of the countertop, but she struggles to find complacency. The tea is quite nice, though, and it helps her to be at peace.

Two men not far away at the bar are engaged in something of an energetic conversation. Their tankards of ale may be getting to their heads. One is an older man, humbly dressed as any farmer or builder may be, and he is growing somewhat rambunctious in the conversation. The other is middle-aged, and he wears the green leather armor of a guardsman. While he is clearly not on duty tonight, he conducts himself well right now. The older man sips his ale, and with a frustrated look, he slams the mug on the bar.

"I'm telling you—" he stops to gather his drunken thoughts. "Something was different about it…" he stammers. "I was only a child, but I remember. The nugget…I remember, Serenus! It was different." He wavers, struggles to stay on his stool for a moment.

The man in armor chuckles. While clearly interested in this story, he is also reluctant to give these drunken ramblings much credit. He reaches out suddenly, catches his partner before he falls off the stool.

"You're such a beautiful drunk." He smiles then stands to help. "Come on, let's get you home and tucked into bed."

He leans in and kisses his drunken partner's head. Together, they stand, both a bit more than tipsy as they move through the cheerful crowd.

Fortia chuckles at them. Her concern over this foreign place begins to fade into the distance. The joyful and energetic song in the background ends, and the atmosphere in the room transitions. A new song starts, one more in tune with the late hour of the night. She smiles at this lovely melody and quietly sips her tea.

Tiler looks back at her from the other side of the bar, again nods his head with a smile to remind her that she is safe. She sips her tea again, and it somehow tastes even better.

~ ~ ~

As the night grows closer to morning, the tavern space has largely cleared out. The music has long since ended, and there are only a few quiet patrons lingering.

Fortia has fallen asleep at the bar, her arms supporting her head on the counter. Tiler sits at the far end of the back bar, busy with the work of closing up. He glances over to her as she slumbers, only to return his attention to the day's inventory. The discipline is obvious, as he seems to always have one eye on the child, though the responsibilities of business cannot be entirely overlooked.

The doorway to the right of the bar opens slowly and Constans approaches his tired daughter with a smile of understanding. As if expecting it, Fortia wakes up and works to regain her surroundings.

"Come with me, Fortia." Constans gently offers his hand in guidance. As Fortia steps down from the bar, she is still working to wake up from her nap. Taking his hand, he calmly leads her through the same doorway.

While passing through this threshold Fortia cannot help but notice that the wall opposite of the door has an engraved wood panel on it. It is the same elaborate design as the one on her headboard at home.

Fortia and her father cautiously descend a steep, winding staircase. Moving deeper into a basement space, the walls and steps are all composed of stone, and the layout is somewhat narrow. These subterranean blocks leave no room for the comforts of natural light, and even with her father guiding her, the tight darkness of this place summons uncertainty. The only light here comes from candles positioned high above them on the center column of the stairs. A single candle, every fifth or sixth riser, is perched on stone sculptures that protrude from the surface around them. They are carved animal faces with the candles resting on a drip pan above each of their heads.

Every few steps, the faces of these animals present a gaze directly into the eyes of the occupant here. One after another, Fortia is confronted by their disconcerting appearance. A suspicious bear considers her presence, followed by the curious gaze of a rabbit and, next, the unsettling snarl of a wolf. The trickle of light from these awkward candelabras does not lend much depth to the stairs. On more than one occasion, Fortia struggles to find the next riser as she moves deeper and deeper into the cellar.

Having survived the staircase, they reach a small dark room at the basement level. There is only a single candle to light this space, which is mounted on the stone wall adjacent to a rather sturdy-looking pocket door. Fortia holds her father's hand tight, wary of the darkness around her and cautious to make sure that he is close by. She has never seen her father behave so mysteriously, and she cannot help but wonder why they are in this gloomy space? Does she even want to know what is beyond that door? Does she really need to be here? Seconds later, he releases her hand and calmly kneels.

"Fortia, in a moment, the doorway will open. I will be on the other side waiting for you."

Feeling small and confused by so much uncertainty, it is a struggle for her to find the right words. Her hands fold over themselves, now missing the safety of his grip.

With one swift motion, her father stands and quietly steps backward. Moving away from her, he is swallowed up by the darkness of this space.

"Papa, wait." Fortia feels the pressure of being alone now. While the door is right next to her, it has not opened, and she is uncomfortable standing here. Even when glancing back toward the stairs, the light from the candles above them seems to have vanished. The stone wall to the left offers no retreat, and the darkness to the right only offers more uncertainty.

"Papa…?" she asks into the darkness, checking for her father. An answer comes.

"Only speak the truth now, Fortia."

She reluctantly steps toward the darkness of his voice. Her motion is interrupted as the doorway quickly slides open, and the candle beside her blows out.

Just through this door Fortia can see another single candlelight originating from a hanging chandelier, roughly a distance of twenty feet from her. The subtle haze of light lands on a polished stone floor, where it illuminates a small yellowish object. Even at this distance she recognizes it, the shard of the Golden Nugget.

A deep and confident voice addresses her from the darkness of that room.

"Come forward, girl. Claim what is yours."

Fortia hesitates but soon moves cautiously through the door. When she has cleared it by a few steps the door closes. The sharp noise of the door panel hitting the frame startles her.

The light ahead of her offers the only hint of comfort here. She can feel the presence of multiple people, but she cannot easily make out their forms. Subduing her fears, she ventures over to the shining piece of nut. She cautiously picks it up, and the voice from the dark room addresses her again.

"Where did this come from, child?"

Fortia looks ahead of her with concern. Her arms gather around her as though they could protect her from a threat she cannot see. She is about to speak, but a harsh female voice from her left interrupts.

"Only speak the truth."

Fortia gathers her confidence. She responds into the void.

"My dog—" she stammers, "—he found it after the prince broke the Golden Nugget."

"Only speak the truth, girl!" a man's voice booms from nowhere and startles her. She can't even tell what direction it came from. Trying to stay strong, she nearly lets a tear fall.

"I am! I swear!" She insists. The voices are not satisfied.

"Tell us what you know of this, child!" Another voice. "Or you may never see the light of day again!"

Fortia trembles. She struggles to get the words out as a sappy brown tear gathers in her eye.

"My dog— he found it— at the ceremony— the ceremony for the king."

"The TRUTH! Only speak the truth!" a new voice booms out from behind her.

"I swear! It was the king's nugget!" She grips the piece of nut tighter, and the fear is almost intolerable.

A noise of heavy steps is heard close by. Another candlelight grows and reveals a knight wearing a blindfold and green leather armor. His ax is lifted in front of her, an immense threat now growing out of the indiscriminate and terrifying darkness.

Fortia gazes upward and trembles at the imposing figure. She steps back as terror fills up her face. Her tears burst out of her as she shakes, never more afraid in her life yet she cannot turn her eyes away from this tall and overwhelming man.

"ONLY THE TRUTH CHILD!" screams another voice from the left. The green knight before her lifts his ax high in the air, moments from striking.

"IT WAS THE KING'S NUT, PAPA! IT WAS THE KING'S NUT I SWEAR!"

The imposing knight advances, and her tears become a pleading shriek of horror. She cannot bear to look again, and the shard of nugget falls at her feet.

The dim light overhead vanishes, leaving behind the single candle in front of her. Out of the darkness, Constans rapidly approaches her. He grabs his daughter and holds her tight as she cries and sobs into his chest.

"It's okay, Fortia. I'm here. It's okay, darling. I'm sorry. I'm so sorry…"

She is paralyzed with fear. There are no defenses left inside of her, yet the comfort of her father's embrace begins to chip away at the moment.

One by one, candles are lit around the two of them. These reveal the presence of numerous other people, six in number. They are sitting in large throne-like chairs arranged in an oblong form which has Fortia and Constans at the center.

Holding his crying child, Constans turns and gives a sincere nod to one of these people. It is the knight clad in green armor, and he nods in return. An agreement, it seems, to some previously discussed topic.

Constans takes a deep breath, glad to know that this event is over. He lifts Fortia and carries her off through the same pocket door that she entered from. He carries her up the dim and disorienting staircase. Fortia has stopped crying, but she has met near total exhaustion.

Even during this short walk, she has fallen asleep in her father's arms.

He enters the tavern area with her and lays her down on a bench nearby. Tiler approaches with a blanket, and he quickly spreads it over her.

"Watch over her for me, Tiler." Constans has a frown of concern on his face.

"Of course, my brother. How long will you be?"

"Before sunrise, I hope. If we can say it has risen at all."

~ ~ ~

Returning to the meeting hall below the tavern, Constans steps through the sliding doorway from the antechamber. With a practiced sense of caution, he closes it behind him.

A few of the people here are standing in a small group as they talk over the event which has just unfolded. Others have already situated themselves in their chairs and are waiting for the meeting to begin.

Positioned under the blazing chandelier at the center of this oblong room is now a flat-topped podium, which is crafted over an ornate wooden spindle. The shard of the Golden Nugget is resting on its leather surface.

With Constans having now returned, the people in this group move back to their chairs. In the chair opposite the pocket door sits the knight in green armor, Matthius, who appears to be deep in contemplation. Tall and relatively young, he has cropped branches of hair and a stern face. Even while deep in thought, he still seems to carry the prideful appearance of a leader. He stands from his seat and briefly waits for calm to settle in.

"Come to order," Matthius says, and any remaining chatter in this group dies down. "Let us begin with a moment of silence for the loss of our great King Serenus."

Everyone present stands from their chairs and they solemnly bow their heads. The time passes, each of them perhaps thinking a similar thought, perhaps with different opinions to voice. The moment is appreciated by each of them, though there is business to conduct.

"Soft and safe to thee, be thy resting place," Matthius says with a sincere tone. "Bright and glorious be thy rising from it." With these words, all present remove themselves from that moment of silence. They all sit, save for Matthius, who remains standing to address them.

"Knights and Ladies of the Ordo Nux Aurea. After the testimony witnessed this evening, there remains no more doubt."

"Are we certain there is no alternative?" This is sternly spoken by Laderas, who is a massive man, easily the largest person at this gathering. Even in his seated position, he is an imposing presence, and his dark red leather armor seems to complement the great girth of his shoulders.

"There must be no doubt!" says an elderly woman sitting next to him. Lady Callidus wears the silky garments and jewelry of a wealthy person. Her dress is ornate and exceptionally patterned. Numerous rings are on her fingers and two expensive-looking necklaces drape over her garments.

"What doubt can there be?" Matthius gestures to the shard of the nugget on the podium. "We have all the evidence. There is a shimmering paint on this piece of nut, and we have a credible witness who found it." He then gestures to Constans. "Even our own Tracker swears that he played no role in the acquisition of that nut. All of this is more evidence than any person could expect to determine that a crime has been committed."

Constans leans forward in his chair, a sincere look across his brow as he speaks.

"I am the only living member of our order who has ever touched a genuine Golden Nugget. While it is possible, highly unlikely, but possible, that someone else could have acquired a Golden Nugget, I tell you on my honor that this is not a piece of the true nugget."

The group of people around him murmur in frustration at this thought, but Constans stands now, still holding their attention.

"None of us want to face the realities that are present today. I give you my word; my girl may be a disobedient sort at times, but she has never failed to own up to the truth."

Constans then sits, but Laderas still seems unsettled. He looks like he has something to say, but Matthius steps forward.

"Our lineage as knights and ladies of this Order stems well past the warring days of our kingdom to a dozen generations of royals. Throughout all of Oakenmeer, every single time a royal has succeeded their predecessor, this brotherhood of knights and ladies has held the responsibility of claiming and protecting the Golden Nugget until such time that the successor to the throne could prove their worth."

There is a rumble of agreement from all present, but Matthius signals for further silence.

"I have trusted my life to each of you on many occasions, and I say to you now, under the penalty of treason, that our great King Serenus has been slain by his own son."

There is a subtle agreement present in the room. Matthius has stated in simple terms what each of them has been thinking all along. He continues, though.

"While this duty falls heavy on our shoulders, it is our responsibility to reveal this truth to our kingdom. I make a motion that we should recover the true Golden Nugget and bring it before the kingdom to prove that Tonitro is NOT worthy of the throne."

With that, Matthius sits down, and a smattering of chatter grows throughout the room. Constans stands again, and the noise soon slows to a silence.

"We have all heard the rumors for years now." Constans speaks with sincerity, and there seems to be a subtle understanding of what he refers to. "Tonitro has repeatedly pressed his father to allow our great army to occupy the Kingdoms of Pignoli and Pecan so he may put an end to the ages-old conflict between those two kingdoms."

This sparks a murmur of distaste in the room, but Laderas stands now, ready to say his piece. Constans sits out of respect for him.

"These are, at best, rumors. Not once have I heard a worthy man confirm that suspicion." Laderas sits down. He made his point clearly and quickly. It appears from the tone in the room that many of the people in this small congregation may agree with him.

Constans glances to Matthius, perhaps a topic they have both already discussed. Matthius gives a heavy sigh, then stands again to speak.

"As Captain of our great army, I have heard Tonitro voice this desire many times." A rumbling of conversation surfaces from this, but Matthius looks directly to Laderas.

"My brother, I have never repeated this outside of Tonitro's confidence, and only now, in your trust, do I place this information."

This has sparked some new energy in the room, and numerous side conversations resurfaced from the group. Laderas has a frown over his face, though. He thinks on this for a moment then stands to speak once more. The room quiets down for him.

"Given this knowledge, I see no reason to delay any further. I second the proposition put forward by Matthius and call for a vote."

Constans quickly stands again to follow this strong statement.

"I vote in favor of the proposition. If there is any chance of harm to our neighboring kingdoms, then we must act now."

"I am with you, Constans!" a skinny and tall woman, Harris, stands and agrees. She is clad in lightweight black leather armor, but she is not a soldier. She appears as something of a rogue and more masculine than her gender might otherwise portray.

One by one, the remainder of the seven people present stand and declare their support for this plan. Matthius finally stands with purpose and steps away from his chair. He moves toward the shard of the nugget, picks it up, and places it in a small leather satchel.

"I will protect this evidence with my life," he says, and moments later, he removes a wooden coin from his pocket. Confidently, he places it heads side up on the podium, then moves away toward Lady Callidus.

Each member of this order soon removes a small wooden coin from their pocket, and one by one, they approach the podium at the center of the room.

Matthius has stepped next to Lady Callidus and is gently assisting her out of the chair. He then guides her to the podium. She removes her wooden coin and, with the uncertainty of a blind person, places it on the table, taking a moment to be sure it is firmly on the surface.

Each of these coins is placed heads side up, and each of them shows the carved profile of King Otenamann of Oak on their surface.

Chapter 3

HAZY MORNING SUNLIGHT rests on Fortia's head as she and Arty sleep comfortably in her bedroom. The pup is sprawled out across the blanket in a ridiculous position, somehow consuming half of a bed that is ten times his size. Sedo opens the door, and the sudden squeak of hinges on wood brings them both awake.

"Good morning, you two." Sedo has the kind smile on her face that Fortia has grown to love. "Time to get up and get ready for—"

"Mama?" Fortia interrupts with a shameful frown. "I'm sorry for sneaking out last night." Arty whimpers with a sad agreement.

"Child, I am glad you are safe." Sedo approaches her with some clothing and lovingly places it on the bed. "You are young, and young people are full of bad decisions. Use them up now so there is room for the good ones later." She smiles at her daughter, and Fortia's grateful eyes eagerly accept her mother's wisdom.

"Come now. I made nut cakes. You need energy for your work this morning."

Fortia and Arty hop out of bed. Ready to face the day.

~ ~ ~

The rear yard of their farmhouse is an open patch of dirt, grass, and brick paving flanked by forest on three sides. The animal run is on the adjacent side of the house, fenced off for safe keeping, with the barn at the rear of all this.

Centered on that open space is a large animal-driven mechanism. It consists of a ring-shaped stone surface, the band of it being five feet wide all around. This ring surrounds the diameter of a twelve-foot-wide tree stump, clearly the remnant of a wooden behemoth long since passed. The top of the stump has been carved to accommodate a wooden arm assembly that is positioned at its center. Spanning past the radius of both the trunk and the stone ring, the arm holds a large stone wheel that is resting perpendicular to a channel in the ring. Finally, this arm assembly protrudes further out to connect with a mount on a steer.

This entire device is arranged well to rotate in a circle around the circumference of the stone ring, and the beast would generally be pulling the stone wheel, though right now, he is resting. Awaiting the command to begin his work.

Constans is wearing a well-distressed leather apron and a sturdy pair of work gloves. He hauls a large sack of nuts over to this device and carefully pours them into the groove of the stone ring. Walking around the perimeter of this whole assembly, he levels the nuts out evenly so they are no more than two layers deep. This assembly is the first press which grinds up the collected nuts into a powdery cake, thus making it easier to heat refine oil from them.

Nearby, this large assembly is another device, smaller in size and made entirely of cast iron. It straddles a bed of hot coals, which appear to have been simmering for some time already. This device functions very much like a large book press but with a bottom and top plate that are slightly convex in shape. The top plate is welded into a circular rotating handle above it. When turned, the top plate will meet flush with the bottom plate, thus applying pressure to whatever is between them. Surrounding the bottom plate is a specialized lip with holes drilled in it. They drain into short iron tubes, which safely guide the newly produced oil into large glass vessels waiting beneath. They are uncorked right now and ready to catch the freshly pressed oil that Constans is preparing.

The coals below the bottom have been smoldering since early this morning, and Constans moves toward this device to toss a few more pieces of wood on it. Maintaining a stable temperature is crucial to the process of making oil. Too hot, and the oil may evaporate or burn. Too cold, and no oil may be produced.

Fortia runs out the kitchen door into the backyard. She is ready to work, having just finished breakfast, and now feeling full of energy. Grabbing a bag of nuts from the sideyard, she carries them to the stone ring assembly. As Constans did moments ago, she spreads them across the circular stone. After making numerous trips back and forth from the wagons, the entire grooved surface of the stone disc is covered with nuts. Constans takes the ox by the reins and gives it a slight tug. They begin walking together, and as the large stone wheel turns, it pulverizes the nuts into a cake-like substance within the groove. Eventually the ox is stopped and let to rest.

Fortia and Constans both pick up hand shovels and together, they scoop the pulverized nut cake out of the channel. The work is typically somewhat boring for Fortia, but today, she has a new energy about her.

Together they make short work of this task as they transfer the nut cake into buckets. These fragments are then placed onto the warm, convex surface of the iron press. Once leveled out to achieve a consistent thickness, the press is ready to use.

Constans detaches the ox from the cylinder and reattaches it to a handle at the top of the press. With a second tug, he guides the oxen in another circle, each rotation around the device bringing the top plate closer to the bottom plate. Eventually, the press becomes harder to move, and the two plates nearly make contact.

Reaching into his pocket, Constans removes a fresh apple and dangles it in front of the beast, almost taunting it. Motivated to pull harder now, the ox gives it all he's got. He wants that apple, and eventually, he will get it. Constans then uses a wooden mallet to strike the handle of the press multiple times. The nut powder must be pressed as tightly as possible if good extraction of oil is to be achieved.

With this equipment, the work is not terribly hard, but it is a long and sometimes monotonous process. Fortia begins loading up the stone surface again, but it will take some time to extract all the oil from that first batch, so there is no particular rush.

Soon enough, though, they can see the fruits of their labor manifesting. Constans tosses another few chunks of wood onto the coals underneath, and the bottom plate of the press begins dripping oil through the holes. Very slowly, the large glass vessels begin to fill up.

Fortia stands at the ready nearby with additional empty vessels. She dutifully inspects each glass jar, watching them closely and waiting to replace any one of them as it approaches being full.

None of the precious oil being made here can be wasted. After settling and aging, it becomes too valuable to let even a single drop go to waste. Constans is not a merchant, though. Like many precious commodities, the sale of oil to the public is controlled by the kingdom. A miller can keep and age as much of their own oil as they like, but they can only sell it to the kingdom. This provides his family a good income, and in times of war, or when trade is particularly good, the value of oil increases so much that the kingdom pays a bonus price to millers who produce higher yields.

This entire assembly here came at great cost. The tree stump that forms the anchor of the first press represents the last vestiges of a wooden giant. It had grown too tall and collapsed under its own weight hundreds of years ago. The resources from that tree were used by Constans's grandfather to build everything on this farm. Their family had previously bought a "Thousand Year Lease" on the land for fifty jars of Median Fire, the most valuable and highly flammable oil ever made. It is said to burn even brighter if doused with water.

The home, the sheds, the barn, even the chicken coop, and much of the furniture inside the home were all built from one enormous fallen tree. The iron used to make the oil press was cast and formed over fires made from its branches and leaves. Nothing went to waste from that tree, for to waste any of it was to waste a gift provided by the Open Forest itself.

As all of this labor unfolds, Arty is at work himself. He paces around the two carts holding the supply of recently gathered nuts. On the lookout, he patrols the territory dutifully until something catches his eye.

A small wooden animal is nearby, a colorful squirrel, which sniffs the air in the direction of the nut supply. Its soft bark is protected by green and blue grass-like hairs, which become even more dense at the length of its bushy tail. Arty stalks the devious creature. That squirrel does not belong here…It will eat the nuts they farmed every chance it gets, and it must be chased off. He growls at the beast for a moment, then sprints at it, barking with all the fury that a twelve-inch-tall dog can muster.

The squirrel is horrified. It moves like lightning into the tree line, and Arty holds just past the boundary of their supply. Having done his duty, for now, he can resume his rounds here, but the price of keeping the nuts safe is constant vigilance. For a moment, though, his ears perk up with curiosity. Noises in the distance?

He leaves the nut supply behind and runs past the front gate of the farm. Looking eastward on the main road, in the direction of the Closed Forest, there are men on horseback approaching. Seeing this, Arty barks out toward the rear yard of the home. Working to alert the family, he has something of an alarming tone in his bark.

Fortia and Costans take an interest in Arty's alert. They make their way over to the front gate and give a questioning gaze at the little pup. Arty continues barking, spinning around with concern and excitement.

"What's happening, boy?" Fortia asks as she tries to settle him with a touch.

Constans glances at the approaching horsemen, and a look of concern immediately builds on his face.

"Fortia," he has a stern tone, "run and get your mother's attention."

"Papa…?" She is confused. "What's wrong?"

"Hurry, child! Go now!" He moves back into the sideyard as Fortia runs to the house. Constans is moving fast toward a shed nearby their nut supply. Swinging the doors open, he quickly steps inside.

In the house, Sedo is sitting comfortably in the living room, knitting a new winter hat for Fortia. She has outgrown the last one and based on how early the leaves changed color this year, the coming winter will likely be a snowy one. A window nearby gives her just enough light to do her work, and she softly hums her favorite tune as the needles cross over.

Fortia bursts in and runs over to her mother, who is surprised to see her in such a state.

"Mama, come see! Papa told me to get you!"

Sedo drops her project and stands quickly, moves to the side door, which is still half open. Growing more concerned, both of them gaze out the door and see Constans emerge from the shed. He has two battle axes now, one in each hand, and he moves with a significant intensity.

Fortia cannot believe her eyes…She has scarcely ever touched a battle ax, let alone seen her father wielding two of them with an obvious fury.

Sedo quickly shuts the door. Confused, though, Fortia protests.

"Wait! What about Papa!?"

"Listen to my instructions," Sedo insists and grabs her daughter's shoulders to hold her attention. Fear grows in Fortia, and her heart beats heavier. She breathes deeper now, but Sedo's calm demeanor helps to restrain her.

"Go to your room, Fortia. Behind your bed is a doorway."

"A doorway? What? There's no doorway—"

"Fortia, please listen! This leads to a ladder. Climb it into the attic."

She appears to understand, but she can hear Arty barking at the door. Opening it for a moment, he rushes in. Fortia is surprised, though, to see six soldiers clad in black leather armor, each in the process of dismounting their horses at the gate. They do not seem very happy as they draw axes, swords, and shields. Constans approaches them, and he is more imposing now than Fortia has ever witnessed. Taking a defensive posture against these men, Constans—

Sedo slams the door shut. "Pay attention!"

Fortia locks eyes with her mother.

"If something happens to your father and I, go to the north-west corner of the attic. Beneath a hatch in the floor is a wood box wrapped in leather. Take that package and go to Tiler's inn—"

"No, Mama! I don't want to leave!"

"Child, you must be brave now." Sedo nearly forms a tear in her eyes. "When you get there, tell Tiler what happened."

Hugging her daughter tight, they can hear Constans's voice becoming more aggressive.

"You have no business here at my home!"

This is answered by another man's voice, equally angry and commanding.

"You are now under arrest! Must we take you by force?!"

Sedo releases Fortia and gives her a smile of concern.

"I love you, my darling. Please go. Now!"

Fortia and Arty dash off toward the stairs. As they approach the first riser, she turns and looks back to the kitchen. Sedo has opened a makeshift hatch under a window near the kitchen door. She pulls from this an impressive metal shield and yet another battle ax. Fortia can barely believe what she is seeing…Her mother straps the shield to her arm quickly, then turns, sees Fortia is still there.

"Go, child!" Sedo commands, then swings open the kitchen door and boldly moves into the backyard.

There is an intensity here that Fortia has never before witnessed in her mother. She has trouble turning away, but Arty barks at her. Fortia snaps out of it and runs up the stairs.

In the second-floor hall, Fortia runs to the end window that faces the sideyard. She can see her father and mother bravely facing down six men who make motions to reposition themselves. They attempt to flank the husband and wife.

Arty barks out, and Fortia remembers there is a task at hand. She sprints through her bedroom door.

Grabbing the right foot of her bed, she pulls with all her might. The bed is dense and heavy. It is made of timber and meant to last forever. She pulls again, nearly slips and falls, but she is able to make a good wedge of space behind the headboard. Sliding herself into this area, she glances around for the secret door. What door…? There's nothing but wood-paneled wall here.

In the distance, she hears the sound of a weapon hitting a shield. The noise of combat ensues, and more weapon strikes quickly follow. A man screams, and a feeling of frustrated panic surges into her.

"Where is the door, Arty?! I don't see a door!"

Arty sniffs around. He spots something. A small space at the bottom of the wall where the wood paneling fails to meet the slats of the floor. Propping himself up with his front legs on the wall, he pushes against it. The wall moves, scraping the floor as it turns inward just a fraction of an inch.

Fortia is stunned, but seeing this, she realizes…She pushes her shoulder into the wall, and it shifts further inward. A section of the wood paneling turns on a hinge at the left, and she pushes harder, harder still. The door opens just enough to fit a person through.

Cautiously, she and Arty slink themselves through the gap into a tight space behind the false wall. It is perhaps four feet wide and three feet deep. There is only darkness above her. The framing of the wall is exposed here, and the wall opposite this doorway is horizontally studded with parallel slats. It forms a makeshift ladder.

Fortia looks up into the space above, though there is only darkness overhead. Feeling uncertain about this, she gathers her confidence. She grabs Arty and rests him on her shoulder, then carefully ascends the ladder.

From a well in the attic deck, Fortia peeks her head up into the attic space. It is very dark and appears completely empty. There is only minimal light available from the gable windows on each end. Seeing these openings, Fortia hurriedly places Arty on the floor and pulls herself fully up the ladder. The roof framing is not far off the ground, and even Fortia needs to crouch when walking under the collar ties.

She moves as fast as she can to the gable window that faces the sideyard, but her panic soon grows into frustration. The slats of the window point downward into the room. They do not reveal much at the ground level.

Hearing the noises of combat outside, she becomes more and more upset that she has no line of sight to her parents. In a moment of anger she grabs the slats in the window and quickly realizes that they articulate. Turning them upward, the sideyard below becomes visible, but a look of fear quickly gathers on her face.

Her parents are in the thick of a fight. Two of the soldiers are laid out on the ground and appear lifeless. One more appears injured and struggles to get back to his feet. Constans is hurt. His left arm dangles now, and he has lost grip on an ax. Sedo covers his weak side with her shield, though.

Another soldier lunges at Sedo with a swing of the ax. His weapon clangs off her shield as she parries his attack, then responds with a strong blow to his weapon arm. Constans jumps from behind her with his ax and finishes that soldier.

Suddenly, a larger soldier tackles them both. His body weight thuds into them, knocking everyone to the ground as they fall out of sight.

Fortia shrieks in terror. Two more soldiers step quickly in that same direction. Tears build up in her eyes as the sound of screaming is heard below. Trying not to sob, she takes a few deep breaths and recovers from this, but she is not sure what to do next.

Arty approaches her, licks her, and nudges her leg. She pets the little pup, comforts herself as her mind fills up with concern. Feeling powerless for a moment, it is difficult to remember why she is even here in this attic, but Arty is quick to remind her.

He sniffs around at a rope attached to a ringlet in the floor, not far from the window. Biting on the rope, he tries his best to pull it, but the hatch is simply too heavy for him.

Fortia grabs the rope and pulls hard. Her hands are shaking, and she struggles to grip it, but soon the hatch swings upward. She overcomes the weight, and it swings backward. It slams hard onto the attic deck.

Dust kicks up all around and obscures everything. As the air begins to clear, Fortia is amazed to see the leather bag her mother spoke of. It is roughly two feet wide, two feet long, and one foot deep. It is very dusty, though, which obscures much of the brown leather wrapping.

She grabs for the straps of the bag but soon realizes that it is relatively heavy for her. Summoning the strength, she gives a strong tug. The heavy parcel slides up the side of the storage pit until it clears the opening. Fumbling with the weight of this object, Fortia loses control of it, and it tumbles hard onto the attic deck.

Two buckles secure the leather over the contents of the package. She unhooks them and pulls back the cover to reveal a rectangular wooden object. The details of it are hard to visualize in the dark, but it does appear very ornate. Squinting in the darkness, she scans the sides of this object. It does not present a keyhole or hinges even.

"Arty, we need to get this to the inn that Papa took me to last night." The pup makes no arguments, and Fortia wraps the chest back up. She drags it back toward the opening where they entered and is about to drop it down, but she stops, a look of concern grows. Arty is sniffing. He can sense something. Fortia leans forward and sniffs as well.

"Smoke?" she says to the worried little dog. They listen close. There are noises below of soldiers in the house, and the crackling sound of wood burning begins to gather from the distance.

Fortia studies the attic for a path to escape, but she cringes at the lack of good options here. Moving back to the gable window, she watches for any motion. Smoke is already rising from the windows of the first floor.

Two soldiers emerge from the kitchen door. The larger man drags Sedo over to the horses. He lifts her up without a struggle and swings her over the back of a horse. Fortia can see her brown sap bleeding from injuries in her arm and trunk. While Sedo appears to be alive and stirring, Fortia cannot help but feel frightened. Tears well up in her eyes at the sight of her injured mother being hauled off like this.

The horses are moving away, and she sees that Constans is tied to the back of another horse. His body is limp and motionless. All the remaining soldiers are leaving, and Fortia counts six. Three still lifeless on the ground. The others, one at a time, pass through the gate on horseback.

Feeling crushed, it is hard for her to overcome seeing this. Even when playing out in the forest, she has never truly been without the comfort and supervision of her parents. In the distance, though, she can hear the sound of the fire consuming more of her home. A window somewhere shatters under the heat, and Fortia snaps back to the urgency of the moment.

Moving back to the ladder, she can see smoke gathering at the base of the attic well. Arty paces nearby her and appears nervous himself.

"We need to get out, Arty." Fortia tries to devise a plan, though Arty cannot help but look at her with concern.

Running over to the gable window again, she kicks at it, but it is too well-built for her to break open. She and the dog are small enough to fit through the window if she could just get the slats cleared. Not far from her on the floor is the chest, and she grabs the cumbersome mass of it. Lifting with all her might, she can barely get it to shoulder level. She slams it against the gable window. Not hard enough, and it is too heavy for her to control. Dropping it, it crashes hard onto the floor.

The smoke is now breaching the top of the attic well, and Arty growls at it with concern. Fortia grabs the chest again and drags it. Stopping adjacent to the well space she steps to the back side of the chest and shoves. It falls into the well space for a moment, only to slam hard onto the floor below.

"Come on, Arty!" She grabs him, props the pooch onto her shoulder, and starts to climb down. Coughing, she descends into the obscurity of the smoke.

It's hard to see anything as they move lower and lower. Even the opening where the smoke emerges is difficult to discern. As she reaches the bottom of the ladder, Arty jumps off her shoulders and runs through the opening.

"Arty, wait!" She reaches for him in fear, but he escapes. Gripping the leather around the chest, she shoves it hard. It is a struggle to breathe, and her lungs burn with every deep inhalation. She maneuvers the chest through the opening into the bedroom before crawling through herself.

Fire is flickering somewhere nearby. Fortia stays low to the floor, but even through the smoke, she can see that the adjacent hallway is already ablaze.

Arty has crawled under the bed. Trembling, he has done well to find a safe spot where it is less smokey. Fortia coughs again, and she can barely see, but she knows where her bedroom windows are. Lifting the chest with all her might, she maneuvers it toward the faintly visible light of the window opposite her bed. With a powerful shove, it crashes through the glass. Smoke immediately escapes through the window as she releases the chest. A thud can be heard in the distance, but she can't see anything as the smoke billows all around.

"Arty! Hurry!" It is difficult to take even small breaths now, but the adrenaline in her sap is keeping her going. The little dog hesitates but soon runs to her. She grabs him and props him on her shoulder. Fortia climbs through the window as swiftly as she can. Now standing on the windowsill, her body is supported by the scarce grip of her fingertips around the wood siding of the home. She can breathe a little better here, but she is not safe for very long.

Fortia looks to her left where only a few feet away is the window of the stairway landing. It suddenly bursts open from the heat behind it. Arty's eyes are pinched shut in terror, and he clamps his legs onto Fortia's shoulder. Now struggling to maintain her grip on the side of the building, she begins to realize she is trapped. With her right hand, she grabs Arty and clutches him to her chest. Embracing the inevitable, she jumps backward.

She is in freefall for a moment, but soon, her body thuds onto the compacted dirt. A sudden crack of pain sears through her left arm. Fortia screams, realizing now that her arm hit hard on the edge of the wood chest next to her. Laying on the ground for a moment, the pain is overwhelming. Even reaching with her opposite arm causes her to cringe.

Arty stumbles up to his paws. He is shaken but still in one piece. Fortia has yet to make another movement, though, and the house is burning beside her. Arty steps up to her, licks her face, and whines with a pleading noise. Fortia is happy to see he is safe, but any movement hurts right now.

He bites onto her shirt and tries pulling her. She moans, turns toward her broken arm, and groans with pain until she clutches it to her chest. Pushing through is a struggle, but she eventually gets to her feet. Biting onto the leather casing around the chest, Arty tries to drag it, but it is too heavy for him. Now on her feet, Fortia groans with every movement. Taking the strap with her good arm, she drags the box away from the house as best she can.

Horses and farm animals are snorting and squealing in the distance. There is a fire on the left side of the barn, and the animals are restless.

Fortia pulls with all her might, slowly drags the box as she approaches the stables. Smoke rises from the front slats now, and soon enough, a blazing fire develops. Animals inside are bellowing and ramming into the walls around them. The barn door cracks open and a horse bursts out, kicking and swinging itself everywhere as the terror overtakes it.

Arty rushes up to it and barks as loud as he can. The horse rears up at him, and the little dog dodges away as the hooves land hard on the dirt. The animal has stopped, but it is still eager to turn away from the fires all around it.

Fortia grabs hold of the reins. She looks the horse in the eyes and sternly holds it for a moment, demanding its attention. As swiftly as she can, she lashes the reins to the leather straps around the chest and guides the horse toward the main road, letting it pull the chest for her.

They move away from the burning stables, but the house nearby is fully engulfed in flames. The horse rears up again and swings the heavy chest forward. It strikes Fortia on the leg and knocks her to the ground. She screams out as her injured arm strikes the dirt.

The horse takes off. Runs toward the front gate and drags the chest along with it. Arty gives chase as the frightened animal charges down the road.

Fortia clutches her injured arm to her chest as she struggles up to her feet. Tired and battered, she moves as best she can toward the road. Arty and the horse are moving too fast, though, and she just can't keep up. Turning the corner through the front gate and onto the road, she watches them sprint off into the distance. An awful feeling of defeat grows in her, and she falls to her knees. Tears well up as she watches the fire rage through her home.

Never in any version of a nightmare could she imagine that this would happen. Her parents taken. Her home in flames. Injured and alone. She kneels there, emotionally and physically exhausted. All she can do is watch as the fire consumes everything that she once knew.

In the distance, a voice. "Fortia!" The noise of the burning building is too loud. "Fortia!" Down the road, she sees a man on horseback who rushes toward her. Who is this?

Frightened, she steps up to her feet then scurries off the road into the brush and trees nearby. Not far into the woods, she finds a small felled tree. A good hiding spot, and she can hear the horse and rider settle to a stop on the road.

"Fortia!" the man yells. "Come out, child! It's Tiler!"

She pokes her head up from behind the tree. Seeing her there, he dismounts and rushes to her. He grasps her with both arms and holds her as she cries and screams into his chest. Unloading the fear and frustration of this event, she just can't hold it in anymore. He hugs her tight, but she yelps out in pain.

Surprised, Tiler pushes her away just enough to inspect her. He now realizes she is injured and gives a deep sigh, glad to see it is only an injured arm.

"Come, child." Tiler lifts and carries her. "There will be time for pain later."

Chapter 4

DAYLIGHT IS SWEEPING through the tavern windows and into the quiet bar space within. Fortia and Arty are sitting at a table with four of the people she saw here last night: Laderas, Matthius, Tiler, and Harris. Her arm has been bandaged up, and she moves with comfort now as she sips a cup of tea.

The gilded and ornate chest that she retrieved from the attic sits in the center of the table, with a few builder's tools not far from it. A warped pry bar and a broken hammer rest on the table nearby. Everyone stares at the box with a sense of amazement.

"Unbelievable…" Matthius is in shock. "Not even a hammer and pry bar could get it open. It must be solid metal on the inside."

"Constans has the key." Harris is certain of it.

"Constans is under arrest," Laderas responds with a harsh and frustrated tone. "Where do you even put a key? There is no keyhole."

"Constans knows!" Harris nearly snaps at him. "Guarding this was his task. Without him, we may never figure it out."

"Everyone, quiet, please." Matthius is studying the form of this box, trying to stay focused on the puzzle it represents. "We will get nowhere with this bickering."

Returning to a quiet sense of amazement, they are each stuck on finding the solution, and it is clearly more of a challenge than they expected. Fortia and Arty are with them in that purpose. The pup is intent on sorting it out. His eyes inspect from one side of the box to the other as he works to put it all together.

The design of it is interesting. The lid shows the same emblem of the oak tree nut that was carved into Fortia's headboard. A single eye within it and rays of sunlight extending from there. The two shorter sides of the box have three obvious vertical boards within the pattern, which are framed by two horizontal boards at the top and bottom. These are all relatively seamless in their construction and were it not for the obvious transition of the wood pattern within these boards, one might think they were all one piece of wood.

The front and back sides are more ornate, though. Their design is complex, with wood slats traversing those surfaces in all directions. Notably, there are four vertical slats on the front and three vertical slats on the back, though each of them is unique. They extend part way across the surface and each of these terminate at a small carving dug into the surface. Those carvings are different from each other, and the mystery of what purpose they serve is yet another perplexing question for everyone involved here.

"This is pointless." Laderas sighs, his growing frustration is obvious as he sneers at this object. "Without Constans, this box is worthless to us."

"We can always help him out of the prison…" Harris says, a devious look in her eye.

"Absolutely not!" Laderas barks at her. "That might land us all in a cell nearby him!"

"Would be a homecoming for me…" Harris chuckles, then smirks at Tiler, who smiles at this lighthearted moment of recollection.

Fortia has not given up her study of the object. The back side of the box is facing her, and a carving at the far-left end rests near the termination of a wood slat. It appears to have the same shape as the oak tree nut on the lid. Suddenly, her eyes open with a revelation.

On the counter not far from them is a large jar full of nuts with a handful of wooden bowls stacked up beside it. She jumps up from the table and interrupts everyone. Pulling the large jar of nuts down, she struggles to unscrew the lid with one injured arm.

"If you are hungry let me help you," Tiler says, as he diligently stands to assist.

Fortia has gotten the lid open. She pours out a handful of nuts on the counter and searches through them rapidly. She finds it: an acorn, the nut of an oak tree. She grabs it and hurriedly walks back to the table, where everyone else appears confused by her actions.

Returning to the backside of the box, she positions the oak nut nearby the carving with the top of the nut turned appropriately. She compares the two, and they appear to be a good match. Placing it inside the carving, the box makes a subtle mechanical noise that is just loud enough for everyone at the table to hear it.

"In the name of Serenus…?" Matthius says. Soon, a look of surprise builds on everyone's faces. They can barely believe that this simple action produced a result in this device.

"How many of these carvings are there on the front and back sides?" Fortia asks as she points to where she has just positioned the nut. They all study it for a moment.

"Seven." Matthius now has a revelation of his own. "One for each of the Great Kingdoms!" A bright smile develops on Fortia's face as Matthius begins to search through the small pile of nuts she had dumped out.

Tiler excitedly jumps to his feet, grabs the jar of nuts and pours them out all across the tabletop. Everyone sorts through them with enthusiasm. They isolate different types of nuts from the mixture, making sure to compare them to each carving for size and fit.

"There, we have it." Matthius pushes six different nuts into a smaller pile.

Slowly, he places a macadamia nut in the appropriate spot, and the box makes a subtle mechanical noise. A chestnut nut then in the appropriate place, and another subtle noise is heard. A colocynth and pignoli in the carvings for these, and more subtle noises are heard. Finally, the cashew and the pecan. As Matthius places these in the final carvings, a subtle noise is heard. It is quickly followed by a series of other mechanical noises.

Each of these seven nuts drops out of their respective carvings. They land on the table's surface and roll a short distance to a stop.

"God in the trees…" Harris says with a chuckle. "This box is tormenting us."

Tiler and Matthius chuckle as well, though Laderas does not appear to be having fun.

"Gentlemen. Lady. We are all fools…" Laderas says with a stern glare, but he soon gives a smirk. They all laugh for a moment and the mood in the room has lightened up some. Ultimately, everyone is still stumped, though. Quietly, everyone ponders what the next step could be.

"I HAVE IT!" Tiler yells. "It's like a strong box. We just need the correct sequence to place the nuts in."

Harris nods her head and smiles bright. She glances at Fortia with an inquisitive look before she begins an explanation.

"Have you learned the history of the five Surviving Kingdoms, Fortia?"

"My father taught me once." Fortia searches her mind. "I can't recall all of it, though."

Harris starts the story and smiles as she engages Fortia's interest.

"In the beginning, all of Oakenmeer was one great kingdom." She gestures the number one with her finger to drive home the point. "The Kingdom of Oak once spanned every stretch of land we now know of." Harris picks up the acorn, places it in the correct carving, and the box makes a subtle noise. "King Otenamann of Oak had twin sons, the Sons of Oak, named Sandia and Markus. Upon his death, the Kingdom was split into Oak and Chestnut. The second of these was named for the Great Chestnut Grove, which is just south of the old eastern border between Oak and Chestnut."

She then reaches for a chestnut, not far from the edge of the table. After manipulating it into the carving that fits this, the box makes another subtle mechanical noise.

Matthius now reaches for another nut, a pignoli. He holds it up for her to see before continuing the story.

"After many years, unrest began to develop within Chestnut, and two factions formed in their army. As a sign of goodwill, King Markus allowed the Kingdom of Pignoli to form, seceding an unpopulated portion of Oak to those people who wanted their own ruler. In doing so he had hoped to gain a strong ally for any future conflict with Chestnut."

He places the pignoli nut in its appropriate place. The chest makes a characteristic noise.

Laderas then reaches for another nut, this time a Macadamia.

"As in all kingdoms," Laderas becomes sincere again, "it is only a matter of time before peace becomes war. Markus of Oak was growing old, and some say he had lost his senses. He waged a great war with his brother that lasted many, many years."

He places the macadamia nut on the space for it, and the mechanism of the chest can be heard moving appropriately. Laderas continues describing the history.

"He had won the war finally and had killed his only brother in the process, but his success came at too great a cost. He did not have enough of a following at that time to maintain such a large kingdom. Oak and Chestnut both were dissolved."

Tiler points to the pignoli nut, which is already on the box, and continues the story.

"Pignoli sustained itself with neutrality, but out of Oak and Chestnut, three other kingdoms were formed. The largest of these was the first to crown their own king. That was Macadamia." He then reaches for a colocynth nut, though. "The second was Colocynth." He places that nut on the chest, and the expected mechanical noise is heard. Then he reaches for a pecan. "The third was Pecan." Again, he places that nut on the carving for it.

Fortia reaches for the last nut, the cashew.

"I remember what my father told me now." She grows excited for a moment, but the thought of her injured parents pushes itself into her mind. Her enjoyment here is swiftly blunted, and a frown gathers on her face.

"The Kingdom of Cashew was formed on the inner coastline by merchants, who had acquired enough wealth and land to demand their own territory. Eventually, they crowned their own king."

She turns the cashew so that it can be aligned properly with the space carved for it, then gently pushes the nut into its spot. On doing this, a rapid mechanical noise is heard, growing louder still as the mechanisms within the chest fulfill their purpose.

At last, the noises stop, and there is silence. The lid has not popped open, though, and everyone waits with bated breath to see what the device will do.

The machine clicks. It seems to have made its last noise, though it does not appear to have moved or done anything more to indicate it is open now.

"Well, this is depressing." Harris frowns at it.

Everyone sits back, again at a loss for words. A moment passes, but the nuts have not popped out of their positions on the chest.

Laderas reaches for it. With cautious effort, he lifts the box and inspects the base of this enigmatic device. As he does this, a smooth metallic bar slides out of the right edge of its base. Dropping on the table with a dense thud, it is clearly much heavier than it would appear.

Fortia retrieves it, and on inspection, it has seven holes in it. The tip of this bar is cut and smoothed at an angle, and when in place, it would appear to be an oval-shaped wooden peg. It now becomes clear that this was one of the components of the locking mechanism within.

Tiler carefully reaches for another oval-shaped insert at the left base, and after touching it ever so lightly, it slides out. Suddenly the entire bottom of the chest appears to come loose. Tiler is lucky to have even caught it.

Laderas helps him lay the entire box on the surface of the table and then slowly lifts the top portion of it again. The bottom of the chest remains on the table, but the entirety of the sides and top slide upward and off.

There is a much smaller and more mundane-looking box resting within it, but this is much less robust in its composition. The walls of the exterior strongbox are very thick on all sides, and clearly, they are made to house the complex mechanism that secures this device. These metal bars are the components that somehow hold the bottom of the device to the sides.

Matthius carefully lifts the lid of the smaller chest. Inside is a blanket that appears to be swaddled around multiple other objects. Unwrapping the blanket then reveals the contents it has kept safe for many years, and Fortia cannot help but be enamored with this moment. Her once sullen mood falls into the background as a host of unique objects are revealed.

Among these is a folded parchment. When opened it reveals itself to be a map. While crudely drawn, it has more than enough detail to show the five Surviving Kingdoms, with numerous geological features represented. Bodies of water, mountains, and valleys are all depicted with pathways to circumvent them. Each pathway begins from the Great Wall of Macadamia, and whichever pathway is followed, it all leads to the same location.

"Kingdom of Roots."

"Interesting…" Matthius studies it. "This is clearly a map intended for one purpose."

"What is the Kingdom of Roots?" Laderas appears confused. "An eighth kingdom is not mentioned in any history book I've ever read."

Silence. They search their minds for an answer, but nothing is revealed.

Next among the items hidden inside is a dagger in its sheath. Very beautiful and ornate, the steel blade has a unique darkness to it that sparks the interest of everyone who sees it.

"That is old Oaken Steel." Harris knows it immediately. "They have not used that for many generations, not since the forges of the Kingdom of Oak were disassembled."

Fortia curiously reaches for a pouch that contains two small gold bars as well as a flexible but metallic-looking glove. It is large enough to fit over a man's hand but has a construction that is very curious. Tiler notices something about it.

"May I, Fortia?" She hands it to him and the movement of it reveals a sound of fluid inside the glove, which piques everyone's interest. Tiler slips it on his hand, though when removed, his hand is dry. The fluid must be enclosed somewhere within the glove's construction. He slips his hand into it again.

"Very cool inside." Tiler is puzzled by it. "Seems like a special glove meant for an iron smith, but it fits me well indeed." He hands it back to Fortia, who tries it on herself.

"It is comfortable." She flexes and extends her fingers to show that it fits well.

"How can that be?" Laderas says, studying the glove with an inquisitive look. Being the largest person at the table, he has a much bigger hand than Fortia, and he is shocked to realize that the glove fits him very well. It becomes clear that the glove is somehow made to comfortably fit whoever happens to be wearing it.

Fortia reaches for another item. It is a small glass vessel resting inside a shallow bowl made of translucent white rock. The bowl is slightly larger than the glass vessel, and the surface of it appears to have the same curvature as its companion. The vial is elliptical in shape and roughly the size of her index finger. There is a viscous and slow-moving fluid inside it, but no obvious opening is present to pour this out.

She is curious about them, but not knowing their purpose, she rests them on the table. A moment passes before she realizes that the vial is moving. The fluid inside it shifts to one end, and soon, the entire vial slowly turns itself until stopping to rest. This appears to be some form of a makeshift compass.

"That is not north," Harris says as she looks at the curious device. "In fact, it appears to be pointing south."

Last but not least, Laderas reaches for the blanket. When unfurled, it is large, light, and thin. It could easily cover an entire adult. Laderas and Harris study the gentle-appearing fabric. Harris takes a knife from her side sheath, pokes the blanket with it. It does not pierce through. Even after applying good pressure, Harris is surprised that the blanket refuses to be cut.

Matthius considers all that has been found here. After a moment of thought, he stands and waits for everyone to bring their attention to him.

"Our task seems clear. As you are aware, Constans held the role of the Tracker in our Order. We must use these items to find the Golden Nugget."

An inquisitive look crosses Fortia's face, and Matthius takes a moment to explain.

"In our Order, your father is a knight. His role is the Tracker, the person who journeys to find and deliver the Golden Nugget when a royal would take the throne in any of the five Surviving Kingdoms."

She seems to understand, though she is still somewhat amazed by all this. Learning that her otherwise humble father is a knight of a secret order was something hard to capture in her mind. It is very uncharacteristic of the quiet and boring man she grew to know, let alone her loving and kind mother who had turned into a warrior before her very eyes. Matthius continues to explain, though.

"Do you recall a few years ago, your father went on a trip for a number of days? He told you that he went to make a delivery of oils in another kingdom?"

"I do remember that…" She searches her memory. "He came back injured but did not say much about why he had been hurt."

"He was delivering the Golden Nugget to the Kingdom of Cashew for the coronation of Queen Cassius but was attacked by a group of highwaymen on the way home."

"Fortia," Tiler clarifies, "we are going on a quest to claim the Golden Nugget and bring it back to Macadamia. We must prove that King Serenus has been killed by his son."

Fortia shakes her head and grows unsettled in her seat. "What about my parents? They are in the prison. Surely, we can get them out, and they can help us."

"At this time, that is impossible." Laderas shakes his head to emphasize. "Finding the Golden Nugget will result in setting them free as well. That must be our focus right now."

"No—" Fortia stammers a moment. "My father and mother can help us! He knows what all these things in the box are for! We need to set them free first!"

"We cannot do it, Fortia," Tiler insists. "Laderas is right. If we get captured, it ruins any chance of us finding the Golden Nugget."

She shakes her head again, standing quickly to confront them all. "We can't leave them there! Who knows what Tonitro will do to them!"

"Fortia, please consider—"

"No! I'm going to get them out! If you won't help me, then I'll sneak in and do it myself. I'm good at being sneaky." She walks off toward the door, but Harris interrupts.

"Fortia. Please wait. Wouldn't your father and mother want you to stay safe with us?"

Considering this suggestion, Fortia is almost convinced, but with a look of disregard, she continues toward the door. Now almost running, she moves out the side door to the front of the tavern, not even waiting for Arty.

She moves fast over to her horse and, with determination, quickly takes the lashing from the post. Gripping the saddle horn with her good arm she makes one swift motion, jumps on the seat, and kicks the animal into a gallop. She rides away with a look of insistence.

Arty barks as he runs out of the tavern, looking worried. His chunky legs are not fast enough, though, and Fortia rides off with disregard.

Harris follows him out and watches as the pup slows his pursuit, howling with concern. Herself feeling worried, she walks over to him and kneels as she offers a few pats of comfort to his frowning little head.

"Don't worry, boy. She'll come back once she cools off."

They watch as the strong-willed child charges off into the distance.

~ ~ ~

Fortia grips the reins with sincerity as the horse moves at a gallop through the dusty road of the Open Forest. Without question this is the best path she can imagine. Her parents are an integral part of success in this plan, and they cannot be disregarded.

Seeing that the Great Walls of Macadamia are not far ahead, she slows the pace of the animal until it comes to a stop. She dismounts and cautiously guides the horse into the thick woods nearby.

Not far from the road rests a small pond in an adjacent clearing with some appreciable trees and foliage nearby. Fortia searches the area and finds an appropriate branch. She lashes the horse to it not far from the water.

"Just stay here, and I'll come back with Mama and Papa. Everything will be okay again." She has convinced herself it is true, and she pets the animal. A reassurance, perhaps for herself instead of the horse. Quickly, she moves through the dense shrubbery parallel to the road and toward the enormous walls. The tunnel entry she went through the night before is not far ahead.

A line of three people is waiting at the entry, some with large satchels on their backs, one with a carriage full of items. A guard clad in dark green leather armor works to inspect each person's cargo, which delays the whole process of entering.

At the head of the line, a merchant carries a large satchel, and he appears very impatient. The guard is busy carrying out his tiresome task of inspecting the parcels. Finally, the merchant becomes frustrated enough to speak up.

"What is this all about? We've never had our goods inspected like this before. The market is already open!"

"Calm down, citizen," the guard says. "A new order from King Tonitro. All parcels need to be inspected.

Only merchants or citizens bearing coin for purchase are allowed entry today."

A look of concern comes over Fortia's face. She turns out her pockets but doesn't even have a single coin on her.

"If you must." The frustrated merchant gives in. "This is unprecedented. We've been selling here for years, and never once have we been treated like this."

"Go on," the guard says as he completes the search. "Next in line!"

Fortia watches as the line moves ahead. Not far from her is the relatively large cart with a tarp over the goods inside. The driver is a rugged appearing man who sits on the front seat of the cart with his back to Fortia. He whips the reins slightly, and the horse yanks the cart forward.

Moving swiftly from the tree line to the rear of this cart, she squats behind it but peeks around to the front so she can watch what is happening.

A farmer ahead of them is having his bag searched, and he can barely sit still any longer. "Is this really necessary?" A scowl of frustration grows on his face.

"Just a quick search," the guard says. "King Tonitro is only trying to keep you safe."

"Safe from what?" the farmer protests. "Macadamia is the most peaceful kingdom in the whole land. What is he worried about?"

"Move along," the guard says as he dismisses another complaint.

The farmer grumbles and makes his way toward the tunnel entry. The cart in front of Fortia shuffles forward as the guard approaches it.

"You there, what are you carrying?" the guard demands.

"Building materials for the shop on Bundleman Row."

The guard walks around toward the back of the cart, ready to begin his inspection. He approaches the rear corner, just inches now from where Fortia is hiding. As he turns the corner, though, there is no one there. Fortia has seemingly disappeared under the tarp.

The guard grabs hold of the back of the tarp, but the merchant interrupts.

"I have a number of trips to make with materials. Can we forego this next time?"

"King's orders." He rolls his eyes, tired of repeating this over and over. Grabbing tight on the tarp, he swiftly flips it upward. Decorative wood columns are stacked neatly in the bed of the cart beside metallic fittings, all of which are bundled together near the back. Fortia must have moved as she is nowhere to be seen.

"All right. Move along," the guard says.

The cart scurries forward into the tunnel, and as it does, it carries Fortia who clings to the side wall of it. Her one good arm holds her horizontally in place with one foot hooked over the rim of the cart's bed. Like a true climber, she found the best foothold she could. She holds tight as the cart rumbles onward.

When it emerges into the light of the Closed Forest, Fortia is no longer attached to its side. It rumbles off into the distance of the adjacent road, and she casually walks out of the tunnel as if nothing had happened. She scans the area, now not sure which direction to go in, but she remembers where the main stage is and darts off in that direction.

As she turns the corner around a building, the market is laid out before her. There are hundreds of merchants set up today, all with tables and blankets and other displays arranged for the crowd of people meandering around. Had she not recently visited the crowded city yesterday this may all feel overwhelming for her, but she is determined now.

Moving through the crowd, her small body weaves between scattered clusters of people. Searching the area, she quickly finds a guard standing nearby and moves to him.

"Sir, please help! A man stole jewelry from our table." She puts on her best sad face.

"What's this? Where!?" The guard is suddenly feeling vindictive.

"In the distance there," she points, "but the other guards took him already. They forgot to give us back the necklace. Please sir. Will they have it at the prison?" giving her best puppy dog eyes.

"The prison is not far that way, child." He points to the street off the far end of the main stage. "Go see if they have it there. I need to stand my post."

"Thank you kindly, sir." She ducks away in that direction. Moving swiftly down the street, she is soon able to see the prison at the end of a diverging road.

It's a foreboding building, half a block wide and maybe three or four levels high. It is hard to gauge the height as there are no windows. The external surface of the walls is made of large square metal plates anchored to a stone substructure. At the street-facing façade is a tall, pointed arch around an armored timber doorway. The bars of this doorway form an array of spikes, much like the interior of an iron maiden. Directly in front of the archway is a stone stage area, only a few steps higher than street level. Upon this rests an empty pillory made of heavy timbers. Unquestionably the place where many criminals have suffered.

She sneaks around the side of the building into an alleyway and looks for another entry point. Not too far along the side wall, there are two large carriage doors, clearly meant for the prison carriage to pass through and circle back into the alley. These doors are open, as if expecting something, and the two guards standing nearby are casually talking amongst themselves.

Fortia hides behind a pile of wood halfway down the alley. Some of the guard's horses are lashed to the wall not far from her, and there are bales of hay here for them to feed on. She isn't quite sure what the next step is to get inside, but she's determined. She has a thought…The guards appear distracted by their own conversation.

"The new king is surely not taking any chances. Been very busy here."

"Too busy," the other guard agrees, "and there's talk of Pignoli wanting to attack!"

His partner is genuinely shocked by this. "I walked our walls for years and never once had a reason to fear our neighbors until now." Both the guards appear to be in agreement that things are changing in Macadamia, and the change is not for the best.

Suddenly, two horses rear up. The animals run down the alleyway at a gallop.

"Kingdoms be!" A shocked guard runs toward them. "I thought you lashed them!"

The other guard joins him in the chase. They run ahead and Fortia sneaks into the carriage port amidst the commotion.

Inside here, it is darker and easier to hide within bundles of hay and other equipment. A side door is not far away, though it is shut. She tests the handle, locked. The two guards are still busy trying to deal with the large wooden beasts, so she knocks hard on the door, then swiftly hides again behind a hay bail.

A moment later, she hears the latches turning, and the door shifts open. Another guard steps out to see the commotion.

"What's going on there!?" He makes his way over to assist his companions.

Fortia sneaks behind him as he goes, then ducks into the adjacent room. It's a small and rather unwelcoming space. Lit only by minimal sunlight from the doorway and a few candelabras on the wall, there is scarcely enough light to work here. Even with the door open, it is rather hard to see. A desk on the opposite side of the room has a closed ledger on it with an ink well and some scattered papers. This appears to be the processing desk, and it is positioned near a metal gate that leads to a hallway. On the adjacent wall is an array of iron prison shackles, all dangling from hooks, but nearby them is a key panel. This small panel is set into the wall with its own gate covering it, keeping the keys safe from prying hands. The metallic rungs of this gate are spaced closely enough that a man would struggle to fit his hand in to reach the keys, but perhaps a child could…

Feeling a sense of panic, Fortia quickly inspects this closer. The key hooks are numbered for every cell, but three of these keys are not labeled at all. In the distance, she can hear a guard.

"Grab her already! Hurry! A prisoner is coming in soon."

Fortia knows she doesn't have much time. She opens the ledger and turns to the last written page. There are only prisoner numbers adjacent to the cell numbers they are secured in. Not knowing which number her father and mother are, she assumes they would be the last two.

"184 and 185," she whispers to herself.

She rushes back to the key panel, and with a smirk, she is pleased to see that her hand fits between the bars. She grabs the keys for 184 and 185, then removes one of the unlabeled keys. Moving fast to the gate of the prison hall, she becomes frustrated when the unlabeled key fails to work. Returning that key to the panel, she tries another. No success.

Not far away, she hears footfalls. The guard is coming, and there is no time left.

"You lash them well to that post. I don't want those animals getting loose again."

Her hands are almost shaking as she grabs the last blank key. She slides it into the lock, turns it and the gate swings open with a sharp creeping sound. Relieved, she quickly reattaches the key to the panel and sneaks inside just in time to close the gate behind her.

The guard steps back into his room, ready to relax again at his desk. He appears not the least bit wiser that two keys are missing now.

Behind the gate, Fortia hides low to the ground. She is thrilled that she succeeded, but she is almost trembling from the adrenaline of the moment. Watching his movements, she slowly sneaks away as quietly as she can.

The guard steps up to his desk. He leisurely sits down and yawns, takes a moment to catch his breath. One of the guards yells to him from the carriage area.

"Captain, a carriage approaches!"

"Unload the prisoner and ready him for processing," he responds, as though he has said those words a thousand times. He turns to his ledger and wets his feather pen. Suddenly, he stops, and an inquisitive look builds. The book was left open…

Fortia moves fast through the candle-lit prison hallway. The cells are numbered and appear to reflect the small amount of light that an intermittent candle provides them. Everything is wet and filthy, and each of the foreboding timber doors has a thin slot for food to pass through. Otherwise, it is hard to tell one door from another, and it feels like a place where very little hope can take hold.

"One-seventy-four.   One-seventy-five," she nervously counts to herself as she passes by each cell. Nearly running down the hall she reaches 184, with 185 opposite this. She moves to the small opening of cell 185 and cautiously whispers through it.

"Mama…? Papa…?"

"Quiet!" a man responds from inside with an equally hushed tone. She does not recognize the voice. He whispers harshly. "If the captain hears anything, you'll be beaten!"

"Fortia?" Her father's voice from nearby. Cell 183…

"Papa!" Excited, she runs to the opening in the doorway.

"Fortia! Kingdoms be…What are you doing here!?"

"I came to save you and Mama!"

"Oh, child!" Even through the small opening, she can hear his frustration. "You need to leave now, Fortia! There is no time to wait!"

"Papa, I can get to the keys! I just need to go back into the captain's room—"

"No, Fortia! You are in great danger!" He is nearly yelling now.

"I can get the keys, Papa!" She has an almost desperate tone. "Where is Mama's cell?"

"YOU MUST GO! Find Tiler! He will keep you safe!"

In the distance, the gate opens. Fortia turns in fear. She sees the captain, and he spots her from a distance.

"HOLD IT!" the guard yells out. "What are you doing here!?" He runs at her with a menacing sneer.

"Go now, Fortia!" Constans begs her. "PLEASE RUN!"

Fearful, she heeds his advice. Turning to run opposite of the guard, she suddenly stops. It's a dead end with a closed iron gate at the end of the hallway. Panic crosses her face, and she trembles. She is only moments from being caught as the guard menacingly runs at her.

She glances at the cell numbers and realizes…Running to door 185, she quickly shoves the key inside and swings the door open.

The prisoner inside steps out almost immediately. He's a hardened man with a thick beard of bark and the rugged clothing of a peasant. Seeing Fortia there, it doesn't take long for him to realize that she has just freed him.

"Run child!" he commands her. The prisoner veers away from Fortia and tackles the guard to the ground. A struggle ensues, and Fortia moves fast to cell 184, shoves the key into the keyhole, and turns it. The door opens swiftly.

It is Sedo, and Fortia is relieved to see her mother, but Sedo doesn't say a word. She grabs Fortia and picks her up. Hurriedly, she carries her daughter down the dark hallway.

"Mama, wait! We can save Papa!"

Sedo says nothing. Even when Fortia struggles with her. They reach the end of the hallway, and she turns into the captain's processing room, but she halts.

The two guards are there with a new prisoner. They all have a look of shock on their faces as this woman and child have appeared out of nowhere.

"RUN, FORTIA!" Sedo drops her and immediately lets out a war cry. She grabs the closest guard and shoves him into the wall. The new prisoner looks at the adjacent guard, snarls, and tackles him to the ground. It is chaos all around.

Fortia finally runs out to the carriage port. The carriage driver is just nearby the door, though. He reaches and grabs her injured arm. She shrieks, struggling to free herself, but his grip is too tight.

"What are you doing here, girl!?" He maintains his grip as Fortia fights him. She slaps and strikes at him, but he has his hands on her. It's too late.

Out of the darkness, a slight, tall, and dark figure appears. Thin and dressed all in black, a single movement is made. Two knives fly through the air, and together, they strike into the leg of the carriage driver. He screams as he falls backward, but Fortia is able to struggle free.

The dark stranger picks her up and carries her to the nearby horses. They throw her on the saddle and slap the horse into motion.

Fortia rides away, still struggling to comprehend who this person is, as she nearly falls off the horse. She grips the grassy hair of the horse's mane, struggling to keep stable as she looks back for a moment.

Harris lifts her mask briefly to reveal herself and smile. Quickly, she covers her face again and disappears into the darkness of the carriage port.

The horse charges forward as Fortia reaches for the reins. It is moving too fast, though, and she struggles to even stay on it. The animal barrels along the alley and into the street. It turns rapidly at a gallop and seems almost out of control. She finally gets a grip on the reins. With a breath of relief, she slows the horse and jumps off, leaving the animal to move along in the street.

Hiding herself behind a barrel in a nearby alley, she breathes deep and struggles to maintain her composure. So much has happened, and it's difficult to think clearly. The adrenaline in her sap tapers off, though, and soon enough, she catches her breath.

In the distance, she can hear the sound of the alarm bell at the prison. A few guards in the street run past her. She regains her wits and moves further down the alley until she turns into the adjacent street. From here, it is easy to disappear into the fabric of the city.

~ ~ ~

Now back in the Open Forest, Fortia woefully approaches her horse in the sunlit clearing by the small pond. The horse is resting quietly, though it turns to see her as footfalls make it alert. She pets the creature on the head, and almost tearfully, she releases the lashing from the tree. Quietly, they walk out of the forest and onto the road. Her every gesture expresses defeat as she plods back to the tavern.

Laderas, Matthius, and Tiler are busy in the front-hitching space. They load up horses with supplies for their journey and have something of a hurried pace about them. Matthius secures a leather rucksack onto his horse, but he stops as something catches his attention.

Fortia approaches from the entry to the tavern drive, still sullen and frustrated, as she guides the horse at her side. Matthius quickly recognizes her awful mood and approaches her with a compassionate gaze. Resting his hand on her shoulder, she looks up at him, almost tearful. He smiles at her with understanding.

"Some tasks are simply beyond the reach of a single person, Fortia. Even for someone as brave and intelligent as you are."

"But I was so close…" The anguish makes her stammer, but Matthius again understands this frustration.

"That is the trick of fate. To touch the prize is common, but only rarely may we grasp it in our hands."

Fortia thinks on this. It is a potent statement. Strangely enough, it gives her some comfort.

Barking with glee, Arty zooms out from the tavern. He's overjoyed to see her safe and back with him where she belongs. He jumps into her arms, and she is immediately broken from her sullen mood. Petting the pup with vigor, she smiles and looks squarely at him.

"I'm sorry I left you behind, Arty." The little dog barely acknowledges this. He is too busy licking and rubbing his nose everywhere he can.

Tiler approaches them, reviews their assembled gear with a quick count of the supplies.

"I think we are ready, Matthius. What of the child?"

Fortia has a pleading look in her eyes, and seeing this, Matthius turns to examine her horse. It appears to be a very capable animal.

"She has a strong horse, Tiler. Ready her for travel."

Fortia realizes the implications of this, and the thought of an adventure brings a bright smile to her face. She props Arty up on the saddle of her horse then runs to help Tiler prepare.

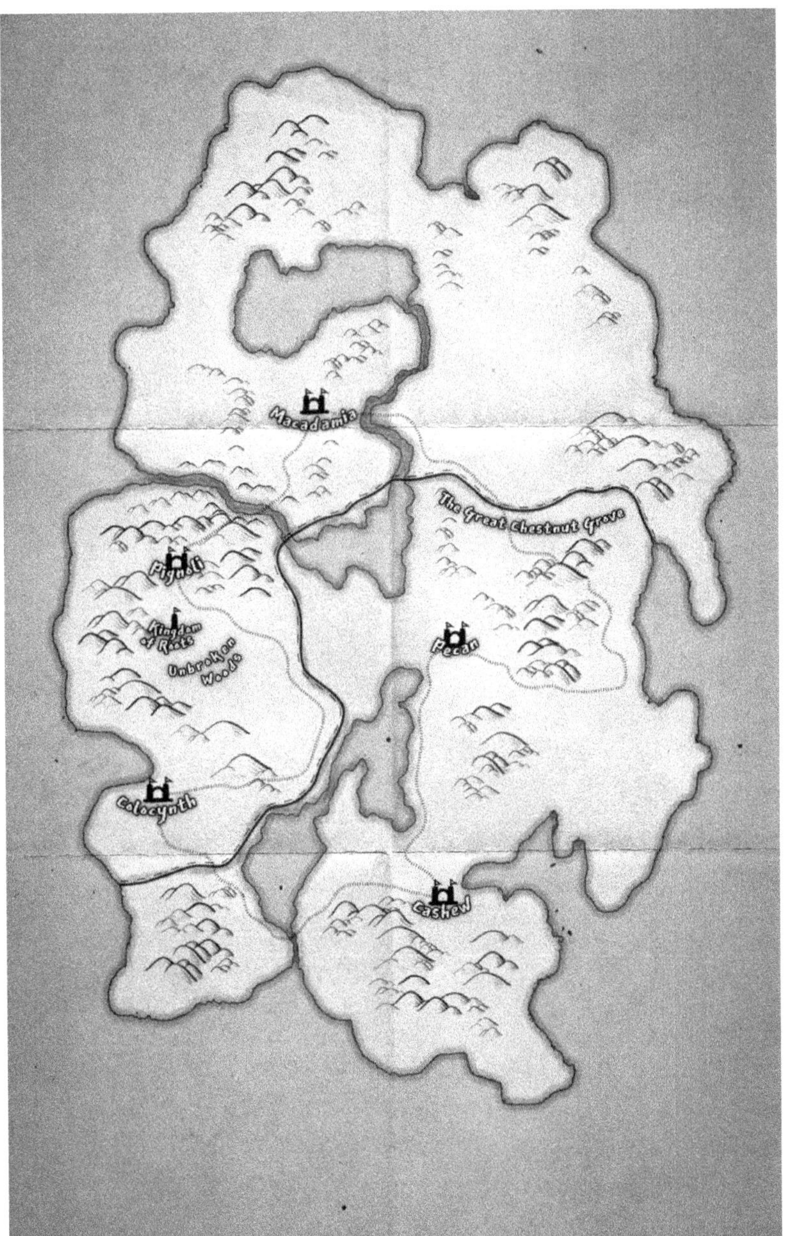

Macadamia
The Great Chestnut Grove
Pignut
Kingdom of Roots
Unbroken Woods
Pecan
Colocynth
Cashew

Chapter 5

THE SUNSET is just beginning. It filters through the foliage of the Open Forest, where the last rays of light reflect off of the various colored leaves and flowers. The band of four travelers make their way along the path in a two-by-two formation. Fortia is scarcely paying attention to the direction of their group. She can't help but acknowledge this beauty of light nearby her. Even Arty seems to have his gaze affixed on the natural wonders here.

"Getting dark, Matthius," Laderas says rather bluntly.

"That is certainly true, my friend. We are a small group, though. We do not need much time to set up camp." Matthius points off in the distance. "I know a good clearing some ways ahead. We can make it there before nightfall." He rides ahead and waves them to follow him. Their pace quickens and Fortia's enjoyment of the sunset is interrupted as she nudges her horse to pick up speed.

At a nearby turn in the path, Matthius directs his horse to the right and picks up his pace even more as he enters the brush of the forest. The party follows as they move further away from the path. Soon enough, they approach a clearing in the woods, and just beyond that is a cliffside.

Fortia is curious to see Matthius standing there, already dismounted from his horse, and gazing into the distance over the cliff's edge. Tiler and Laderas are quick to start arranging camp. She approaches Matthius, and it soon becomes obvious what has his attention. The sunset view from this cliff's edge is breathtaking.

The southern expanse of land before them is dense, full of a rich variety of colors and geography. Mountains lay ahead of them, spanning to the east and west, with another mountain range still flanking those to the west. An enormous lake rests between the mountains, and huge patches of trees reveal themselves in swaths of colors. The light from a faraway city on a hill is hard to see, and well beyond that, to the east, is an inlet branching from the ocean. Misty light dances over parts of the land nearby them, and the sunset is just off to the west of the view, still lending significant light to the remaining day.

Matthius points to a large grove of trees just barely visible past the range of mountains to the west. They are so far away that they almost touch the horizon.

"There, that grove of trees, just past the Closed Forest of Pignoli, beyond the western stretch of the

Pedrian Range. That is our destination." He has something of a warning to his tone.

Fortia inspects the area where he is directing her, though she struggles to know for sure what he is referring to.

"All I see are more mountains," she says, not sure what he is pointing at.

"They look like mountains because they are some of the largest trees in all of Oakenmeer, but if you see, they are a different color than the mountain range nearby them."

She appears to see it now, and a shock begins to grow on her face. Matthius smiles at her, quietly acknowledging the amazement that she is experiencing.

"Those are the Unbroken Woods, Fortia. More pristine than any other grove of trees in all of Oakenmeer and more mysterious still. Save for your father. Nobody I know has ever visited them and returned to speak of it."

Fortia regards him with a look of intrigue. The terror associated with what he has just said is obvious, but her sense of adventure remains.

"Has your father told you how the land of Oakenmeer first came to exist?"

"No, I don't think he ever did." She smiles, looking forward to another lesson.

"There is an ancient text hidden within the vast library at the University of Heights. It speaks of many stories but briefly discusses how Oakenmeer is thought to have been formed."

Fortia is keen to hear this and she gives all her attention to him now.

"An enormous fire fell from the sky. It burned massive holes into the ground. They eventually formed huge lakes of water. Over many millions of years, though, the land moved. Upward, outward, and caved into itself. Mountains and valleys formed in this way, and eventually, our grand forests emerged. From these behemoths, our people were born."

"It seems almost too much to imagine…" She is stunned just thinking of it, and she again takes a moment to regard the incredible view here.

"Fortia, the journey you have embarked on with us will be both awful and wonderful. Your father is a man who is braver than any I have ever met. He would undertake this journey himself. Alone, he would traverse this amazing land and face all the dangers of it."

Fortia struggles to comprehend that. By now, she has begun to understand that her parents were not average people, but it seems that nearly every new day reveals more and more of what they are capable of. Matthius continues, though.

"You will come back from this adventure a different person. Stronger than you are now, I assure you of that, but I cannot promise you success without further injury."

Fortia receives his words with a solemn look, but she still appears optimistic.

"My arm is already healing well." She moves it around some. Clearly regaining some capacity with it. Matthius smiles at seeing this.

"It is wonderful how quickly we heal. A gift that we cannot explain." Matthius reaches into the rucksack attached to his horse. He removes the Oaken Steel dagger and hands it to her.

"You will need to learn how to use this. I will teach you some crucial movements." He swings it swiftly and displays good skill with the knife himself. "Your first lesson will be tonight, but for now, we should help arrange camp."

Fortia and Matthius join Tiler and Laderas, who are busy nearby. Tiler is working to build a fire, and she gathers some wood to assist him.

The sunlight is nearing its end for the day, and the land in the distance shimmers with so many colors. Such a beautiful world all around them. It is such a shame that so many dangers await within it.

~ ~ ~

The prison cell is damp, dark, and cramped. It is barely large enough for Constans to stretch himself out and lay on the uncomfortable stone floor. Sitting on the floor in the corner of this tight space, his head is slumped forward with a defeated posture. There is only a bit of light from the opening in the timber door, and while that light is somehow comforting, it also feels like a source of torment.

In the darkness, he can hear feet shuffling toward his cell. Keys jingle, and the bolted lock shifts. The door swings wide and the room is greeted with the scarce light of the hallway, not at all abundant, but enough to make Constans alert.

"Up," the guard barks. "The king wants to speak to you."

Constans slowly stands, tries to get his bearings. He hasn't walked for some time now in this cramped space, and getting his balance will take a moment.

"Let's go, prisoner," he snaps out with impatience. "The king is wasting his time with you, I suspect."

Constans ignores that slight but does make progress getting out to the hallway.

In a quiet and well-appointed room, Tonitro sits in a comfortable padded armchair and sips a cup of tea. There is a small window here with bars over it that provide a welcome bit of moonlight. Opposite him is another chair of the same make, and a short wooden console table stands between them with a lit candelabra on it. A steaming pot of tea rests on the table, and a second cup waits nearby for a visitor to embrace it. Curiously, a single scroll of paper is rolled up next to all of this, with a small inkwell resting adjacent to it.

Were this not a prison, you would think a fireplace might be nearby, a cozy thick rug to warm the feet, perhaps a shelf with various books to enjoy. None of those other niceties are available, though. This comfortable furniture feels somewhat out of place in an otherwise bleak room composed of stone and a heavy iron gate.

Tonitro sips his tea gently. Clearly, his mannerisms suggest that he was raised in polite society, though none of that fully betrays his commanding nature. He has been giving orders to people all his life, and this forms a degree of insistence for everything he does.

Soon enough, the gate opens, and a guard guides Constans in. The shackles on his legs and arms scrape and clatter with every movement. Wasting no time, Tonitro stands, rapidly places his cup on the table, and approaches them both.

"Thank you, Arturo." Tonitro dismisses him with a gesture. "Please leave me with the keys to his shackles."

Arturo dutifully hands the noisy keys to Tonitro, then exits, leaving the gate open.

Tonitro takes a moment to size up Constans as though he is considering something. Constans seems unsure what to make of it, but he is too tired and uncomfortable to really care. Soon enough, Tonitro uses the keys to unshackle Constans's arms. He places the shackles on the floor nearby his chair and the keys on the table. Sitting again, Tonitro resumes his cup of tea. Constans remains standing, though, now feeling somewhat awkward until he realizes that Tonitro is still gazing at him quietly, pondering something.

"Please." Tonitro gestures to the opposite chair. "Sit and have some tea with me."

Constans shuffles his shackled legs over to the chair, and with great relief, he sits. It is odd how sitting in a chair is so comforting when it has been denied for long enough.

Tonitro pours him a cup of steaming tea and pushes it close to him. Constans slowly sips it, and the warm flavors summon a sigh of relaxation on his face. Having essentially been without food since he arrived here, the taste of this tea is phenomenal. He cannot help but cherish it for a while.

"My grandmother's recipe for fragrant nut tea," Tonitro says with an air of pride.

"Thank you. It is delightful." Constans tries not to show too much excitement.

"Please don't be bashful." Tonitro gestures to the teapot. "I can have Arturo bring more."

Constans takes another healthy sip of tea, not willing to waste that offer.

"You must be wondering why I had you brought here?" Tonitro hints at him.

"Honestly," Constans sips his tea again, "it may be some time before I have another cup of tea or sit in a comfortable chair, so I'm just going to enjoy this."

Tonitro laughs. Caught by surprise with this comment, it prompts a curious smile.

"Yes, you are quite right to do so. However, I would be remiss if I did not stay on task myself. You see, there is much at stake, and we need your help."

"My help...?" Constans chuckles. "Your men attacked us, burned our house, and imprisoned us. How can you think I would want to help you?"

"If I may, I must apologize for that. I did not order the burning of your home. The soldiers did that to spite the confidence in battle that you and your wife displayed. They had been deployed there peacefully, simply to bring you to me for questioning. You met them with a rather unexpected violence."

Constans is not convinced. It's difficult to believe anything this man says.

"However," Tonitro continues, "please let me stay on task. It is not at all just me making this request, Constans. Your kingdom needs your help."

"If that were true, then you should release me."

"So you can acquire the Golden Nugget and attempt to dethrone me? No…We are past that right now."

Constans is about to speak, but Tonitro interrupts.

"Something you are not aware of is that we have received countless reports of the Kingdom of Pignoli plotting a grand attack on Macadamia."

Constans is forced to smirk; he almost chuckles.

"They would be mad to even try."

"Nonetheless, that is our reality. They have already murdered my father, and—"

"Murdered?" Constans is very doubtful.

"Yes, with evidence left behind." Tonitro's tone is absolutely sincere. "My own mother has seen this with her eyes and swears to it."

Constans considers this, but he remains very skeptical. He continues to sip his tea, though.

"It is for these reasons," Tonitro says, "that we again ask for your help."

"What precisely do you need from me?"

"The map," Tonitro says. As the words are uttered, Constans looks directly in his eyes.

"What map do you refer to?"

"Tempus fugit. Playing the fool will get us nowhere. My mother is very aware of your role in the Ordo Nux Aurea, and we need that map."

"As you have burned my home, you have likely burned the map with it."

"This is a possibility that I have considered…" Tonitro places his cup on the table and lifts the roll of parchment. He slides a wooden pen out of it and removes the lid from the ink well. With quickness and slightness, he unfurls the paper and lays it flat on the table. Constans looks it over with a smirk.

"If I knew the way by heart, then what need would I have for a map?"

"Your best effort, please." Tonitro stares intently at Constans. He is not really asking…Regardless of Tonitro's insistence, Constans does not make a move to begin drawing the map. Tonitro soon realizes that more effort will be needed.

"You see, Constans, the Kingdom of Pignoli will stop at nothing to acquire the map. If they were to somehow conquer our kingdom, they would need the nugget to show our people that King Potilius was worthy of the throne. Similarly, were I to take power over their kingdom temporarily, I would need the nugget to show their people my worthiness. My little display last night worked once, but it will not work forever."

"Did it really work though?" Constans sips his tea as that remark settles in.

Tonitro ponders this for a moment, an implication that he has perhaps not fully considered. "Well, it's a good thing we have taken steps to mitigate that."

Constans does not like hearing that, but he is also unsure what it really means. Tonitro lifts his teacup once more for a sip, then gently places it on the table nearby.

"Unfortunately, I must be going, Constans. As you can imagine, I have many tasks to address each day. I will leave you here with these items." Preparing to exit, he grabs the noisy keys Arturo gave him. "Should you wish to assist your kingdom further, please draw the map. Otherwise, efforts are already underway to acquire it elsewhere."

Tonitro stands and begins his approach to the door, though Constans interrupts.

"It is more than likely that the Order has the map, and you will never get your hands on it or the Golden Nugget."

Tonitro turns and smiles to him; he seems to be aware. "There was a time, Constans, when I would threaten people to achieve my goals. That time is largely past in my life, so I will not say to you that I have your daughter."

At the mere mention of Fortia, a fury falls over Constans's face. He almost loses his composure, though with a moment of consideration, he regains himself.

"I will tell you, though," Tonitro continues, "should we capture her with the map, she may need to be treated as any other traitor." Tonitro continues out the door—

"No." Constans halts him. The look of fury he had a moment ago is now blunted by something of a plea for mercy. "Please, have your guard come back in five minutes, and you will have your map."

Tonitro smiles and swiftly leaves Constans there with a feeling of uncertainty.

~ ~ ~

As night has set in, the fire at the center of camp is burning well. Tiler works to prepare dinner with a small pot positioned over the fire on a swing assembly. Laderas has his usual scowl of sincerity as he sharpens his sword near the edge of the camp. He glances in various directions as he does, a watchful eye on the perimeter. In a clearing close by, Matthius and Fortia practice with her dagger.

With an uncertain gesture, she slowly lunges at him with the weapon. Matthius moves away to deflect it. He captures her arm and bends it inward, redirects the blade toward her. She halts with fear as she realizes her own weapon has been used against her.

"The failing, Fortia, was that your arm was straightened as you reached to strike me. This makes it easier for me to capture and redirect your attack."

She seems to understand as he continues his instructions.

"Do not reach for your enemy. If you are worried about being hurt, then you cannot win the fight. Move closer to your enemy, and this will move the dagger into range for you."

He repositions her body just a few inches closer to his, then allows the dagger to softly touch his chest plating so she can observe the angle of her own arm.

"Keep the elbow closer to your hip and slightly bent. This will improve your control of the weapon." He repositions her arm, bends it slightly, and closes the angle of the shoulder.

"Until you are more experienced, once you strike you should never hesitate to rapidly open the gap between you and the opponent. As my own instructor would say, 'All combat is a fight for territory.' If you control the space between you and your opponent, you control the outcome of the fight."

She nods to show an appreciation of the point he has made, then steps back to try again. This time, she strikes with better form and rapidly moves back out of his range.

"Good! Again." He watches her as she practices this maneuver. "You are smaller than us for now and faster as a result. Use that to your advantage, and you will survive."

Fortia continues her practice, though she cannot help but feel unprepared for all this. This part of her parent's life was hidden too well from her, and now, when she needs them most, it feels easy to resent that. After some additional thrusts of the dagger, she stops, feeling uncomfortable with the weapon. There is something of a distaste for it in her gestures, and a moment of uncertainty passes as she regards the sharp edges of its blade.

"I'm afraid of it, sir. I'm afraid of the knife." The dagger suddenly feels heavier in her hand, and her grip loosens.

"You are right to be." He is sincere as he approaches her. "Remember, though, the dagger is only truly dangerous from the front. Striking yourself by accident on the side of the blade—" He slides his arm up hers and pushes the surface of his forearm up against the side of her knife, "—will not hurt you very much." He pushes even harder on her dagger with his arm, and the entire weapon comes loose from her grip.

He grabs it as it falls and swiftly slashes her leg with the edge. Surprised by this, Fortia checks her leg for injury. In one quick motion, he disarmed and struck her without harm.

"The tip of the dagger is where the danger resides." He shows it to her and pushes his finger into the tip. He draws some sap from his finger, just long enough to regain her attention, then swiftly hands the blade back to her.

"Try again, Fortia. Practice until you feel like it is easy, and then we will put you in front of a target so you can learn to grip the blade properly."

After some more practice, the group settles in around the fire. They eat dinner as the night proceeds and Fortia plays with her bowl of nut stew, as she would even when at home. Arty is busy chomping on raw nuts beside her, somewhat oblivious to her sullen attitude. Tiler sits beside her and gives a curious smirk to her as she avoids eating.

"My stew is not good?" Tiler's smile grows with a wink of his eye.

"Sorry…" She realizes she is being rude and eats a hearty spoonful.

Matthius and Tiler chuckle a bit, but Laderas does not seem amused.

"You should eat up girl." Laderas has a calm but often scolding demeanor. "We have the luxury of a hot meal now, but we may not be able to enjoy this each night."

"It's true." Matthius nods in agreement. "Each night will not be like this, Fortia. In the coming days, we may need to fall asleep with only a cold wrap and some raw nuts."

Fortia considers this, and she begins eating more heartily. A rugged lifestyle in the Open Forest is not at all foreign to her, but she has not yet embraced the pressures of this current situation.

There is something else in her mind, though. Unable to define it as yet, the fire seems to command much of her attention tonight. This is the first time she has been around fire since her home burned down around her. With even a simple look at the flames for a moment, a rush of memory invades her. She almost forgets where she is, forgets that there is a bowl of food in her hand, forgets that she is with friends.

A moment passes until Arty interrupts. He is perhaps the only creature alive who could remind her that there are still reasons to be happy, and he nudges her leg with his face. His chunky little body then lays next to her foot, just long enough to grant her comfort. Fortia snaps out of it and quickly smiles at her little pup. She suppresses the thought of these harsh memories, and soon enough, she eats another spoonful of stew.

As the meal carries on, the subtle noises of the forest are everywhere. A chirping of birds, the swaying of trees and leaves. From that peaceful setting, a sharp cracking noise comes out of the dark forest around them.

The group all looked up from their food, gazed at each other, and wondered what that was.

Matthius quietly looks at Laderas, then glances off to the distance. A silent command that Laderas understands, and he places his bowl on the ground. He stands and prepares himself.

"Nature calls, my brothers. I will find a private spot." He quietly moves into the tree line.

Fortia is not sure what to make of this, and she looks at Matthius for reassurance. He nods his head with a calming smile as he hopes to put her at ease. Tiler stands as well. He casually walks over to his belongings and picks up his bow.

"Matthius, I noticed my bow was not notching correctly. Can you look at it with me?"

He pulls an arrow from the quiver nearby, then mounts it on the bow as he shows it to Matthius. Placing his bowl of stew on the ground, Matthius pretends to inspect the bow with curiosity. Moments of silence pass as they inspect the weapon, and Fortia eats her food. It seems that she has set aside anxiety for the moment.

In the forest, Laderas moves through the rough terrain, not so far away from the campsite as yet. He moves swiftly, as quietly as a large man can, and makes a quick search with intention. Drawing his focus onto something ahead of him, it quickly halts his progress.

Back at the camp, Matthius and Tiler are still inspecting the bow.

"Here's the problem," Matthius says, showing something on the arrow to Tiler. A purposeful sound of knocking comes from the forest, a signal from Laderas, no doubt.

Matthius and Tiler both swiftly make their way toward the forest line. Fortia is now visibly concerned, though, and Matthius takes a moment to address her.

"We will be just a few meters into the tree line," he whispers with a calming smile. She nods an understanding, though she glances around with concern.

"Stay here, Fortia, and mind your dagger."

The look of concern on her face grows, and her hand slowly moves to the dagger. She draws it from the sheath mounted on her belt line. Matthius vanishes into the woods soon after, leaving her and Arty to wonder where the danger will come from.

In the dark woods, there is barely any moonlight to give a sense of place. Laderas squats quietly in a thatch of bushes. His sword is drawn. In the distance, through the trees, a subtle moonlight is cast over a large horse with a saddle. It wanders somewhat aimlessly until it stops and chews on the greenery below it.

Matthius slowly appears behind Laderas, a heightened alert on both of their faces. He makes a brief clicking noise, and Laderas turns to him, directs his attention to the horse. Tiler appears from his hiding place behind a nearby tree. Matthius gives him a hand gesture in the direction of the horse, and Tiler quickly disappears behind the tree again.

A few moments of quiet darkness pass before Tiler reappears some twenty feet ahead, now just adjacent to the horse. Relaxing his bow, he uses his free hand to remove something from the saddle. A canteen. He uncorks it then pours some water from it.

Laderas looks to Matthius, a moment of confusion.

"Where is the rider?" Laderas whispers. For a moment, they both consider this until their eyes suddenly open wide. "The camp!"

The firelight of the camp flickers rapidly and Fortia is nervously holding her bowl with one hand while clutching her dagger with the other. She tries to remain still and silent. Her gaze is fixed on the woods nearby, which leaves her back turned to the fire.

From the forest line behind her, a dark figure emerges. The fire light barely illuminates his form at all. He is clad in black leather armor but has no mask on. His face has a swirling variety of black and gray colors on the left side, almost as if burned that way. His flexible branches of hair are trimmed closer to the root, something of a military cut. Approaching the camp in silence, the light now reveals more of his face, which clearly has been burned on the left side at some time in his life. His features are partially masked by it, but not enough to hide his true nature. There is very little good in this evil man…

Fortia and Arty are too focused on the forest line in front of them, where the knights had stepped away. They hear nothing as the man maneuvers around at the opposite end of the camp.

The shadowy figure searches through Tiler's sack on the ground near his tent. Then moves quietly to Laderas's tent and searches it as well. He steps behind the tent, and just as he does, Fortia turns to look behind her. Who knows what might be lurking there?

Soon enough, she turns back to watch the tree line. Her anxiety builds, and she has trouble sitting still as she waits and hopes for someone to reappear.

The dark figure emerges from behind the tent and now approaches Fortia. He steps around the fire, closer now.

Arty's ears perk up. He turns quickly and barks at the threat behind them.

The man lunges and knocks Fortia to the ground as she shrieks. Her knife falls into the grass not far away.

Quickly, he grabs her and lifts her light body off the ground. Arty lunges and bites an exposed part of the man's leg. He shrieks out, but with a quick shove, he throws Arty off. Striking a large rock nearby, the pup yelps out.

"ARTY!" Fortia struggles to free herself, but the man draws his own dagger and places it directly up to her neck. She freezes. Struck with fear.

"Tell me where the map is, girl! Quickly!" His eyes are menacing and sincere. His smile is toothy and reveals his awful cracked and jagged root wood teeth.

Fortia is too scared to say anything. She doesn't even know where the map is.

Laderas and Matthius jump out of the tree line with their weapons drawn and ready.

"Let her go!" Laderas orders, but the man is determined.

"Another move, and her sap will drain! I swear it!"

Fortia can barely even take a breath as the tip of the knife is already pressing into her soft young bark. Any movements and he might easily cut into her.

Arty hobbles to a standing position and shrugs off the abuse he received. He focuses on the man in black, snarls at him again with a growl.

"We will die before we give it up." Matthius takes a step toward Fortia. The attacker lifts his knife, now seconds away from stabbing her.

A hollow thwack echoes out as an arrow strikes him in the shoulder. He shrieks with pain and instinctively drops Fortia. She scurries to grab her knife.

Tiler emerges from the tree line, already working to mount another arrow in his bow.

The attacker swings his knife with his other hand. Launching it at Tiler, who expertly swats it out of the air with the bow. His view of the target is lost momentarily.

Laderas pounces on the man with a war cry and swings his sword. The man dodges away toward Matthius who also swings his ax at him. This enemy is well trained, though, and nimble on his feet. He dodges yet again.

Tiler fires another arrow, this one striking him in the arm. He bellows with pain. Quickly the man begins to realize he is outmatched, and he ducks into the tree line.

Arty is about to give chase, but Laderas halts him. Steps in front of the pup.

"Give your king a message! His days on the throne are numbered!"

With a look of confusion, Fortia holds her dagger at the ready. "Why don't we capture him!?" Frustrated, she almost wants the fight.

"It is better this way," Laderas says, moving back to his spot. Matthius does similar and lifts his bowl of stew.

"We want Tonitro to know that his henchman failed," Matthius explains. "It's good to make your enemy angry. They make more mistakes that way."

Fortia realizes the intent, and she cautiously slides her dagger back into the sheath.

"You did well. Both of you." Laderas pets the little pup. "She is lucky to have you, Arty." The pup seems proud to receive this encouragement.

He and Fortia move to sit by the fire again. Fortia makes an attempt to finish her dinner, but the adrenaline of the moment is still in her. Knowing that the worst of it is past, they all resume their evening at camp as best they can.

"He has seen you now, Matthius," Tiler says with a look of concern on his face.

With frustration, Matthius nods an acknowledgment. He continues eating while his food is still warm, though it is hard to suppress the knowledge that his involvement in the Order has been uncovered.

"I do not recognize him as one of my men," Matthius admits. "Perhaps he is one of the operatives with Harris."

"He moved very well." Laderas appears impressed. "Only a coward or madman threatens a child, though, and he did not seem like a coward." They all agree on that point, and the meal quietly continues.

Fortia finally eats another spoonful of stew. It tastes better somehow, and perhaps that is what life will be like from now on. The small things that she took for granted will now have more value as the space between herself and her childhood is rapidly growing wider.

Chapter 6

THE ROYAL RESIDENCE of the Kingdom of Macadamia is humbler than one might think, though it is still grand in its appointments. The ancient builders knew that if you want to build something that lasts forever, you should use the materials that are already present where you want to build. For that reason, all the stone that was used to erect this structure carries a slight pinkish hue to it, a result of mineral deposits within a large adjacent quarry. It gives the entire structure something of a uniqueness relative to the wood and brick structures nearby it. Over generations, this has become a defining feature of this palace.

Like many castles it has its own forms of defensive refinements. There is a residence for the royal family and their caretakers, which is flanked on all sides by towers and battlements. These serve both domestic and defensive intent. Adjacent to this is a bailey where soldiers and guardsmen are engaged in practicing maneuvers, and a large gateway leads to this area from the space of the Closed Forest. While there is no moat surrounding this castle, there are ground-level fortifications in the form of a stone wall with a channel space behind it that runs the perimeter of the castle. This is an excellent source of cover during an attack, and if needed, this channel can be flooded with highly flammable oils and tree cuttings, which allows the defending army to make it into a moat of fire around the castle. This wall also serves as the rear wall of the royal stables, which are at ground level with the rest of the Closed Forest.

The hustle and bustle of the city is all around this structure when Tonitro and his complement of two royal guards approach on horseback. They ride toward the gate at the bailey and slow their pace as it opens for them.

~ ~ ~

The dining hall is somewhat vast and well-ornamented. There are countless relief sculptures carved into the stone walls here, which are adjacent to grand timber doors. Thick and ornate timber columns are positioned around the large dining table, which makes up the centerpiece of this room. There is a generous fireplace here, and adjacent to it is a smaller staging table just a few steps away from a threshold. A rather generous-appearing kitchen is immediately accessible from this area, and a handful of caretakers are working not far away.

Julianna is dressed in all black and sitting at this small staging table, enjoying a breakfast of tea and nut cakes with sweet oil. Holding herself well with an upright and composed posture, you might think her husband was dining with her this morning. There is another chair and place setting waiting for an occupant, though.

While this was all arranged and served to her by caretakers of the residence, it is something of a humble meal and a humble choice of seating for a woman of her stature. Her mannerisms are those of someone whose heart is holding the weight of mourning but still working to retain the dignity of nobility.

Tonitro enters from a door across the room. He moves with his usual swift and purposeful pace. In his hand, he has the roll of parchment that was left with Constans, and he begins to untie it as he approaches Julianna.

"Good morning, Mother." He kisses her on the head. "I spoke with our friend in the Order, and I believe we have what we need."

"Good morning, son." She still uses the commonalities of a mother to her child, and for a moment, Tonitro is distracted by this. He frowns but quickly shakes off that perceived slight. He unrolls the parchment fully and lays it out on the table for her to see. Inspecting it in front of her, the queen is rather reluctant to even look at it.

It is a very abbreviated version of the map from the trunk. While the original map showed various routes leading from multiple kingdoms to the location of the Golden Nugget, this map appears to only show major features of the seven kingdoms and one route from Macadamia, which leads to the words "Crystal Tower."

Tonitro sits and serves himself a few nut cakes.

"Our source has obviously not seen the original, but from what they know of previous reports, this does seem to be accurate."

"I am worried for you son…" She is almost trembling as she says this.

"There is no reason for worry, Mother. Constans was reluctant to help, but once I made him aware of the potential prosecution of his daughter for treason, well…"

Julianna pauses while eating her breakfast as a flash of sadness crosses her face. "It is never kind to threaten a child," she says with dignity, though after this unpleasant thought, she may have trouble finishing her meal.

Tonitro lets this wash over him. Ignoring the impact of his mother's scrutiny, he eats the nut cakes in a rush.

"Mother, I'm sure that Father would agree when I say kings do not always have the luxury of every moral precept." Tonitro is too fixed on his path to take any advice it seems. "I will deploy Matthius and a party of our best men to catch up with Malleus."

In the distance, a caretaker approaches from another entry across the room.

"My king, a rider is here to see you."

"Send them in," Tonitro orders, still eating his breakfast in a rush.

Soon enough the man in black from the campsite, Malleus, enters the room. He has bandaged his arm and still appears to be hurting, but he does not waste time approaching them to give his report. As he does, there is an obvious feeling of discomfort from Julianna. Something about this man rubs her the wrong way, and even a look in his direction summons an unsettled feeling in her.

"They have the map," Malleus reports with a disciplined tone. "I have failed to acquire it, though. We will need a few more operatives to achieve this goal." With a brutal lack of decorum, Malleus reaches into the plate of nut cakes and grabs one. He chews on it with disregard for any form of table manners.

Tonitro frowns and looks him over. He has become accustomed to this brutish behavior from Malleus, but Julianna remains quiet. She is not at all willing to engage in conversation with this harsh and impolite man.

"Malleus," Tonitro stands and gives him a sincere look in the eyes, "you will have all the support you need, but another failure cannot be tolerated."

Malleus has a constant sneer of hatred on his face, and even with that disposition present, Tonitro knows he must command him sternly. An unflinching look is shared between them, and Malleus receives this as intended. He quickly realizes that obedience is necessary, and his head bows for a moment.

"Go see the Generalist and tend to your injuries," Tonitro commands. "Prepare yourself for a journey to gather the Golden Nugget."

Malleus looks up at Tonitro with some confusion. Seeing the map on the table, though, he rapidly finishes his nut cake and picks up the document. After reviewing it, he smiles at Tonitro, and the wickedness of his toothy grin would scare most anyone. If Tonitro is intimidated, though, he does well to hide it.

Without another word, Malleus turns to march out of the room but stops for a moment.

"There is one more piece of news. Matthius is with them."

On hearing this, a look of fury begins to build on Tonitro's face. His mother, still feeling sheepish but wanting him to keep his polite disposition, places her hand on his. Tonitro seems to calm himself after a period of silent contemplation.

"Thank you, Malleus. You will lead the men on this journey."

Malleus exits the room, and Tonitro turns his frustrated gaze to his mother.

"Did you know Matthius was in the Order?"

She continues eating, still avoids eye contact, though she soon finds the right words.

"Our source never made mention of that."

Tonitro stands, and with an unsettled mind, he begins to pace the room. "This changes things...The troops have always trusted him more than me."

Julianna gathers her strength and stands. She approaches him and takes his hand again.

"Cross that bridge when you need to," she says, and Tonitro seems to know she is correct. "No matter who leads the army, you will struggle to keep order over two kingdoms if you do not have access to the nugget. That must be your goal for now."

Tonitro feels reassured by this. He kisses her hand in gratitude, and with determination, he turns to exit—

"Son?" Julianna stops him, almost afraid to speak, as he turns back to listen.

"When your father died, did he speak of me? Did he give you any message for me?"

Tonitro looks away shamefully, struggles now to look her in the eyes. With a deep breath he straightens his back.

"The arrow was too sudden." He coldly turns and exits, leaving her saddened by these parting words.

Julianna sits quietly and attempts to continue her meal. She lifts her teacup, but the trembling of her hands is too much. Returning the cup to the table, she attempts to compose herself. The troubles in her mind must be more than even a queen can bear.

Chapter 7

TRAVEL FOR ANY GREAT PERIOD of time becomes monotonous. Trees that hold so much beauty, when seen in similar form over and over, will begin to all look the same. The sparkle of sunlight on leaves even begins to feel like a burden at times.

Fortia sees squirrels everywhere. They are the natural-born enemy of the nut miller, and after years of training she and Arty are masters at spotting them. Many animals, though, are new to Fortia. For as much time that she has spent in the woods, the proximity of their home to the dense collection areas of the forest limits her exposure to larger wildlife. They avoid civilization, and rightly so. The noises of a residence and frequent trips by people to forage for nuts would push most any wild animal far away. The occasional fox has crossed her path, though, as the fox is the natural enemy of a farm-raised chicken, but Arty is skilled in that arena.

The caravan of four travelers slows as Matthius extends his arm. He has spotted something in the distance up ahead, and signals to Tiler.

Fortia looks as well but can't seem to see anything of note. She glances to Laderas, who signals for quiet.

Tiler sees it now and signals as much to Matthius. He quietly dismounts his horse and hands Matthius the reins to keep the animal steady. Silently, he removes his bow and quiver, notching an arrow as he sneaks off and disappears into the tree line at the left. He reappears a good distance ahead of the caravan, having quickly repositioned himself in silence.

"What is it?" Fortia whispers to Laderas.

"Deer," Laderas responds with a gesture to hush her.

Fortia smiles bright at the thought. Now wishing she could see it, she attempts to gaze past Matthius and improve her view. Only once before did she cross paths with a deer, but it left a definite impression. It was a doe walking swiftly across the road not far from her house. It became startled by her cart and moved very fast out of sight. She recalls it being very tall, with thick multi-colored bark across its hide. Regardless of the brief encounter, she remembers that beautiful animal very well.

Up ahead of the group, Tiler stops beside a smaller tree along the path. He remains still a few moments, only moving to slowly raise his bow.

Fortia is eager to see the animal and she leans slightly left for a better view. Her horse senses the excitement and shimmies slightly to the side. Gripping the reins tight, she attempts to control the animal, but its hooves are large and noisy.

A large buck bursts from the tree line opposite Tiler's position and charges along the road toward the horses. Seeing this, Fortia's eyes widen with amazement as she finally gets a good look at this amazing creature.

It is perhaps as tall as any horse she has ever seen but moving much faster. The colorful bark on it looks almost as thick as armor, and the enormous wooden branching of its rack adds to the truly imposing nature of this animal.

A hollow thwack echoes out as an arrow strikes the deer in the side. The angle is perfect, just behind the musculature of the front legs. This is an expert shot that likely punctured a lung. The beast stammers, but it is full of adrenaline, and a creature this size could easily run for miles. It charges forward.

Tiler quickly moves into the road and notches another arrow as he goes. The deer has slowed, but it is still closing fast. Now barely thirty feet from the horses, the quiet domesticated animals see this wild creature coming, and they begin to grow frightened. Matthius grips Tiler's horse tight to keep it from running.

Arty's fearful whining becomes more evident. Fortia now realizes the danger but she is still so amazed by this animal.

Another arrow strikes the hind leg, and the animal stumbles. It has lost good use of much of its right side and cannot maintain balance. It falls and an enormous thud shakes the ground as it slides into the dirt and gravel, now stopping only a few meters ahead of the horses. It is not dead, though. Writhing and thrusting its limbs around, it swings the imposing rack as it works to regain footing.

Laderas dismounts rapidly. He draws his sword with intention and marches forward as the deer moans out with suffering. They cannot let this go on for long.

Laderas approaches cautiously, careful not to be struck by its hooves. The deer swings its antlers at him, attempts to defend itself. With a swift movement, Laderas shuffles forward and around the antlers. He raises his sword upward and thrusts, pierces into the animal's left lung and deep into its thorax. It becomes rigid from the pain and struggles to get the air in as Laderas holds the sword tight.

Fortia watches in absolute awe. For her, this moment is as overwhelming as most anything she has seen in her life. Arty hides though, not sure he can tolerate it. She dismounts her horse now. Feeling somewhat safer and still wanting to see more of this animal.

Laderas is kneeling next to it now, and the creature has no more fight in it. The sap pours from its wounds but is also filling its lungs. It gasps for air again, perhaps the final attempt.

"I've never seen one this close." Fortia remains stunned by this incredible animal.

"Your father is a quiet man," Tiler says, now nearly upon the animal himself. "He taught me everything I know about hunting."

Fortia cannot help but confidently breathe in that thought as a moment of pride lifts a quiet smile onto her face.

"He will teach you someday, Fortia," Laderas says with certainty. "For now, let us acknowledge the good fortune that this animal will be to our journey."
The deer is lifeless. Tiler and Laderas kneel just next to it. They both place their right hand on its barky hide. Laderas motions with his left hand for Fortia to join them. She kneels, moves to place her left hand on the animal.

"Your right hand," Tiler gently instructs her, and Fortia obliges, caressing the thick bark of the animal.

"Touch the animal, but be still," Tiler says. "Stillness is reverence." She heeds this advice, and the three of them hold the animal in silence.

The wind blows around them, and the leaves rustle in the distance. The sunlight sparkles as it ever did. Branches rub the bark of their grand companions as the trees creep and shift in the distance. The forest has lost one of its creatures, but it does not protest. The sap of the animal is absorbed into the stone and gravel of the road. The rain will move this into the soil and water below. The roots and other creatures beneath will take from the sap what they need and leave the rest to everything around them. Just as the death of a tree can give life to a whole farm, perhaps this deer can help save a whole kingdom.

~ ~ ~

The next morning the four riders are still on the same road. A few things have changed, though. Laderas's horse has a large deer pelt folded and draped over its backside. The bark having been stripped off, and the rest dried overnight. It has a consistency that is much like leather but slightly more rigid, with a wood grain inherent to it. A deer hide of this type is excellent for both armor and warmth.

Tiler has a pile of broken branches bundled on the backside of his horse. On closer inspection, it is obvious that these are the broken pieces of the deer's rack. When stripped and dried out, these pieces of antler are unlike any other form of wood. They burn long, slow, and purposeful while producing a magnificent heat. A single piece of this material can keep a camp warm for an entire night, with no other wood added above it.

Fortia's horse now carries a large leather parcel full of dried deer summerwood, a jerky of sorts that can be made overnight from the natural salt of stones found in the forest. This meaty wood will sustain itself for many weeks of travel, and while the taste is somewhat gamey and salty, the nutrition within it is unmistakable. As any good dog would be, Arty is interested in getting some jerky. He sniffs and maneuvers his snout closer to the parcel.

"Leave it, Arty." Fortia smiles and repositions him onto her lap. "Don't make me put you on another horse."

Laderas and the others chuckle. They can't blame him.

"Look up ahead," Tiler alerts them to a waypoint ahead.

Fortia notices a clearing with a small building at the far edge of it. As they make their approach, she can see it now. It is a small house on the opposing end of a chasm. The home is large enough for two rooms and only a single level.

The edges of the chasm are at most sixty feet apart, but they preside over a hundred-and-fifty-foot deep gap with a rapidly moving river at the bottom. Bulky stones and felled tree limbs litter the bottom of the chasm, but in the center of all this is a large assembly of tree trunks, which form a single thick column. This is braced by other trunks protruding horizontally into the walls of the chasm. The entire assembly supports a large but rudimentary swing bridge, which is currently positioned parallel to the cliff's edge. This is not a vast canyon by any means, but it is clearly a landmark that needs to be traversed.

Matthius steps down from his horse and approaches the cliff's edge to address the bridgeman. Fortia, Arty, and the others join him on the ground, and they all approach the cliffside to assess the situation.

"Hello there!" Matthius uses the firm tone needed for his words to reach across the gap.

A rugged middle-aged man steps out the front door of the home with a large wrench in each hand. He inquisitively looks across the cliffside to the sound of Matthius's voice.

Being another seasoned person of the Open Forest, he has a solid trunk and bark displaying some age. He wears the usual beard of a man who needs to stay warm and a work bib with loops sewn into it, each of these hosting a variety of tools. Various keys with unique shapes, a hammer, some wrenches, and a pry bar are positioned strategically on his garments. It is all easy for him to reach and replace during his efforts to maintain this large bridge.

"I am Gruff of Pignoli. Do you seek passage?" This man has no inside voice. He has been speaking across this precipice for most of his life, and his voice comes with a similar tone needed to carry the words across the void.

"Yes, please," Matthius returns. "What is the fee here?"

"None for citizens." Gruff has something of a chuckle in his voice. "At this moment, though, no passage can be given."

"What's this about?" Laderas is curious.

"First off, the wretched thing won't turn." Gruff chuckles, references the mechanism nearby him that controls the ropes and turns the swing bridge. Frustrated, he walks over to it and kicks it. "Been working on this cursed thing all morning with my tools. She won't budge."

Matthius considers this dilemma. He knows the closest crossing point from here will add days to their trip, days of travel they cannot afford. Any compromise they can make here will benefit them.

"Perhaps my friends and I can assist you? If we can somehow cross…"

"That is appreciated." Gruff seems agreeable to this, though he is still somewhat suspicious. "Good King Potilius has had second thoughts of late when it comes to visitors from Macadamia." He gives a pause as he looks them over again. "I'm afraid I don't recognize you."

"We are citizens of Macadamia," Matthius clarifies, "but we mean you or no other Pignolian any harm. We are not an envoy of King Tonitro."

"Somewhat the opposite," Tiler whispers to Laderas. They both hold in a laugh. Laderas's mood seems to have changed for the better since that deer was taken. Perhaps for good reasons.

"We are all skilled climbers," Matthius proposes to Gruff. "We have some rope. If we can toss it to you, one of us can cross and try to assist you with repairing the bridge."

Gruff considers this, but he remains hesitant. There has been too much talk about King Tonitro lately, and the poor intentions he has for his neighbors. Still, this has been a very pleasant exchange here.

"You have shown much kindness already." Gruff is convinced. "Throw the rope over, and we'll make a go of it."

Tiler opens a rucksack strapped to the back of his horse and removes a coiled length of sturdy-looking rope. It is thick enough to be useful for supporting a person but not so heavy that it is a burden to carry. He sees a decent-sized rock nearby, grabs it out of the dirt, and ties one end of the rope around it a few times. There is an appropriate weight on the end now to carry the rope across the chasm.

He begins swinging the rock. As the rope becomes tighter during each rotation, he loosens his grip, and the circumference of the swinging rock becomes wider and wider. Finally, he lets it loose, and the rope flies partway across the chasm. It misses the other side.

Laderas and Matthius chuckle at this as Tiler sighs. Frustrated, he regathers the rope.

"A wager, perhaps?" Laderas jokes to Matthius. "He misses a second time?"

"I'll take that bet." Matthius chuckles.

"Very funny…" Tiler is slightly embarrassed. Having finally gathered the rope, he begins swinging the rock again. He builds up the momentum to make his second attempt and quickly releases it. The rock strikes the ground a few feet on the other side of the chasm. Gruff tries to reach for it in time, but the weight of the rope drags the rock back into the chasm.

Matthius and Laderas look at each other with an uncertain gaze. They are not at all certain who won that bet.

On his third attempt Tiler is successful, and Gruff has snagged the rope. He works to tie his end of the rope to a nearby oak tree. Tiler moves to do similar, though he now realizes the rope will come short of their needs. He turns to Laderas and Matthius.

"Tell me we have another rope?" he says, feeling doubtful even as the words are spoken.

Matthius sighs, and he yells over to Gruff.

"Perhaps there is a branch closer to the edge that you can tie onto?"

Gruff realizes the situation and searches around. He spots one and drags the rope over to a tree not far from the bridge. He ties it to his belt line and skillfully climbs up the relatively thin tree trunk. Making his way onto an upward-reaching limb that spans a short distance over the chasm, he ties off the rope midway across the branch. There is no joining point to fully secure it, though. Gruff yanks the knot as tight as he can, though they will need to rely on the upward slope of the branch to give the rope stability.

"Will this do?" Gruff clarifies.

Tiler gives the rope a few good tugs. Seems like it will hold. He moves over to another tree and seems satisfied that he can tie the rope off there.

"I'll go first," Matthius says, not wanting to risk anyone else in his group.

"Perhaps I would be better," Tiler offers, "to help him with the bridge, that is. We will need it for the horses, and I may have a better sense of how to get it moving."

Matthius nods in agreement. He knows that Tiler has more experience with engineered devices like this.

Tiler rubs some dirt into his hands, prepares for the climb. He again holds the rope, just enough to suspend his weight on it while over land. This all appears sturdy.

"Wait." Matthius unties the leather belt under his armor and lashes it around the rope. He attaches it to Tiler's belt and runs it securely back into the buckle.

Tiler gives him a nod of appreciation for that idea. They both recognize the risk inherent to this and briefly exchange a moment of acknowledgment between friends. Soon, Tiler begins his treacherous climb out across the chasm while Matthius holds the other end of the rope. Attempting to add a bit more stability to it as his friend climbs further out.

Fortia watches with something of a look of familiarity on her face. She has had her share of risky experiences on unsteady ropes and does not seem phased by the idea of this.

As Tiler scurries across the rope, Gruff has returned to work on the bridge mechanism. He is busy banging on it with his tools when a young boy roughly the age of Fortia approaches him with a mallet.

"Thank you, Angelus." Gruff repositions and strikes the device with the mallet. Almost with hatred…

Angelus is much like his Uncle Gruff, as he has lived all his life in this forest. Climbing, hunting, working with his hands to stay alive, or just to meet the needs of the day. While he is slightly older than Fortia and nearly as tall as he will grow, he is still very much a young man who relies on the tutelage of a mentor.

For a moment, Angelus seems impressed as he watches Tiler scurry across the rope. For someone older, Tiler displays great skill and dexterity. Having reached the halfway point, he continues to move quickly across the chasm with a rhythmic pace. Feeling more confident about this now he seems to even speed up a bit.

Just as he does, though, there is a sudden shift in the rope. He freezes, a moment of fear passing through him like lightning.

Matthius is watching closely. "What's the matter?"

"The rope shifted. I felt it." Tiler's voice shakes for a moment.

Angelus grows concerned as he has seen Tiler stop moving. Walking quickly to the tree, he climbs up, using the various branches to move swiftly up the girth of the trunk. Now shuffling across the branch supporting the rope, he can see the area where the rope is tied on. The bark has been torn back some by the movement of the rope.

"It has moved," Angelus says with certainty. "I will brace it for you." He climbs down, then runs over to his uncle's tool belt. Rapidly grabbing a hammer and nail, he climbs back up to the limb and positions the nail at the front of the rope. After hammering it into the wood, this creates a peg for the rope to apply pressure to, but regardless, he remains on the limb and assists by holding the rope as steady as he can.

Taking a deep breath, Tiler shuffles forward with some considerable speed. He is now ready to end this crossing, and he moves far enough over the opposite edge to be safe. Confidently, he unlatches the belt harness and drops down to make an easy landing. Rather glad to have his feet on the ground again, he takes a moment to breathe before attaching both his own and Matthius's belts to the rope. With a strong shove he slides them both across to the other side, then moves toward Gruff to assist.

On the other side, Matthius grabs the two belts as they slide across. He turns to Laderas.

"The child next?" Laderas says, and Matthius seems to agree that is best.

"You and I should stay back with the horses anyhow, in case our friend returns."

"I can make it across." Fortia confidently strides over to grab hold of the rope. "My father and I have made a living on dangerous ropes. It would be easy."

Matthius unlatches the belts and loops one of them around Fortia's waistline. She has a relatively thin fabric belt on that will not hold her weight well. He attaches her to the rope, and she bounces up and down some, testing the weight on it.

"Sorry, Arty." She frowns to her pup. "You'll have to wait and cross with the horses."

Arty huffs at this as he prefers to be at his master's side.

She begins to scurry her arms and legs across the chasm. Not at all intimidated by this height, she makes very steady progress. The view down into the chasm is somewhat surreal from this position, though the height itself remains far from concern. If anything, this is the one risky behavior in her life that she is not swayed by. Soon enough, she is nearing the center of the rope, and the rushing noise of the river below becomes more pronounced.

Angelus is working to steady the rope when he hears a slight creeping noise. He looks intently at the nail in the branch below him. The limb was weakened by the damage from the nail, and it is starting to crack.

"TURN BACK!" he screams to her.

Fortia can't hear him well as the rush of water beneath is too loud. She stops, though, and turns to him, tries to get a sense of what he is saying.

"What was that?" She is confused, unsure if there is any reason to worry.

"What's happening?" Matthius yells over to Angelus, a look of concern growing.

"The nail is breaking the branch!" Angelus screams. "Turn back!"

Fortia looks to Matthius, who hurriedly waves at her to return. Realizing that something is wrong, a hint of fear sets in. Keeping her senses, she scurries backward toward him.

More and more, the branch starts cracking. Angelus lays his entire weight on the area of the limb behind the nail and grabs the rope. He pulls it. Trying to relieve some of the weight from the front end of the branch. It helps some, but soon enough, the limb is giving way, and Angelus is doing all the work. A snap echoes out, and the limb breaks free.

Fortia feels the sudden shift of her weight. She drops briefly and freezes in terror.

Angelus has the rope, though he struggles. The weight of both the branch and Fortia is too much for him. Feeling the rope slip from his hands, he pulls with all his might. The movement of Fortia's swinging inertia is too great. His face fills with fear as the rope slips out of his hands.

Fortia's terror intensifies as she feels herself in freefall. Clutching for the rope she is desperate to keep a hold of it. Hitting the rear wall of the cavern could easily knock her loose. Matthius holds the rope tight and leans back, preparing for the coming weight.

Fortia watches the trees around her grow distant for a moment. The feeling of freefall is terrifying, but suddenly, something massive appears underneath her. The swing bridge is finally moving.

Tiler and Gruff hurriedly push and turn the gears. With everything they can muster, they shove their weight into it and move as rapidly as they can.

Fortia lands hard on her back, striking the platform of the bridge with a wooden thud. She belts out a scream. Not understanding what just happened, she lays on her back in a tense state. The panic of the moment is still very real to her.

Soon after, she realizes she is not falling anymore and glances around for a sense of place. The swing bridge continues moving for a moment more. The timbers of it screech and crackle until it delivers her back to the rear edge of the cliff.

She continues to lay there as Arty sprints over and checks on her. It was a horrible experience for him to even watch. Fortia pets him, now beginning to show signs of recovering. He halts for a moment, though, looks at something on her shirt just above her torso. Fortia notices his gaze and begins to focus on it herself.

Two small blue and red sappy beetles emerge from a fold in the top of her romper and scurry onto her stomach. Fortia and Arty look at them, not sure what to make of it. For a brief moment she recalls what her mother said.

"Good luck…"

As though in unison, the two beetles fluff out their small wings and lift off into flight. They leave Fortia to recover from this trauma on the bridge, and she slowly sits up, not yet ready to get moving.

Matthius arrives to check on her, then quickly helps her to her feet. He looks her over and smiles, almost laughing at the outcome of this scenario. Laderas arrives shortly after as he is guiding the horses across the bridge.

"I will tell stories of this." Laderas smiles as he passes them with the animals. "Not a single person will believe it, but I will tell stories of this."

~ ~ ~

Once everyone is situated on the other side of the chasm, Gruff is in the process of addressing the group and explaining the need for a visit to King Potilius.

"The people here are very tense," Gruff explains. "King Potilius has never said an unkind word toward your kingdom, but somehow, all the people of Pignoli are now concerned about your new king."

"As are we, Gruff." Matthius definitely understands this concern. "If you feel that the king will want to address us directly, then we will certainly not resist that advice." Regardless of Matthius saying this, Gruff has a look of confusion. He scans Matthius's armor, and with a questioning look, he cannot help but ask.

"Are you not a soldier of Macadamia?"

Matthius frowns in response, certainly frustrated by a thought running through his head.

"When I started this journey, I was the Captain of the Army of Macadamia." He has an uncertain tone, now feeling doubtful about his position in the world.

"Regardless…We are not an envoy of King Tonitro, but you would be wise to expect such a party, perhaps not far behind us."

Gruff considers this, though he frowns at the idea of a confrontation.

"Angelus will show you the way to the city. The travel is half a day on horseback."

Laderas removes some deer jerky and a piece of antler from the horses. With a smile he hands them over to Gruff, who inspects them a moment.

"Some jerky and antler. Thank you for the assistance, my friend." Laderas shakes his hand firmly.

Parting salutations are shared, and the travelers begin mounting their horses. Angelus grabs a backpack nearby, unlashes a horse at the edge of their home, and mounts it.

As they all ride away, Matthius stops for a moment and addresses Gruff once more.

"Beware of a man in black leather armor with a burn on the left side of his face. He cannot be trusted."

"Thank you," Gruff says with a look of concern. "I will do my best to slow them, though it may not be possible to prevent them from crossing."

Matthius nods to him, then nudges his horse forward.

Gruff makes his way to the gear assembly and begins cranking the surly old mechanism. He rotates the bridge back to parallel, then casually enters his home.

On returning moments later, he is carrying a rather large crossbow, an arbalest, and a sleeve of very long arrows. Within a short period of time, he has managed to mount this weapon onto a wooden tripod near a chair at the front of the home.

Resting his achy body into the chair, he removes a wedge of the jerky. It is as good a time as any to enjoy some meat, for who knows what the future will hold.

Chapter 8

THE KINGDOM OF PIGNOLI at this region is very similar in appearance to Macadamia, though being further south, the ambient temperature has not yet reached the cold of Autumn that is common to Macadamia at this time. The trees have yet to transition their leaves to the bright colors seen just a few days north of here. Regardless, had an imaginary line not been formed throughout history, there might be no reason for Fortia to think that she was in a different kingdom at all. Everyone speaks the same language here, and when the occasional traveler passes by, there is really no discernable difference between the citizens.

The enormity of the trees all around masks them from seeing the grandeur of mountains that reside to the west of this road. Pignoli is one of two kingdoms where much of the Open Forest is composed of highlands and mountains. Pecan is the other, and their proximity to one another geographically is a large part of the reason why, at least historically, they have fought over their resources.

Angelus has taken the opportunity to make small talk with Fortia. They ride side by side at the center of the party, with Matthius at point a few paces ahead.

"Your home sounds like it was an amazing place." Angelus seems impressed by Fortia's description of her life back in Macadamia.

"We will rebuild. I am certain of it." After her experience on the bridge, Fortia now seems more confident about this whole adventure.

"My Uncle Gruff and I have lived in that small home for much of my life. He has taught me everything he knows, and someday, when I'm ready, I will take over his post."

"I am certain you will make your uncle proud." They share a mutual smile, and Fortia appears to be enjoying this brief portion of time they have shared. Laderas and Tiler are close behind them, and as Laderas passes his canteen to Tiler, he interrupts the pleasant chat ahead of them.

"Should we consider finding camp, Angelus?" The sun is indeed getting low.

"We are just an hour out, sir. There will be ample food and shelter in the city."

Fortia's eyes smile. She is somewhat excited by the idea of seeing another city. It was somewhat rare that she had the opportunity to visit the Closed Forest of Macadamia. Seeing another kingdom such as Pignoli would, until now, have only been a distant dream.

"How large is the city?" she asks Angelus, trying not to show too much excitement.

"To me, it is as large as anything I have ever seen. My uncle, though, he says it is but a fraction of what the Closed Forest of Macadamia is."

Fortia can see it in her mind's eye, and the adventures ahead of her now feel limitless.

~ ~ ~

The sunset is nearly giving way to darkness when Fortia and her companions approach the main gate of Pignoli. Unlike Macadamia, there is no enormous brick and dirt wall surrounding this place. The city wall appears to be composed entirely of massive felled trees which are standing vertically on end. All of these have been manually erected into an upright position, and there is seemingly no remnant of their stumps or roots nearby. The wall they form is no less than thirty feet high and ten feet deep. There are gaps occasionally between these trunks, which make for convenient defensible positions from the opposite side of the wall, but they are not very large and often are distant from one another.

War is often unkind to any great achievements that existed before it. This is particularly true of any civilization after a war changes that landscape, and this was certainly the case for the Kingdoms of Oak and Chestnut when they were dissolved. New cities are often built from the old, and the great structures that existed are taken apart piece by piece in the name of progress. Perhaps those changes unfold for other reasons, though, as an unspoken intention is always lingering.

Remembering everything as it was before a war is sometimes too great a trauma for a country to carry into the future.

After the territory of Pignoli was seceded from Oak, the City of Pignoli was built in a similar style as the main cities and castles of Chestnut and Oak had been. For this reason, the appearance of the city of Pignoli now would be as close a representation for anyone of how the Great City of Oak would have appeared.

The city gate itself appears at first to be made of rather mundane timbers, only connected by metal straps and bolts. Though this is somewhat elusive. Were one to inspect closer the depth of the gate would become more apparent. While the timbers are spaced rather generously for what a fortification would need, the depth of the gate is easily ten feet. It is hard to imagine how this gate would even rotate to open, though it clearly must have some functional capacity.

Unlike the walls of Macadamia, which have an enormous space in front of them to reveal any approaching attackers, the walls of Pignoli rest directly against the Open Forest around them. While this may seem to have its disadvantages, the greatest benefit shown by history is the lack of open space for the assembly and the effective use of siege weapons.

Fortia and her group are waiting on the road about twenty meters from these walls, and their visibility is obscured by darkness. The composition of the wood used for the city walls appears unique, and she is unsure what type of tree it would originate from. Angelus rides ahead for a moment but stops just short of the gate in order to address the guards.

"Good evening, sirs," Angelus says up to the top of the walls. Soon enough, two guards appear from behind a parapet and look over the edge.

"Announce yourself," one of them orders, not wasting any time.

"I am Angelus, nephew to Gruff, a bridgeman at the Northwest Chasm."

The two guards take a moment to confide in each other, then one of them makes a motion with his hand. Moments later, the gates begin to shift. Strangely enough, only half the gate is moving. Like a deck of cards overlapping each other, the gate is shifting to the right and overlapping the adjacent portion of door. A horrible, screeching mechanical sound accompanies every movement of these doors. It is almost too much to bear when standing near it, so Angelus directs his horse to rejoin the group not far away.

As Fortia watches the gate, she realizes that it is actually hung from a rail built into the haunches of a large archway above it while also being guided by another rail below. It is only after some patience observing its movement that a space to the left opens, making enough room for men and horses.

Approaching the opening on horseback, she finally gets a better look at the wood that forms this wall. She is surprised to see that it has the consistency of stone.

"What is this wood?" She is confused, but Angelus is happy to share what he knows.

"This is petrified wood," he explains. "It dates back to when the kingdom was first established. My uncle says it was transported here from the dry beds that made up part of the Lost Kingdom of Chestnut, though no one I know has ever seen this place."

Soon enough, they emerge on the other side of the main gate. The expectation of a grand cityscape before them is blunted by the realization that they have entered a pit of sorts. They are all standing on a large wooden platform which is roughly twenty feet below the level of the guards above them. Flanked on three sides by stone walls, this would be a precarious spot for any attacker who had breached the gate.

Soon enough, the platform begins to rise, and after a time, they find themselves approaching ground level of the city. Guards in brown leather armor stand by cautiously, and one of them approaches the edge to address them.

"Who leads your group?" He seems to be the captain, and Matthius dismounts his horse before answering him.

"I am Matthius, Captain of the Army of Macadamia. We come to you as travelers, though. We are not here on King Tonitro's orders."

The guard considers this, and he frowns with reluctance. In times like this, it is best to defer to royalty. "King Potilius will want to speak with you. Everyone, please follow me to his residence."

The group dismounts and follows him into a moderate bailey space, which is flanked on all sides by tall, heavy timber walls. There is another timber gate here, which is already open, and something of the cityscape beyond this can now be seen.

~ ~ ~

The hour is late at Gruff's home. Still sitting beside the large mounted crossbow, he has started a generous fire not far away. Since he is expecting company, he attempts to stay awake as long as he can, but the comfort of the fire is taking its toll. It is easy to slip off into sleep for a moment.

"Bridgeman!" a voice comes from across the chasm.

Gruff starts awake. He slowly rises from his chair and stretches, calmly looking across the dark chasm to address the startling voice.

"Hello there." He struggles to see them in the dark and can't quite make out the number of people present. "Do you seek passage?"

"Yes," the voice says. "What is the toll?"

"Light some torches so I can see you." Gruff is right to be suspicious. "If you are merchants, the toll is five pieces. If citizens, then there is no toll here."

After a moment, some sparks of flint are seen, and soon, a torch at ground level is ablaze. A man lifts it up. Gruff can now see the burned face of Malleus, still in his black armor with his arm bandaged in a sling. He has six companions, each of them standing beside a horse. They are all in black armor with only a minimal variety of color elsewhere. Other than their uniform leather armor, there is nothing to reveal them as soldiers or part of some larger organization. Malleus moves the torch across his group, so Gruff can see how many people are there. Harris is with them.

Gruff looks over the group and recalls Matthius's warning.

"What is your business?" He keeps a straight face, trying not to reveal too much.

"We are here on the order of King Tonitro," Malleus says. "By the Treaty of Serenus and Potilius, we have a right to passage."

Gruff considers this. He knows they have a right to ask for passage, but he needs to find a way to delay them at least. Stretching his old joints, he moves over to the large wooden mechanism that controls the bridge and begins cranking it. In the process, he uses his foot to move a concealed rock into a position so that it catches a gear. A practiced maneuver that has yet to fail him. With its next turn, the mechanism halts. It has only moved the bridge halfway into the rotation across the chasm, scarcely of use to anyone. Gruff pretends to push on the mechanism, acting out the struggle for a time.

"Let me get my tools." Feigning concern over the device. "I think I can fix this with a bit of oil and ingenuity." He turns and walks back toward his home.

Malleus has a sour look of frustration as he consults his group with a thought.

"We have no time for this. Which one of you can make that jump?" Referencing the dark leap to the edge of the bridge, which is now only partly facing them.

A few of them stare warily at him, unsure they can safely maneuver that leap without falling to their death.

"I can make that," Harris offers. "Perhaps I can help him get the mechanism moving."

Malleus nods to approve. Harris readies herself at the edge of the chasm. She steps back a number of strides and digs her feet in. Swiftly, she sprints forward. Nearly at full speed when her feet push off the edge of the chasm.

It seems like almost too long a leap. The grouping there watches with a hint of concern.

She lands safe. Rolling to a stop on the bridge's surface. After a brief moment recovering, she readies herself to jump again at the other side. With just as much skill, she makes the landing on the other edge of the chasm. Dusting herself off, she approaches Gruff who is at the mechanism pretending to have a go at the problem.

"Harris," she introduces herself with a kind smile. "What seems to be the issue?"

Gruff was not expecting this…He stands, fumbling for an excuse only to remain silent.

Harris bends forward and inspects the mechanism. She stops as she realizes the presence of this very obvious stone holding up the gears, but she does not react right away. Gruff sees her studying it, and his brow furrows with confusion.

Harris glances back at him, shares a bit of the smirk on her face. Soon enough, Gruff realizes that she is not going to reveal his ploy here.

"I think we will need some time to work on it," she says aloud, projects her voice enough so that the men across the chasm can hear her.

Malleus gives a frustrated sigh, but he has resigned himself to the idea that Harris is working on it. He commands to his party, "Lash the horses and gather wood for a fire. Somebody cook me some meat." He proceeds to tie up his own horse.

Back at the bridge mechanism, Gruff kneels down next to Harris, who is busy inspecting the broken device.

"Do you know Matthius?" he whispers to her, still a bit confused by her reactions here.

"We are allies," Harris whispers with a smile in her response. "How long can we make this ruse last?"

"It has worked for a good long while before, but we won't be getting any rest in the process." Gruff pulls a tool from his belt and makes a go at wedging it between two meaningless parts of the mechanism. It looks like work is being done here, but really, nothing of value is being achieved.

Harris glances over at the crossbow nearby. She notices something about the arrow mounted there. It has a rather thick head on it, perhaps more than is ideal for good aerodynamics, and it is only crudely shaped like an arrow.

"Interesting choice of arrow," she whispers to him.

"Yes." Gruff smiles. "It will make for a good show if they get a fire lit."

Harris stands, walks over to the ledge, and addresses the men on the other side.

"Captain, I think we can get it moving, but it may take a bit of time. The large gear connected to the pully adjacent here will need to be reseated and per—"

"There's no time for this, Harris," Malleus interrupts. "Work quickly. We'll bring some hot food to you both once the bridge is open." He arranges wood for a fire as another man prepares a grill swing for the group.

Harris kneels down next to Gruff, again whispers to him.

"You can hit that fire with one shot?" She has a doubt.

"I rarely miss," Gruff responds confidently. He removes a hammer and a triangular wedge, places it under the largest gear, and has a weak go at hammering it. Harris considers the plan. She knows that this will unfold with some uncertainty.

"Once we get this moving, I'll need to put on a good show for them."

Gruff understands. He taps on some armor plating near his right shoulder, showing her that he has a good area of leather just underneath that portion of his vestments.

Harris nods to him with understanding and continues making an effort to pretend they are repairing the device.

The men on the other side have rapidly lit a campfire using the torch. One of them is already cooking something on the grill swing. Malleus sits on a large stone nearby and sharpens his knife. He seems to be healing well and removes his sling. Moving his arm around, he feels like he can do without the extra support, so he folds it up and stores it in his rucksack.

Malleus looks across the chasm to Gruff and Harris. They appear to be hard at work. Gruff is hitting something with a hammer, it seems. One of his men approaches Malleus from nearby, hands him a wooden skewer with some meat on it. Malleus takes it without a word of thanks, almost as though it was owed to him.

He eats the meat and wanders a bit, looks around the area of the chasm. He can hear the sound of the water below, though the moonlight is unable to pierce deep enough down the cliff to see the rapids. A few moments pass as he eats, but Malleus notices the dirt around the edge of the chasm is disturbed. He realizes these are horse hooves and footprints scattered in the area where the bridge's edge would join the cliff side.

"Has someone crossed recently?" Malleus projects across the chasm to Gruff, who stands quickly to respond from behind the mechanism.

"Surely. Numerous people." He ducks back behind the device, continues his subterfuge at repairing the gears.

"Was there a group of men with a child?" Malleus almost expects the answer he knows.

Gruff freezes at hearing this. He looks to Harris, a silent request for advice. She sighs but nods, suggesting he should respond truthfully. Gruff has a look of frustration, feels like this may be the start of something painful. He stands up again.

"Yes, much earlier this morning. They said they were heading toward Colocynth."

At hearing this, Malleus signals to his men, swings his hand in a circle to suggest that they need to wrap it up. The men finish eating their meat and start disassembling the grilling swing.

Gruff kneels again and whispers to Harris. "I think we are out of time."

Harris leans to the side some, shows Gruff the knives on her belt line. He seems to understand. Standing up, he takes a deep breath in preparation for this act of subterfuge.

"Have another whack at it with that hammer," he says to Harris, projecting his voice still. "I'll grab some more oil, and we'll get this moving."

Gruff moves away toward the house, and Harris continues hammering on the wedge. Just as he approaches the house, he swiftly changes direction. He grabs the stock of the crossbow, aims it quickly across the chasm, and fires.

Malleus has turned his back on them, now busy preparing his horse to move again. The fire nearby him shuffles suddenly, and a few embers fly up. Malleus notes the disturbance and quickly realizes there is now an arrow sticking out of the fire. He and his men look confused for a moment. Where did this come from?

The fire explodes into the night. Embers and burning wood light up the area as they are launched in all directions. The horses rear up as three of them scare and sprint down the nearby road. One randomly veers off into the woods.

Malleus recovers from this, gets to his feet, and glares across the chasm. He sees Harris jump up from behind the mechanism as she pulls a knife from her hip and throws.

With a sharp crack, it sticks into Gruff's shoulder. Hitting right where the armor is. Making a show of it, he falls backward. Shuffling up to his feet again, he quickly leaps over a small tree stump. His horse is nearby, and he jumps onto the animal then gallops away into the darkness of night.

Harris makes a movement to chase him, but—

"Harris, stop!" Malleus halts her in her tracks. She turns back to see the men near Malleus chasing after their horses. "Finish the repair! We need to get moving."

Harris moves back to the mechanism and continues hammering for a few moments more. Soon enough, she removes the meaningless wedge that she was banging on and reaches into the device to dislodge the stone. She reverses the mechanism a moment, and it begins moving, then pushes forward, and the bridge redirects toward the perpendicular.

Crossing the bridge back to the other side, she pretends to look frustrated as Malleus waits for a report.

"Sabotage, I'm sure of it." She feigns a look of anger. "I suspect that he damaged the gear to prevent it from moving easily after Matthius and his men crossed."

"Foolish old man..." Malleus sneers with frustration. "You were fast on the draw with that knife, though. Excellent work." He gives her a sneer of approval, and it seems this is the best gesture he can make to compliment someone. Harris smiles in thanks, but her attention is on other things.

"If King Potilius knows we are coming, it may complicate things for us."

Malleus ponders this. He is not entirely sure how this will change their mission.

Harris moves to her horse and the animal is still shaken by the explosion. She calms it with a reassuring hand, then removes some nuts from a satchel and eats a quick handful.

"I'll help them gather their horses." She swiftly moves off into the woods nearby, leaving Malleus there with a snarl of anger on his face.

Chapter 9

THE FIRST IMPRESSION Fortia has of the Closed Forest of Pignoli is that it is very different from Macadamia. Most noticeably, while there are countless trees here, nearly every structure is built from brick and stone. Additionally, the city is built on a large hillside, and most buildings are situated on a different level than the adjacent structures. When the city was first established, the parcels of land were rather small and disorganized. There are no predominant straight lines in the urban fabric as a result, and the streets that developed around those landlines took similar form. Stairs or ramps interrupt every path, and it is rare that you walk in a straight line for very long as the streets turn and wind regularly. At times, the person taking a stroll through the city can see numerous buildings ahead of them, though, at other times, they feel like they are surrounded by retaining walls and staircases.

Much of the city is built upon a stratum of bedrock, which has formed a large hilltop landmass. This geology is occasionally visible in the form of a garden wall for a residence or a small outcropping of an undeveloped area. Were one to have a bird's eye view, they would see a moderate highway of sorts that runs adjacent to the city walls in the form of gentle slopes and valleys. To traverse the city at its cross-section, though, requires a tolerance for climbing and descending stairs or ramps, but if you are not in a rush, the beauty of the city can be easily appreciated. The frequent changes in level while ambulating through the urban fabric will grant the viewer something of a picturesque event at the top of every staircase or at the turn of every building's corner.

The single greatest appreciation of this city's construction, though, is the occasional elevated viewpoint upon which the Open Forest and much of the city's varied levels can be appreciated. These are scarce to find, and they do require some hiking to get to, but they are breathtaking once located.

The residence of King Potilius is one such location. As Fortia and her companions approach the main entrance, this viewpoint is immediately apparent. The moonlight shows it to be situated upon a cliff's edge, overlooking much of the Open Forest to the south and a glorious mountain range to the west. At the same time though, this viewpoint is situated at nearly the highest point in the city, which provides many excellent angles to see the roads and structures all around.

The front doors are at least twice the height of the average man and are decorated with a beveled pattern that fits this picturesque city well. The walls adjacent to these doors are composed of polished brown stones, many of which catch the moonlight with a subtle radiance, but others have a curious pattern within them.

A caretaker approaches Fortia and takes the reins of her horse. He guides it away as Arty hops off and into her arms. As the rest of their horses are moved to stables by other caretakers, the party of travelers gets situated to make a more formal appearance.

Fortia, however, examines the brown stones of the wall nearby her. As she looks closer, she sees a variety of impressions within some of them, patterns much like shells and even shellfish at times scattered within these stones. They appear to be a form of fossil plate, revealed during the process of refining these stones for the structure. Seeing her give attention to this detail, Angelus approaches her.

"They are remnants of dead creatures. In the days before men and animals as we know them, every living thing was said to have a hardened shell of stone around it."

Fortia can hardly imagine this, let alone believe it is truth. The look of amazement she has on her face is contagious, and Angelus cannot help but smile at her.

The door of the residence opens to reveal a rather grand caretaker who wears an elaborate and colorful dress. The uniqueness of this woman is apparent immediately. She has an enchanting and stunningly dark bark, almost as though made of ebony wood. Her hair is flowing and thick, full of curls of foliage. Elegantly stepping forward, she greets the group with a gentle smile.

Almost immediately, Matthius is taken by her. For a moment, he cannot look away, and as she notices this, she gives him a pleasant smile in response. Tiler nudges him to break the moment, though, giving a chuckle as he does.

"Welcome," she says. "I am Salamena, First Caretaker of this residence. I am at your service." A subtle bow is given to her guests.

Fortia watches as Angelus and the knights bow in response. Not knowing what else to do, she bows herself, though somewhat awkwardly. Matthius steps forward to respond but clears his throat briefly, not wanting to give a bad first impression.

"I am Matthius, Captain of the Army of Macadamia. With your guidance, we would be honored to greet the king and alert him to our purpose here." Salamena appears very interested in him, and for a moment, she is caught off guard by this rather handsome visitor.

"The hour is late…The king and queen are dining, though we will inquire about their availability."

She makes a slight head gesture to her right side, and another Caretaker, who was concealed behind the edges of the portico, makes a swift turn, moves off into the residence.

Soon enough the others in the group have announced themselves to Salamena. At last, Fortia steps forward.

"I am Fortia of Macadamia, daughter of Constans and Sedo of Macadamia."

With this, Salamena's smile grows brighter and her eyes light up.

"Constans! How is that excellent man? Has he traveled here with you today?"

At this point Fortia is not surprised to learn that Salamena knows her father, but the thought of her parents in that prison has interrupted this pleasant exchange for her. The intrigue and excitement of this new place have been blunted by thoughts that are difficult to dismiss. Matthius, seeing her distracted somehow, quickly responds for her.

"Would that he was here, we would all feel much safer." His solemn tone is not lost on her, and Salamena, being the excellent host that she is, recognizes this as a topic that should not be discussed in a doorway. Pleased by these introductions, she gestures to them, welcoming them to enter.

They are guided into a vaulted foyer with a large skylight and an elaborate staircase. Elegant sculptures are chiseled into the stones all around them. By the time everyone has entered, the caretaker who had run off to speak with the king is on his way back to the foyer. He whispers to Salamena.

"First one, if you feel there is urgency, the king and queen are open to company."

Salamena is pleased to hear this and she makes a quick count of their guests before responding further. "Please notify the kitchen staff to prepare for five."

The caretaker runs off. Laderas and Tiler are somewhat intrigued by this woman. If they didn't know better, they would have thought she was the queen herself.

~ ~ ~

Even after more than a century of his reign, nobody knows how old King Potilius is. A number of years ago, a 152-year-old Pignolian citizen named Mendax died after a horse fell on him and cracked his trunk. This man was something of a local legend in more than one kingdom, and as older men are prone to do, he frequently told stories in taverns about being young. One of these was about witnessing the grand coronation of a young King Potilius, and as he told it, Potilius was older than him at that time. Whatever the actual number may be, nothing about King Potilius masks his age. He appears old in nearly every way that an old man can be.

Sitting at the head of a long but not too grand dining table, he is wearing thick and comfortable nighttime garments. His sturdy old trunk fills up much of the chair's platform. Some might say he is a fat man, but in truth his girth is simply the result of exceptional age. His hair has grown past the woven foliage of most people and has developed into dense branches. The thick bark of his face is composed of various knots, and a handful of scars adorn his right cheek. Time has been both good and bad to him, but nonetheless, he seems content. For this reason, it is rare that his sappy brown eyes do not smile, and when they do not, it is for good reason. At this grand old age, though, the arms become too stiff for the body. As Potilius dines, he slowly reaches for his cup of tea, almost as though struggling to get a grip on the handle.

His queen is much younger and far more attractive than he is, but anyone would be a fool to think she is the first queen to share his dinner table. Sitting not far from his side, she sees him making an attempt to pick up his tea. She spares him the struggle and moves his teacup closer to him. As he grabs it, he gives her a soft smile of gratitude. She returns the same to him, and her smile is as lovely as that humble moment was.

Neither of them is dressed for company, but she is certainly the more elaborate of the two. She wears a comfortable but intricately decorated dress, golden jewelry suitable to her position, and her soft, grassy hair is well-maintained. While she is his queen, in a sense, she is also his caretaker. As he returns his teacup to the table, she is eager to refill it from the adjacent teapot. Eventually, a handful of caretakers enter the room from the kitchen.

They carry numerous dining and serving plates, all that is needed for the table settings, as they begin to arrange this near the king and queen. Shortly after this, Salamena enters, and she subtly bows to them as she approaches the dining table.

"Thank you, my king and queen. May I present four travelers from Macadamia." As she says this, they each approach from behind her and make themselves more visible as they bow near the table.

"Laderas, a merchant and retired Lieutenant of the Second Division. Tiler, owner and operator of the Cowan's Eaves Tavern and Inn. Matthius, Captain of the Army of Macadamia, and certainly not the least, Fortia, daughter to Constans and Sedo of Macadamia."

At hearing Fortia's name, the king's eyes light up.

"Fortia!" He quickly makes an attempt to stand from the table. The queen rises to assist him and Salamena is not far behind her. They both make an effort to support him as he struggles to his feet.

Having never seen someone quite this old, Fortia cannot help but be concerned for his well-being. Her grandparents had both died before she was old enough to separate herself from the support of her mother's trunk. It is difficult for her to imagine how life would be enjoyable at such a late age, regardless of the obvious comforts inherent to this residence.

Once he is upright, though, Potilius takes a moment to kiss his wife's hand, then smiles to her with thanks.

He turns his attention to Fortia and waddles over to greet her.

"Many, many times has your father graced my table with stories of you, child. Why he even once told me how you and your faithful pup Arty once saved him from a boar."

Fortia smiles as she recalls this event. This endearing man has seemed to almost instantly charm her and put her at ease.

"Arty was fierce that day." She is very proud of her friend and companion.

"I am certain he was." Potilius pets the pup. He reaches into his pocket and removes a nut, which he quickly tosses to the side. As Arty shuffles out of Fortia's arms to retrieve it, Potilius leans in to share a secret with her.

"It is said that every dog in Pignoli loves their king, and now you know why." He smirks, and Fortia responds with a chuckle. He gestures to have her sit at the table next to him, and Salamena guides the rest of the men to place settings.

Potilius returns to his chair, and with Salamena's help, he sits. Soon enough, food and tea are served to everyone as caretakers from the kitchen staff plate out a hearty meal.

"An interesting assembly of travelers." Potilius looks at Matthius, an air of suspicion in his otherwise gentle voice.

Matthius takes a sip of his tea but soon turns his attention to Potilius.

"Would you like me to speak freely, good king?"

Potilius raises an eyebrow, suddenly more curious about the conversation to come.

"Like Constans, we three men are knights in the Ordo Nux Aurea. Fortia here witnessed the coronation of Tonitro. She found a shard of the nut he crushed, and it was clear—"

Potilius stops him with a gesture. He turns to his wife for a moment.

"Suavis, would you please ask Salamena to send a messenger out to General Certus? I will likely need to speak with him in the morning."

She stands, leans in, and, with an endearing smile she kisses him squarely on the lips before removing herself from the table. Potilius watches her walk away, enjoys the view as she goes, but also appreciates the opportunity to speak with the guests alone.

"A wise man once said, 'It is good to be the king.'" He says with a smirk. Tiler and Laderas hold back laughter for a moment, and Potilius smiles brightly at them both. He soon returns his attention to Matthius again.

"Are you still the captain of your army?" Potilius has a rather cunning wit.

Matthius is taken slightly off guard by the question. It is perhaps an elephant in the room which has not yet found a room to be discussed in. With a sincere frown, though, he reveals that this has been a question at the back of his mind for a few days now.

"I know that nothing Tonitro says can make my men truly turn away from me."

"Hear, hear!" Laderas cheers. Everyone at the table appreciates that confidence it seems.

"However," Matthius continues, still feeling uncertain, "I would be a fool to think he has not started to sully the waters of my reputation. We met an operative and crossed blades with him not far from the border. He was well trained, and he would have recognized me."

Potilius listens, but he is deep in thought. There is a moment of silence following this. Everyone at the table continues their meal within that quiet, and Fortia is truly enjoying this array of fruits, nuts, meat and sapling cheese. Potilius, though, is still deep in thought. His eyes close for a time as he considers what he has heard thus far.

Eventually, Tiler takes an interest in Potilius and looks up from his plate with a growing concern. He studies him, unsure what to make of this moment. Save for breathing, Potilius is nearly motionless. Tiler looks to Laderas and Matthius with a questioning gaze, and they both appear somewhat puzzled.

Suddenly, Potilius's eyes open wide. He smiles, and something of a revelation is present.

"Peace…" he says, and everyone at the table looks away from their food. They wait for his next words, but he simply stares across the table, far across the room, to an elaborate painting on the wall.

Everyone follows his gaze, and when they see the painting, they become interested. It depicts a sort of diagram of a tree. It is a large, detailed, and colorful design that takes up much of the wall space between the two columns. At the various parts of the tree, the roots, the branches, the trunk, the leaves, etc. there are symbols. They are very old symbols, and even King Potilius scarcely knows all their true meaning.

"Fortia, do you know that tree?" Potilius directs her, though even after gazing at it for some time, she struggles to recognize what type of tree this would be.

"No, sir," she admits, not even sure she understands this as a painting of a tree.

"Before I was crowned King, my grandmother made that painting to commemorate an important moment in my youth. It is a very old tree, not far from the southern walls. The roots of this tree form a natural labyrinth, and walking the labyrinth was once a rite of passage for the young people of Pignoli."

Fortia has taken more of an interest in it now, and as she leans in to see more of the painting, Potilius continues.

"Angelus guided you all here, yes?" Potilius is perhaps planning something now.

"He wanted to stay with his horse tonight." Fortia almost wishes he was here, though.

"A good horse requires that type of loyalty at times." Potilius smiles at the thought, perhaps remembering some time in his life years ago. "After dinner, I would like you and Angelus to accompany us to this tree. If you are brave enough, perhaps you will learn something new about yourself."

With that, King Potilius cautiously shuffles his chair back and begins the struggle of standing up. Fortia quickly stands to assist him. Once upright, though, Potilius takes a moment to address Matthius again.

"You will have all the support you need from Pignoli once you find the Golden Nugget. If my general is successful in the coming days, perhaps we can even come to rely on people who we now call our enemy."

Matthius has a confused look on his face. He is not really sure how all of that will manifest from what was said at the table just now. However, the king has made a bold statement in support of their mission. Matthius and the others quickly stand and bow their heads in gratitude. Potilius nods in acknowledgment. He turns to exit and leaves the guests to finish eating. Shortly after this, Salamena enters and gracefully addresses the table.

"Please take your time and enjoy your food. In one hour, King Potilius requests that you meet him at the entry of the residence. We will all journey down to the Dry Woods." She gives a brief bow before she exits and steps away.

Tiler looks over to Fortia, notices that she seems a bit uncertain about all this. She is normally the first to embrace a challenge, but so much has already happened on this journey.

"Worry not, Fortia." He has a calming tone. "Every rite of passage is designed to be survived. If not, there would be no passage."

She seems to understand, but she remains weary of the unknown. Arty jumps up on her lap, and after a moment with her best friend, she begins to feel comforted by his presence. Perhaps it is this place, the food, or simply the result of good company, but a feeling of renewed strength begins to settle in.

~ ~ ~

There are many places in Oakenmeer that can only be described as haunting, and the location of this enormous tree is certainly one that Fortia would designate as such. Perhaps it is just the grandeur of the tree that stands before her, though, as things of this size are best described as sublime.

The trunk of this tree is so wide that if she doesn't turn her head, she can't even see from one side of it to the other. It is not a very tall tree, though, and many details of the canopy are easily visible from the ground. Perhaps the most haunting aspect of it comes from the strange whiteness of the bark. The unique bark on this tree almost appears to be composed of small crystals. Perhaps coincidentally, or perhaps it is just the nature of this place, but there is a bit of fog creeping by tonight. The haunting nature of this dark, foggy location and this enormous, foreboding tree would be justification enough for even an adult to feel unsettled here.

Fortia and her traveling companions stand adjacent to King Potilius and Salamena. All the visitors to this place are similarly in awe. They have never seen a tree with white crystalline bark, let alone one as expansive as this. While there is fog in this area, Fortia cannot help but notice that, unlike other surrounding trees, there is no fog actually in close proximity to this one tree.

Not far from them are the lateral roots of it. There are two large openings in the roots here, natural archways that are positioned side by side. Visible beyond them is only slightly more wood of the roots, with open space above. In the daylight, more channels of root space might be visible beyond these openings, though in the dark of night, they are not easy to discern.

Angelus is cautious as he approaches Fortia and Potilius.

"We have to go in there?" Not too humble to admit that he feels uncertain, his confidence shrinks as he takes in the weighty presence of this enormous tree.

"I was about your age when I did." Potilius seems to recall it in his mind's eye, fondly remembering the experience. "I died that day and was reborn."

Fortia does not like the sound of that. She looks at Potilius with something of distrust now. He knows this place well, though, and understands her thoughts in this moment. Some words of preparation for the forthcoming experience are warranted.

"This is a labyrinth, Fortia. Not a maze. If you enter from one archway, you will exit from the other, every time. There is only one path and no way to get lost as the path always leads to the one exit or the one entrance."

She and Angelus both feel reassured by this. They seem to take more of an interest in the idea of this challenge now.

"However," he continues, and that word strikes Fortia, "the Dry Woods are not without danger. If you successfully walk the whole labyrinth, you will never again be the same person you are today."

Fortia looks to Angelus again, once more feeling uncertain. Without hesitation, though, Angelus offers her his hand and lends her a sincere smile. He feels ready to guide her into this challenge, and this alone seems like enough to convince her.

She hands Arty to Tiler and gives the pup a brief hug goodbye as she embraces the sense of adventure here. Reluctantly, she takes Angelus's hand, and together they approach the leftmost archway. Still somewhat uncertain but also very curious, they step into the void.

Tiler and Arty watch them enter, and Arty groans out a concern that is mutually felt. Once they have crossed the archway, a left turn is made, and they are quickly out of sight. Tiler comforts the pup with some gentle pets on the back, though soon he turns to Potilius.

"How did you know they would go?" His curiosity gets the better of him.

"The brave will always be tempted by a chance to shape their own fate."

~ ~ ~

Fortia and Angelus walk at a steady pace on a silty dirt path between the lateral root walls of this mysterious white tree. Above them, the canopy is largely still visible for the majority of the time. It is eerily quiet, though, as though no sound outside these lateral roots is allowed to enter. Fortia cannot help but take note of the dry air here. Just taking a few deep breaths she can smell and taste the absence of any humidity around her.

Together, they pass under the occasional archway or traverse a short tunnel space as they make progress. If the foreboding quiet and darkness were not so present here, it might otherwise be a very scenic experience. A lovely evening stroll or perhaps an opportunity to become better acquainted.

Now feeling less worried about this place, Fortia gazes at the roots around her with an inquisitive pinch of the eyes.

"How is it that these tree roots have grown into such a perfect pathway?" A fair question, almost suggesting to Angelus that the tree must be aware of its own growth.

"It seems impossible, doesn't it? As impossible as the luck that a sap beetle might bestow upon us." Angelus has made a good point, which Fortia has received well. It somehow feels very potent, given everything she has experienced.

"What an interesting man, King Potilius," Fortia says, now making conversation on this somewhat slow walk.

"Yes, he has never failed to guide his people well." Angelus crouches down, offers his hand to help balance Fortia. Together, they maneuver themselves under a low archway of roots only to continue on the path beyond this.

"How old is he? He must be at least one hundred seventy years old."

"Truly, nobody knows. My uncle has never known a time when Potilius was not his king. I would have to ask him if even his parents spoke of another king during their lives."

"You've met him before?" She ducks under another low archway with him.

"On a few occasions. He has stopped at the bridge to visit with my uncle."

Occasionally, the passage between these walls of root wood becomes very narrow, and they are forced to clear it by walking one in front of the other. During one of these occasions, Fortia notices something. As she exhales a breath, the bark of this tree seems to react to this.

"Look at this," she says, and she breathes out again, this time purposefully blowing on the bark. As she does, they both see the white crystals of the bark appear to absorb the moisture of her breath. Any water vapor from her breath quickly crystalizes onto the bark of these roots.

Angelus is tempted. He reaches his hand forward, and with a fingertip, he touches the bark.

"Ah!" He withdraws quickly with a look of shock on his face. "It burned me…"

Fortia watches as the bark he touched seems to crystallize a small amount, and a worrisome look grows out of them both. She is eager to get moving now.

"This has been a nice walk. Any idea how much further?"

Angelus glances at her with concern, but they push forward into this subtle challenge.

~ ~ ~

Back at the entry to the Dry Woods, Matthius and Salamena stroll through the area adjacent to the tree. Together, they take in the stars and the moonlight. Reduced as they are by the fog around them, it is still a nice night nonetheless. Matthius appears to be somewhat enchanted on this walk, and Salamena has just finished telling him a story about herself.

"And you've lived here with Potilius ever since? Ten years now?" Matthius appears amazed by what he has just heard, and his curiosity is piqued.

"Yes. He has become like a second father to me. I learn as much as I can here." Salamena smiles with sincerity.

"A truly incredible story…I often wish I had more opportunities to work closely with King Serenus. He was a great king, but he was not overly interested in matters of the military."

They wander in the moonlight together, and not far ahead of them are the other members of the party. Potilius is engaged in play with Arty, tossing him nuts from an endless supply in his pocket. Tiler and Laderas are relaxing on large stones nearby, engaged in their own conversation. The fog and darkness of this place have fallen into the background, and it is clear that Salamena and Matthius are very comfortable around each other.

Salamena cautiously turns to Matthius and stops their pace. She looks at him with the gentle gaze that Matthius has become accustomed to seeing from her.

"Do you have family back in Macadamia?" A curious question… "A wife?"

Matthius smiles. "I often wish my life could be that quiet and warm."

Salamena feels those words deep inside her. She cannot help but want to reach out and take his hand, and she almost does. Her hand nearly touches him. Instead, it clenches into itself. The thought of her duties here to Potilius makes an intrusion when they truly should not.

~ ~ ~

Back within the lateral roots of the Dry Woods, another narrow tunnel is not far ahead of Angelus and Fortia. He takes the lead as they move through it, and Fortia cannot help but take a deep breath. She has begun to feel somewhat fatigued, almost lightheaded.

"Are you feeling well?" She shakes off a momentary feeling of dizziness.

"It does feel harder to breathe…" He is definitely feeling unsure of this place now.

"Should we turn back?" She again feels dizzy, and a moment of frustration grows.

"I'm not sure it would help. We may be closer to the exit than the entrance."

Fortia knows he could very well be right, though this feeling of fatigue is becoming very prominent. She is beginning to have difficulty keeping her eyes open.

"Maybe we could…" she is woozy, "…just rest a moment?" She leans to the side, instinctively extending her hand to support herself. "Ah!" The burn quickly sets in, but for a moment it helps to wake her up.

Angelus grasps her, supports her at the shoulder to guide her forward. As he does this, he notices that her face has become particularly dry, almost as though the space between her young bark and sapwood is separating and cracking. He looks at his hands, and similarly, he is drying out.

"The air is just too dry here…Our sapwood cannot breathe." He struggles to walk, balancing her on his arm during subsequent steps. Continuing to move forward as best he can, he attempts to guide her. She is very fatigued, though, not even acknowledging his comments.

"We need to keep moving, Fortia. I think we are more than halfway around the tree."

Fortia slumps in his arms, almost unconscious now. It's getting harder and harder for Angelus to carry her, but he keeps pushing himself. He stumbles, almost falls as he becomes so very dizzy and lightheaded. Rapidly blinking his eyes and shaking his head, he tries to keep himself alert. Determined, he drags her as best he can.

Finally, he can't advance any further. He falls to his knees but supports Fortia and helps her to the ground. Barely able to keep himself awake, he lays her down, and she is now fully unconscious, prone on the dirt. She is almost lifeless, though still taking very shallow breaths.

Angelus looks at his hands and they are deeply cracking now. His bark and sapwood are almost flaking from the lack of moisture and oxygen around them. "The bark must breathe." It is a lesson learned early in life when anyone learns to swim, but the tree they are within must be absorbing all the water vapor and moisture into itself. Very little has been left behind for them to survive on.

Rolling up his sleeve, he can see the bark on his arm becoming parched and brittle, almost frightening to see. He removes his knife, and with a swift stab, he punctures deep into his arm. He shrieks out, but he is too weak to truly react to the pain. Positioning himself above Fortia, he lets his sap begin to drain onto her. Slowly, it pours out onto her exposed arms and soaks into the adjacent clothing. Eventually, Angelus falls unconscious, and they lie in this horrific state.

Fortia's eyes are shut, but they appear to be moving rapidly. She is dreaming for a time, but this does not last very long. The sacrifice Angelus has made begins to take effect.

Her eyes flutter open, and she works to regain her senses. Seeing what he has done, she is overcome with sadness. Her bark is absorbing the oxygen in his sap. A tear comes into her eye, though it evaporates quickly in this terrible dryness. She is still too weak to truly weep or protest. If only Angelus had realized that she had a canteen strapped to her belt.

She reaches for it, struggling to grasp it in her weakened state, but she finally gets a hold of it. Pulling the top off, she immediately pours water all over her face. Very rapidly, she becomes more alert. Pouring some water on Angelus, she awaits the same response, but he does not seem to be recovering. Rising to her knees, she grabs his arm and presses it against the bark. A squeal is heard as the crystals absorb any remaining moisture on his hand, but he does not react.

Fortia gets to her feet. She can feel herself much more awake now, but she pours some more water over her face and arms. Returning the canteen to her hip, she grabs Angelus's lifeless arms. She drags him through this awful place, and every exertion now strains her in agony.

This continues through one turn after another. Dipping under archways, tugging him through narrow passages. She is beyond physically exhausted, but with determination, she continues to move him steadily through the labyrinth.

At times, she feels lightheaded, and sparing the water, she instead runs her arm over the bark. There is a good burn, and it raises her adrenaline some, giving her enough motivation to keep going.

Finally, after one last turn, Fortia sees the exit not far away. With the end nearby, she rallies once again and pours more water over herself. Empowered by this, she pulls Angelus forward, forward again. The last stretch feels like a mile. Finally, they are through the exit, and she steps out of these horrible roots, collapsing beyond the archway in exhaustion.

Limp and drained of energy, she lays there and looks up at the canopy overhead. She takes deeper breaths. The moisture of the air here feels very welcome in her lungs.

Potilius and Salamena move quickly to them.

"Tend to the boy, Salamena," Potilius orders, and she rapidly applies a sap-like salve to his arms and face.

"He is alive," she says, still examining his condition. "He is still in the dream, though."

Potilius slowly kneels beside Fortia. A difficult position for him to achieve at this age.

"Did you have a dream, Fortia?"

Almost angry at him, she is reluctant to answer, but she is surprised to hear him ask this.

"A storm." She pours water over herself as she recovers.

"Was there someone in the storm?" he asks, and Fortia looks at him sincerely.

"My mother. She was wearing leather armor."

"Think, Fortia. Try hard to remember the image." He gives her a moment before he continues. "Are you absolutely certain about this dream?"

Fortia closes her eyes, still struggling to recover from the harrowing experience but also trying to follow the guidance of this king.

She thinks hard. In her mind's eye, she recalls the image of the storm. A rocky shoreline is adjacent to a wild and tempestuous sea. Dark clouds are overhead, and an unrelenting wind moves the sand and foliage as it blows. Amidst all of this, a woman in dark red armor is clad with weapons. She stands on the rocks of the shoreline with a look of contemplation as she confronts the sea. Cresting waves break all around her, but she is unafraid.

"No." Fortia's eyes burst open with a sudden realization. "It was me…"

Potilius smiles wide, almost laughs with joy at hearing this. He takes a deep breath of satisfaction, letting her have a moment to appreciate that realization before he speaks again.

"Hundreds of years ago, I threw myself out of that same exit. Just as you are, I laid myself here. Exhausted, frustrated, and certainly dry as a tinder." He recalls every detail, it seems. A moment so many years ago that is still very real to him.

"In my dream, I saw myself wearing the crown of a king, standing in a valley between two great mountains."

Salamena kneels beside Fortia and begins to apply the same salve to her as she did to Angelus. Potilius continues the explanation.

"There will be a moment on your journey, Fortia, not long from now. You will need to choose between remaining who you are today or taking a single step into the uncertain world of that person you saw in your dream."

Fortia hears him say this, but she is still so exhausted. He extends his hand to her confidently, and she wearily reaches for it. He helps her up, but she soon looks with concern to Angelus as he is still unconscious.

"He will recover." Potilius is confident. "The liniment Salamena has put on you both will help to renew his sap."

Fortia is more than ready to leave this haunting place behind, but she is reluctant to leave Angelus there. She and Potilius stay with him, just at his side.

Arty moves to take his favorite spot in Fortia's arms, and she is glad to have him there.

The abundance of misty fog is nearly unrelenting here. It is a peculiarity of this place that has helped sustain this enormous tree for more than ten thousand years. In those many generations, the fate of a thousand lives has been foretold. Had anyone ever documented such experiences, they would perhaps have solved a great mystery.

At least this much can be known about fate…A hundred and sixty years have separated those two nights, but a young girl and an old king have now shared the same incredible experience.

~ ~ ~

The next morning Fortia wakes to sunlight in her eyes. The bed she is in is not much smaller than her bed at home, and the comfort it provides is fully welcome. Blankets and pillows are always appreciated by the weary, and Arty is taking his share of the comfort, as though he had lived here for many years already. It has been a while since she slept in a bed, and Fortia is in no rush to give that up right now. Embracing that comfort a while longer, it is only interrupted by a knock on the door. Sitting up slowly, she is still reluctant to embrace the morning.

"Come in." She knows that the day is starting around her.

Salamena enters with Fortia's clothing. They have been cleaned overnight and she places them on a bureau nearby.

"Good morning, Fortia. I trust you slept well?"

"Yes. This place is very comfortable, thank you."

"Excellent," she says with a smile. "Please join everyone for breakfast. Matthius told us of your fondness for nut cakes, and the chef has prepared his finest batch for you."

Salamena smiles and gracefully exits into the hall. Fortia reluctantly swings her legs out of the bed, still struggling to accept the daylight into her eyes.

The guest rooms of this residence are abundant in space and furniture but not overly lavish. Were a full tour provided, one would see that while the king and queen have a very fitting bedroom for their residence, they are not at all showered in luxury. If it were not for a history of significant warfare with their neighbor Pecan, the city might have even expanded outside of its original medieval walls, and this residence may be even more lavish.

Unfortunately, Pecan has not fully found its peace in the world, and they are constantly skirmishing to challenge the lines of demarcation between themselves and Pignoli. Every now and then, tensions develop on their border, and King Potilius must reluctantly respond.

It is this topic, in part, that he and General Certus are discussing in the dining hall this very morning. Certus is much younger but still not at all an inexperienced leader. He has clearly made the effort to look presentable to his king, but a warm pair of slippers betrays his comfort here. For him Potilius is not just a king who he bows to, but a lifelong friend who he knows will not lead him astray. They sip tea while they sit side by side at a small console table near the entry of the dining hall.

"I believe this will work, Certus." Potilius appears confident, as always.

"I would be a fool to doubt your judgment, good king," Certus responds, though his gestures betray a touch of uncertainty regarding this discussion. "I am simply reluctant to place my faith in the Kingdom of Pecan. They have harmed many of our citizens. Fully trusting them will take time."

Potilius understands. He places his teacup aside, and with both hands, he grips Certus's free hand, an effort to drive home the coming advice.

"This is an opportunity for all three of us northern kingdoms to unite. An opportunity like this has not presented itself often, not even in my long lifetime. Should it all go wrong, I would give my own sap to the battlefield in order to grant our citizens a lasting peace."

Certus smiles at hearing him say this. He places his teacup down and swiftly stands, now feeling fulfilled by this exchange. Potilius reaches for a folded parchment nearby. It is sealed in wax, having used the seal of his kingdom as proof that it originated from his desk. Certus takes it, already knowing what he needs to do.

"My best to the queen." He bows a moment and swiftly exits the room.

Potilius begins an effort to stand up. Simple things often feel like a struggle when aging. While the girth of age can be a burden, it is also a mark of distinction. It can take command of a room as quickly as any other force.

He moves to his position at the dining table. Place settings are laid out appropriately for everyone, and a variety of cold foods are already displayed.

As Potilius positions himself and prepares to sit down, Fortia approaches from behind.

"Please, let me help, sir." She moves eagerly toward him and helps him get comfortable in the chair.

"Your parents have raised a fine girl." With a smile, he gestures for her to sit beside him.

Soon enough a caretaker enters from the kitchen with a large platter full of nut cakes. Fortia's eyes are full of interest in those cakes, and on the floor nearby, Arty begins to whine for his breakfast.

Moments later a caretaker enters with a small plate, two nut cakes resting on it. They position it on the floor nearby Arty, and he shamelessly begins to eat.

Potilius and Fortia both watch him. A laugh grows between them as they observe his furious chewing. He gets as much food on the floor as he does in his mouth.

Moments later, Matthius and Tiler join them. The makings of a pleasant meal are coming together. Fortia smothers a stack of nut cakes on her plate with sweet oil. She has always said her mother's cakes are the best, but eating nut cakes at a king's table makes them even more delicious.

~ ~ ~

In the bailey at the city gate, Fortia, Tiler, Matthius, and Laderas ready their horses for the next leg of their journey. Soldiers of Pignoli are out and perform drills in the distance. The sunlight of a fine day is all around.

Salamena and King Potilius stand nearby, and Angelus has just jumped onto his horse, already prepared to begin the ride back to the Northwest Chasm. Potilius turns to him.

"Please give your uncle my regards. I hope to enjoy a cup of tea with him soon."

"It would be my pleasure, good ki—"

"A rider approaching!" a soldier interrupts them, and not far away, they can see the gate slide open to allow someone in. Soon enough, they see Gruff enter on horseback, and the platform adjacent to them begins rising. Potilius approaches the edge of the platform with a smile.

"Gruff! It is a pleasure to see you again."

"My king." He jumps off his horse, protects his injured shoulder with his opposite hand.

"What has happened, my friend?" Potilius turns to Salamena. "Check his arm, please."

"A party of six soldiers from Macadamia have crossed the bridge. I was able to stall them some, but by now, they are not far behind me."

"Without question," Matthius interrupts, "they have a similar goal as we do."

Potilius thinks it through. He considers for a moment whether this changes anything for his larger plan. He turns back to Matthius with a thought.

"I wonder if they have everything they need to succeed?"

"It is possible they have a map," Matthius considers this, "though the other items they would need to steal from us. That will not be easy for them…"

Potilius leans into Matthius, wanting to share a suggestion with him.

"May I recommend you give those items to Fortia? She will be more valuable to this quest than you may know."

Matthius nods in appreciation and shakes Potilius's hand before he mounts his horse. Tiler and Laderas are not far behind, but Potilius takes a moment more to speak with Fortia.

"Should you wish, Fortia, Arty can stay safe here with us. It may be difficult to care for him as you travel."

Fortia considers it, but one look at her faithful companion and she can see that Arty is ready for action. He wags his tail and seems eager to resume the adventure.

"I'm certain he would enjoy the comfort of this place, but I suspect he would be too angry at me if I left him behind."

Arty barks in agreement. She rests him on a blanket behind the saddle then mounts her horse.

"I envy you both." Potilius shares a sincere smile.

They all turn their horses onto the platform nearby, and Angelus soon joins them.

"I will tend to the bridge, Uncle." He speaks this with absolute confidence.

"Thank you, son." Gruff has a swell of pride on his face.

The platform slowly lowers them to the level of the gate, and Angelus is quick to position his horse next to Fortia.

"I will miss you, Fortia," he says with a gentle smile. She blushes in return, too bashful to receive a charming compliment. Angelus is bold enough to gently take her hand, and she does not protest.

"When we meet again, I will tell you about my dream." He kisses her hand, perhaps revealing something of the dream even now.

Fortia's smile has never been wider than in this moment. Nobody has ever been this flattering to her, and having this chance, she grips his hand a little bit tighter.

Chapter 10

AMIDST THIS SUNNY DAY, the small caravan of four travelers continues their journey south toward an uncertain destination. It is a day of consistent travel without interruption or worrisome events. Peaceful, quiet, and one could even say rhythmic.

The weather has been agreeable for much of this journey, and it is rather serendipitous that the season is good for this type of travel. Had these uncertain times made manifest a few months later, the burden of winter would complicate things.

While the fall colors have yet to fully blossom here in Pignoli, there is evidence in the subtle yellowing of leaves that a change is coming. Such colors represent a form of sacrifice. A chemical change is occurring within every tree and shrub, and it sets them on a path toward renewal. Autumn is the season when all natural things, which do not exist with the delusion of commanding their own fate, are confronted by an opportunity to begin a process of rebirth. It is in their nature to seek out such a path. To die and be reborn again later… Even if the path ends early for one of them, they must walk it. There is no sadness or shame in dying on this path, as such burdens of the mind do not exist in nature.

~ ~ ~

In the darkness of night, the exterior of the prison of Macadamia is a particularly harrowing place, but tonight, it is even more so as a rather extensive crowd has gathered in front of the building. These are not simply citizens, though. The crowd consists of soldiers from the Army of Macadamia, hundreds of them clearly have been summoned here. The front gates of the prison are open, and a handful of guards are positioned along the front façade. The moonlight is obscured by the surrounding trees tonight, and torches have been positioned well. It appears that an event is planned, and things will be getting underway soon.

In the dimly lit hall of the prison, three guards march toward Constans's cell. They unlock it, and one of them steps inside to retrieve him. Guiding him by his chains into the hallway, Constans struggles to keep his balance. He is almost too weak to stay upright without help. They all move toward the far end of the hall, then through another door that is already wedged open. Dim torchlights seem almost blazing in this bleak hallway.

They enter a foyer which is immediately adjacent to the front gates of the prison. A murmur of noises from the crowd outside is obvious. Guiding Constans by his chains, they move through the gates to the outside.

Once out on the patio, the crowd in front comes to a hush. The guards pull Constans over to the front of the patio and force him to his knees. He is too weak to resist as they shackle him to an iron ring that is embedded in the stone of the patio. They turn back into the prison.

For a time, there is near silence. Constans is scarcely able to keep himself upright on his knees. The awful dryness of his bark speaks volumes of his mistreatment. His hair is tossed about, and his clothing has become filthy. Clearly the Kingdom of Macadamia does not currently show much mercy to their prisoners, and until now, perhaps everyone who received such treatment had deserved it.

Soon enough, Tonitro approaches on horseback with a small entourage of his royal guards. The soldiers all make room for his approach, and when he reaches the patio, he swiftly dismounts. He moves with the energy and resolve that he has always displayed. After a few swift steps he has positioned himself in the center of the patio, not far from Constans or the pillory that is central to this area.

"Soldiers of Macadamia," Tonitro projects his voice well into the crowd, "I come to you today with frightful news. Via the operatives of our kingdom and other reliable resources, we have learned that the Kingdom of Pignoli plans to attack our great kingdom!"

The soldiers all around exchange verbalizations of surprise and frustration at hearing this. The sound of their chatter becomes too great, though. Tonitro signals for silence.

"This man, a nut oil miller from our own Open Forest, is a member of a secret order who is actively plotting against our fair kingdom."

The crowd here boos and bellows at Constans. Tonitro is selling this well, it seems.

"However—" he silences them with a gesture again, "—he has seen the error of his ways and has shared with us crucial information that will help to prevent the coming attack. For that reason, his sentence will be greatly commuted. He may at some time taste freedom, but never again will we call him a citizen of Macadamia."

The crowd cheers at hearing this, but for Constans, these words hit like lead. He had very little strength left even before that, but now he falls into tears as he drapes his head in misery.

Moments later, Sedo is guided out by her chains. She is equally battered and worn out. The guards position her behind the pillory. They open it, push her forward and she is locked into the awful wooden structure.

"His wife, though," Tonitro gestures to Sedo, "has not been as cooperative, and for this reason, she will remain imprisoned without any opportunity for freedom. Worse yet, she will carry the mark of a traitor for the rest of her life!"

A guard approaches quickly from behind. In his hand is a red-hot brand. He swiftly moves over to Sedo, and the brand is forced onto her exposed left arm.

Sedo screams out at the pain, and seeing this, Constans becomes enraged. He lunges at the guards in protest.

"NOOOOO!"

The chains are too short. He is yanked back to his knees quickly. Constans pulls on his chains as hard as he can, but they are unrelenting. Even screaming is difficult for him to maintain in this weakened state. He collapses…Only hate and tears can fill his face now.

The guards pull back the brand, and it has left behind a "P" on her arm, the mark of a traitor in any land across the Surviving Kingdoms.

The soldiers all around are unsettled, some of them yelling at Constans. Others throwing nuts at Sedo, who now cringes from the pillory as she recovers from the pain.

Tonitro steps in front of Constans, blocks the crowd from seeing him.

"Soldiers, I regret that I have yet more bad news to share." They quiet down to listen, and Tonitro holds their attention a moment. "To my own shame, I must make an admission to you all." Pausing, he gives added weight to his words. "One of our closest compatriots is a member of that order. Matthius, the captain of our great army, has betrayed us all."

At this news, the troops can hardly muster a word. Just a single glance in their direction, and Constans can tell they may or may not even believe what Tonitro just said.

"Our sources have reported that Matthius himself is leading a group of traitors, destined to join the forces of Pignoli in their attack against us."

The soldiers are still stunned by this, but soon enough, chatter among them quietly resumes. Perhaps his report of this is not falling on deaf ears after all.

"I have deployed some of our finest operatives to intercept this group of traitors, and with some good fortune, we will be successful. However! I am not willing to wait only to be placed under siege!" The soldiers appear to mumble an agreement between themselves as Tonitro continues.

"As we speak, both I and our highest-ranking officers are drawing up plans to pre-emptively invade Pignoli and eliminate the threat they pose to us!"

The soldiers don't seem opposed to this concept, though they have not yet cheered for this path of action either. Regardless, Tonitro quickly turns and signals to the guards. He points to Constans as a command to them. They unshackle him from the metal ring in the patio and begin dragging him back to the prison.

"This traitor," referencing Sedo, "will remain here for our whole kingdom to observe. Her shame, on display here, is a great triumph for us."

Tonitro is about to walk off stage when suddenly—

"MURDERER!" Constans screams out. The guards halt at the front gate of the prison as he yells out with all his remaining energy.

Tonitro glances behind him and sees Constans embrace one more moment of strength.

"MURDERER!" Constans bellows out again. Able to muster the strength to voice that one impactful word.

For a moment, Tonitro seems concerned, but his work is done here. He waves the guards to continue moving Constans inside, then moves swiftly toward his entourage.

The crowd is silent as Tonitro mounts his horse. From his saddle, he looks to the soldiers all around him. They return a quiet gaze at him, a look of confusion and internal conflict.

Regardless of everything said aloud, Tonitro can see that they are not entirely convinced by his words. If he were a wiser king, he might already know that men and women of good conscience can never fully ignore the truth that they feel inside, no matter what a leader may tell them.

~ ~ ~

Fortia and Matthius sit on a pair of large rocks in a dark camp, secluded well within the woods. With the threat of operatives from Macadamia nearby, they cannot risk lighting a fire or arranging large, easily visible tents. Not far away, Tiler and Laderas are already asleep. They have wrapped themselves in blankets and found a comfortable patch of grass to lay in. Arty is sawing logs nearby, not wasting any time to rest.

Matthius has spread out on the grass the items from the chest that Fortia recovered. He opens up the blanket, lays the remaining items on top of it and wraps the blanket into a flat square shape. He ties it shut with a short length of rope and places the entire assembly into his own rucksack, which he then hands to Fortia.

"You now carry the burdens of a knight, Fortia." He offers her a look of sincerity.

Fortia feels empowered by these words. She pulls the straps of the rucksack over her shoulders as she firmly takes possession of it. The confident gaze on Matthius's face suggests a feeling that he has put these items in good hands.

Soon enough they both lay down to rest as they wrap themselves in blankets. Fortia snuggles up to Arty and gives him cover from her own blanket. Even as she lies to sleep in the darkness of this cold forest, she is wearing the rucksack.

~ ~ ~

In the morning, the four travelers are all back on the main road, their horses moving at a decent pace through the sunlit forest of Pignoli. Fortia still carries the rucksack full of unexplained treasures. She chews on a handful of raw nuts as they travel, a subtle meal for the person on horseback. Reaching behind her, she shares some nuts with Arty, not forgetting that her loyal pup is undoubtedly hungry as well.

After a ride through much of the morning, the terrain around them has begun to change considerably. The dense forest has begun to thin, and there are large areas of plains with tall grass all around. The grass is so tall that they can scarcely see over it, even while on the back of a horse. Were it not for the overall enormity of trees in this land, even the top canopy of the forests surrounding the grass would be obscured.

Up ahead, the gravel road turns to the left and a crudely shaped wooden sign is posted, the word "Pecan" written on it. The only suggestion being that they are now approaching the border between Pignoli and Pecan.

To the right, though, leading away from the road is a scarcely beaten path into the tall grass. This path being thin enough for only one horse to traverse at a time, Tiler takes the lead. Slowly, the three other travelers follow him into the uncertainty of this poorly defined channel.

Fortia watches as the road behind her moves further and further away. The well-developed path between multiple kingdoms that has guided many travelers will no longer be there as a source of security for them.

The grass around them seems to have grown taller, even more so the further that they venture away from the road. Soon enough, there is nothing to see but a scarcely formed path beneath her and endless amounts of tall grass all around. Were it not for the horse in front of her that Matthius is riding or the horse behind her controlled by Laderas, it would be easy to feel entirely isolated in this place.

Fortia notices something unique about the ground in this grassy plain. The soil itself seems to grip the horse's hooves. It is muddy but also slightly gelatinous in quality. She is unsure what to make of this, though, as the horses do not seem to struggle much with maneuvering around in this muck. The progress of their group is rather slow though.

Suddenly, Matthius halts. He has done this because Tiler in front of him has stopped. Fortia pulls her horse to a stop and tries to look around Matthius, wanting to get a sense of what is going on. Tiler dismounts his horse then walks ahead a few feet in the sticky soil. Crouching down to examine the ground ahead of him, he sees something he does not like. He moves back toward Matthius and Laderas, who have both dismounted to approach him.

"Report," Matthius says with a firm tone.

"They are ahead of us," Tiler responds, and he shows them the impressions from numerous hooves on the path.

They return to Fortia, now needing to make a decision. Matthius takes a moment to consider the options, but he doesn't seem to like any of them.

"If we continue on the path, we may be ambushed. If we go off the path into the grass, we may become lost." He shakes his head, struggling to feel confident either way.

"The path is best," Laderas says. "According to the map, it should be less than a half day before we arrive at the Unbroken Woods."

Matthius is still considering options, though. He looks around and feels uncertain about the situation. For a moment, they are silent, unsure if the risk of an ambush is enough to abandon what little guidance this path provides for them.

The tall grass around them sways with the breeze, shifting the sunlight and shadows around as it moves. It is a rather nice environment, and if there was not so much at stake, then riding quietly in this otherwise mammoth field of grass could be somewhat relaxing. Matthius takes a deep breath as he knows he has to make a decision for everyone.

"We stick to the path." Matthius is perhaps feigning confidence. "We should spread out, though, to minimize the impact of any potential ambush."

Everyone seems to agree. Soon enough Matthius and Tiler have mounted their horses and begun moving forward again. Fortia cannot help but notice that when she nudges her horse to resume walking, the animal struggles to pull its hooves out of the ground. Perhaps standing still in the muddy soil had made their hooves sink slightly?

Everyone is feeling a rather heightened sense of alertness now, though. The idea of being ambushed has been in the background throughout much of this adventure, but now, approaching closer to their goal, this seems to be a near certainty.

~ ~ ~

The Grasslands are impressive in their dimensions, and in some areas, they could be a kingdom to themselves. On this crude path, though, there is the occasional glimpse ahead of another enormous forest not far from the horizon. The distance they have to traverse here does not feel very overbearing, but somehow, it seems they have been riding here for too long.

The journey continues, though, and their horses trod through the sappy mud between massive walls of grass. Even at a distance of five feet off the path in any direction, the density of the grass obscures nearly everything beyond it.

Far overhead, Fortia hears a curious humming noise. On looking up, there appears to be a swarm of colorful bugs that are crossing the Grasslands. The sun must be hitting their wings at just the right angle, and it makes these creatures twinkle with light as they fly past. They are high up enough that there is no considerable sense of a threat here, and the shimmering of their wings is rather beautiful as a result.

At this moment, Fortia realizes something…She has become more worldly in the last few days of travel than she had become after a decade of living on a farm. Even more so, she now realizes that she has been correct all this time, that the life of a farmer is truly not what she wants. With her parents in prison, though, she cannot help but feel that the cost of these experiences is much too great.

~ ~ ~

The monotony of the Grasslands continues. The tall brush all around limits the appreciation of the grand landscape that would otherwise be visible in the distance. Arty has fallen asleep on the back of their horse, and Fortia herself is feeling somewhat weary from travel at this point. Her other companions have maintained the discipline of their distance from one another and appear alert to the potential for an ambush.

Suddenly, though, Tiler stops his horse. He dismounts again, and as Matthius approaches him, he appears confused by what he sees on the ground.

"Look here," Tiler says, and Matthius dismounts.

Again, Tiler is looking at hoof prints. A cluster of them appears to trail off into the tall grass instead of following the path they are on. He and Matthius are perplexed by this. Why would the operatives leave the very reliable path they were on? They take a moment to ponder this, and Tiler looks around them as he considers the possibility of danger that they have not yet recognized.

"I have a thought…" Matthius says, and he signals for Tiler to follow him.

They follow their own hoof prints backward. They approach and pass by Fortia, then move further and further backward on the trail. Passing Laderas at the rear, they continue further back. Just then, Matthius sees it. His suspicion is confirmed, and he can barely tolerate the idea of it. Their own hoof prints appear to vanish into the tall grass behind them.

Tiler and Matthius gaze at this in amazement, both of them hardly able to imagine how this is possible. Soon enough, they regroup with Laderas and Fortia, but they are still struggling to comprehend this, let alone explain it.

"The grass appears to be moving," Matthius says, still rather uncertain how to voice it.

"What do you mean, moving?" Fortia asks, herself confused. "With the wind?"

"No. I mean, the grass is changing the trail. As though it wants us to stay here, on a path that never ends."

Just as this concept is sinking in for everyone, Tiler signals for silence. He hears other voices, and as the group quiets down, the whispers of a man can be heard not far away.

"Just there. Over there." Someone speaks from the tall grass, barely audible but definitely coming from the left of Fortia's position.

Matthius and the others can now hear the movement of horses, the sound of leather armor brushing onto itself. The operatives are close by.

Tiler quietly moves toward his horse and retrieves his bow. Matthius moves similarly toward his ax, and Laderas draws his sword from the mount on his horse.

Just as everyone is preparing for an ambush, Arty begins to wake. He stands on the back of the horse, stretches a moment, and yawns. Getting his bearings, he realizes that something is amiss and sniffs around. The scent angers him as he recognizes Malleus. He growls…

Fortia turns to him in a panic, hushes him with a finger to her lips, but Arty knows the threat is nearby. He barks at it.

Everyone freezes just long enough to hear hoof beats rapidly move toward them.

A horse bursts into the clearing with Malleus mounted on it. His ax is drawn, and he sneers, immediately looking around for a victim to attack.

Matthius is just nearby and swings his own ax, but Malleus is too fast. Turning away, he jumps off his horse, which rears up and causes a commotion for the other animals.

Moments later three other operatives on horseback enter the clearing. They immediately confront Tiler and Laderas. Tiler fires an arrow fast and it strikes one of the operatives in the side. He falls off his horse, hitting the ground hard as he screams at the pain.

Another operative charges Tiler, and the horse rams him, knocking him hard into the ground. He loses his grip on the bow and scrambles to regain it.

Laderas and an operative are locked in mounted combat. They clash axes and swords with one blow after another. Each one struggles to get the upper hand from the other.

Fortia is unsure what direction to go in, but she steadies her frightened horse. Another mounted operative appears from the grass, and he charges at her with his ax drawn. She pulls out her dagger and instinctively jumps off the backside of her horse. Hiding behind it, the attacker cannot see her to strike clearly.

The operative is brutal, though, and he strikes at her horse with his ax. It rears up, and Arty is tossed off. The pup strikes the mushy ground and is stunned for a moment.

Fortia gains some distance from the operative and grips her dagger tight. She stares him down with a look of fury. Ready to strike, the operative turns his horse toward her now just moments from charging.

Boldly, she stands her ground, but the advantage that a mounted rider has was never taught to her. This is not a confrontation she can win with just a dagger.

Laderas is still locked in combat with the other operative, but seeing Fortia in danger now, he gives the operative a great shove. They both fall off their horses.

The mounted rider charges Fortia, and Laderas quickly scurries to his feet. He raises his sword high and throws.

It whirls through the air and lodges itself into the back of the mounted rider. He is stunned and freezes as the pain seers into his back. He soon falls dead to the ground.

"Hide, Fortia!" Laderus commands her for a moment, but a hollow noise clangs out from behind him. Laderas is stunned as he realizes…

The operative behind him has taken the advantage and struck an awful blow with his ax. Laderas stumbles to the side and falls backward, lifeless at the edge of the path.

Fortia watches in shock as her friend collapses. Realizing now what he did, the thought of his death fills her with anger and terror. She screams with all her power. An instinctive and enraged war cry directed at the operative.

His eyes widen in shock as a fierce young girl charges him. He is about to reach for his secondary weapon, but it's too late. Fortia's knife pierces his chest. It stabs clean through his armor and into his heart.

She screams at him again, releasing all her fury at once as she looks with madness into his pain-struck face. He drops to his knees, clutching his chest from the searing pain. For a moment, he looks into her tear-filled and intense young face, then collapses at her feet.

A brief moment of quiet passes and Fortia is held there in her fury. The adrenaline of the moment begins to give way, and finally stepping back from him, she surveys the three men lying nearby her. It feels as sublime as anything she has experienced on this journey, and it is difficult for her senses to recover.

Slowly, her wits come back to her, and an overwhelming sadness rushes forward. More than anything, she wishes she could hear the voice of her mother, telling her that everything will be okay. She wants to hear the voice of her father counseling her, confirming that this was a necessary evil.

Suddenly, Harris appears from the grass nearby and grabs Fortia. She pulls her into the tall foliage and holds her hand over her mouth for a moment.

Realizing who it is, Fortia turns quickly and hugs Harris as she struggles to hold back the frustration. Knowing what has just happened, it is difficult for Harris to leave Fortia alone. She holds her for a moment longer, but soon, she pushes her backward just far enough to lock eyes with her.

"Wait here, Fortia."

Harris jumps into the clearing with two throwing knives drawn, entering the fight with stealth and power. Ahead of her, Malleus and Matthius are locked in combat. Each one swings and dodges axes as they expertly do battle. Matthius appears to have taken a blow to the leg already, as the armor on his left thigh is torn with sap running from it.

Not far away, two other operatives are overwhelming Tiler. One of them gets a strike into Tiler's arm with a sword, and he shrieks. Harris launches two throwing knives at the operative. They both stick into his trunk and he drops his sword, falls immediately limp. She quickly pulls two more knives from her beltline and throws them.

One of them hits Malleus in his arm wielding the ax, while the other strikes the leg of the second operative still looming over Tiler. Malleus screams and drops his ax as the pain sears into him. The operative near Tiler bellows with pain as he tries to grab at the knife lodged in his leg. The angle is too awkward, though, and he can't quite grasp it.

Matthius takes the advantage. He swings his ax, and it sticks into Malleus's thigh. Shrieking again, Malleus turns away to flee, but he quickly realizes. It was Harris who attacked him, and he immediately becomes enraged.

"TRAITOR!" He charges her. Even with an ax stuck in his leg, this furious man is unrelenting. Matthius attempts to grab him but the pain in his own leg holds him back. He stumbles to a knee.

Harris doesn't have time to launch another knife as Malleus tackles her. They both fall to the ground, and he screams as the ax dislodges from his leg. Now on top of her, he grabs her head. With a swift and furious motion, he smacks it into the ground. Again. Again. Until Harris falls limp…

Tiler is injured, but he scrambles to grab his bow. It is a struggle to draw back the string, but he pushes past the pain in his arm and aims at the shrieking man with a knife in his leg. An arrow strikes deep into the chest of the operative, and he collapses nearby.

Malleus soon gets to his feet and sees his last operative fall to the ground. Cringing with pain and anger, he sees Matthius stand and reach for the knife on his belt. Tiler pulls another arrow to rapidly load the bow. In just a matter of seconds, they will both attack.

He may be the murderous sort, but Malleus is not a fool, he knows this battle is lost. He limps into the tall grass, disappearing into the thickness of the foliage all around.

Matthius limps to Harris as best he can. Full of concern, he checks her for signs of life.

"She is alive," he announces to Tiler, who approaches from behind but soon runs to Laderas. Tiler kneels next to his body, and Matthius can see a sadness pouring through him.

Matthius's leg is not in good condition. Losing sap fast, he has trouble even bearing weight on it. He stumbles to his horse and reaches for a pouch on the saddle, where he removes a moderate-sized wooden vial with a cork in it. After opening the cork, he pours a thick, black, viscous substance over the wound in his leg. It burns him, but the sap begins to clot up quickly. It is still very difficult for him to walk, but he hurries to Tiler and pours the same substance onto his arm.

"Fortia!?" Matthius yells, glancing in every direction.

"We are here!" she says, and soon enough, she emerges from the grass carrying Arty.

"Are you hurt?" Matthius checks her for injuries.

"No. I think Arty got a little stunned, but we're okay."

Matthius takes in the carnage of this place. They have won a victory, but it seems the cost was too high. He again must consider their options, and soon, he resigns himself.

"We need to turn back. King Potilius will help us."

Tiler seems to agree, and he begins to gather any horses that remained nearby during the fight. Matthius swiftly turns and moves back to his own horse.

"No," Fortia says, and she looks sternly at them both.

Matthius is somewhat shocked by this declaration from her…Regardless, he tries to calmly explain the situation.

"I can barely walk, Fortia. Tiler has one good arm, and we need to get Harris to a Generalist. We have no idea how bad her injuries are."

"Arty and I can continue," she says with sincerity. "We have everything my father would have on this journey, and we are closer now than ever."

Matthius takes a deep breath at the idea. He does not like this plan, but Fortia seems entirely determined to do this.

"What direction should you go in, Fortia? Do you know how to get out of this grass?"

It's a good question, and for a moment Fortia is unsure how to answer it. A thought develops, though…She takes the rucksack off her back, opens it, and removes the small glass vial with the stone bowl. Positioning the vial for use, she holds it steady. The vial slowly re-aligns itself. It turns in the direction in which the fluid inside the vial has moved.

"This will guide me." She seems entirely confident that she understands the purpose of this device now.

"Kingdom's be…" Tiler removes a compass from a small pouch mounted on his belt. He turns it, aligns it to north and confirms for Matthius that Fortia's device is not facing north. It is not simply a makeshift compass.

"She's right," Tiler continues. "It must be what Constans uses to guide himself through this awful grass. If you and I guide the horses north, we will find the city of Pignoli behind us. The road should cross in front of us even."

Matthius is still not convinced, but he has no choice. As he turns to Fortia, she is already putting Arty up on the horse. With the rucksack on her back, she jumps up onto the saddle, not wasting any time.

Matthius hands her the wooden vial with the cork that he used to seal his injured leg.

"Take this. If you are injured, it will help clot your sap."

She understands and places it into a pouch on her saddle.

"How much water do you have?" Matthius works to prepare her best he can.

"My canteen is nearly full," she says, but Matthius limps over to his horse and retrieves his own canteen. He brings it to her and attaches it to a strap on her saddle.

"We have Tiler's water, and we will soon find more."

Tiler takes a few large pieces of deer jerky and wraps them in a rag with a few pieces of antler. He conceals them in a pouch on her saddle.

"Thank you," Fortia says as she attempts to form a smile on her troubled face. She's not happy about going off alone, but the idea of going backward while her parents are still in danger does not sit right with her. She lifts the reins with one hand and readies the device in her opposite hand.

"If needed, Arty and I will turn around and go the opposite direction of this device."

Offering a confident look at them both, a smile almost develops again, but this is blunted quickly. With only a short glance at Laderas's body, she becomes sincere. Determined, she nudges the horse forward, only this time she ignores the path. They head directly into the wall of grass in front of them.

Tiler and Matthius watch, amazed by her bravery, as she forages ahead. With just a few steps into the grass, she is almost entirely concealed, swallowed up by this elusive and confusing landscape.

Chapter 11

SLOWLY, FORTIA AND ARTY move through the tall grass on horseback. It is a tedious process, but Fortia is very focused. She seems to not even be interested in where the horse is going. Instead, the effort must be made to closely watch for any subtle movements of the vial in her hand. Holding it as steady as possible, she works to redirect the horse every time this device makes a turn in any direction.

She and Arty cannot help but feel nervous, and rightfully so. The source of this device's power is wholly unknown to her, and to blindly follow it without any understanding of why it works as it does requires something of a leap of faith.

Over some time, though, it becomes apparent that she has made progress. The tall grass begins to thin considerably, and in the distance ahead of them, the

Unbroken Woods becomes more and more visible. For a moment, she feels more hopeful, but Arty has taken note of something. He stands up, and his ears become alert, as though a threat is near.

Whatever it is, Fortia struggles to see it. She can at least make out the tree line of the forest ahead, and the closer they get, the easier it is to make out the enormous height of these trees. Once the form of the forest has become more visible, it is apparent that the Unbroken Woods is a very unique place.

Most notably, the ground here is grassy and full of wildflowers. There is a complete lack of detritus on the forest floor. No leaves have fallen here with their compacted decay forming new topsoil over generations. No branches are lying about, having cracked under the weight of snow and fallen to become the breeding ground for new mushrooms. The bark of all these trees is pristine, no deer have scraped their antlers into them during the rut, and no evidence of seasonal shedding even exists.

These trees are massive, and from nearly all angles, they are large enough that the tops of them cannot even be seen. Regardless, every tree here appears to be nearly perfect. Almost as though they have grown without limitations and have remained fully unscathed by the passage of time.

Fortia and Arty venture forward, and while she takes in the grandeur of this place, Arty still seems very unsettled. There is definitely something in the distance…

"What is it, boy?" She is again becoming concerned by his behavior. "It looks so beautiful, huh?" She subdues her anxiety for a moment and takes in the forest again. As she follows the movements of the vial and continues to redirect the horse appropriately, their approach has kept them close to the tree line.

Arty barks out with insistence now. He is no longer just nervous but stares off at something with intention.

Fortia looks in that direction, and while nothing is visible yet, she feels something changing. Arty has never led her astray, so his behavior is worth investigating. Inspecting the area keenly, her quiet curiosity soon pays off. She can hear something different. It's a buzzing noise similar to the one far overhead in the grass.

Moments later, she sees them. A loose cloud of relatively large insects is moving toward them. Fortia recognizes the sparkling of their wings in the sunlight. Unsure what to do, she immediately holds the horse steady.

The insects are nearing closer, though, and Arty snaps at them. They get close enough to land on the horse, and the animal immediately becomes unsettled. One of them lands on Fortia's arm. This single bug is slightly larger than her fingertip. Its exoskeleton is plated and shiny, with intermittent red streaks.

"Ah!" It bites her. Termites…She swats it away, but a hoard of them grows nearer. The swarming noise is almost all that is audible now.

Arty growls and snaps at them as they approach him. The horse gets bit, again and again. It attempts to shake the bugs off each time but to little avail.

Finally, the horse veers toward the Grasslands. Fortia struggles to control it, swatting at the termites as she does. She lets the horse guide them back into the tall grass, though, and moments later, it becomes evident that the termites are shedding off. They fly back into their forested area. Strangely enough, they do not land on the grass below either or on the tree trunks nearby. Some of them return to the higher areas of the trees above, but many of them stay hovering nearby, almost as though warning the travelers not to enter.

"They must not like going into the grass, Arty." She sighs, unsure how they will make progress now. The vial in her hand only points in one direction, insisting that they take a path into this hoard of bugs.

She jumps off the horse and helps her pup to the ground. Pacing for a moment, she tries to think. How can they survive this swarm of bugs without being eaten alive? She thinks on it more and soon opens the rucksack in an effort to assess whatever options she may have.

Removing the glove, she looks it over. It does not immediately seem useful here. Next she removes the blanket and considers this. Eventually, she drapes it over herself, lets it rest on her shoulders for a moment.

"Remember when we found the blanket in Papa's chest?"

Arty is too busy huffing at the insects to really have a conversation right now.

"Harris tried to pierce the blanket with her knife, but it wouldn't cut." She is figuring this out on a whim here. "I think this blanket is meant to protect us, Arty." Quickly, she realizes that it is not big enough to cover the horse, though it clearly can cover her and Arty.

"We'll have to continue on foot for now, boy." Arty huffs at this, not at all liking the idea of leaving the horse behind.

Fortia leads the horse over to a small tree a brief distance away. She lashes it there and reaches into the pouches of her saddle, where she removes the ointment, food, and antlers. After placing them neatly into the rucksack, she latches the other canteen on her belt. The weight of everything is beginning to feel like a burden, but not so much that she is overwhelmed.

She picks Arty up off the ground and rests him on her shoulder. The pup lays his weight over her and uses his feet to maintain balance as best he can.

With a swift movement, she throws the blanket over herself. It is meant for an adult, so it is a generous size for a child. A portion of it drags behind her as she moves around.

Once inside the blanket, she is surprised to find that she can see through it reasonably well. It is not at all perfectly translucent, but with the sunlight outside she can see enough of the surrounding trees and forest that she could guide herself visually if needed.

Soon enough she removes the vial device and levels it. The fluid shifts in the direction of their destination. With one hand holding the blanket steady and the other hand on the vial guiding her, she begins to approach the forest line again.

The noise of the swarm nearby grows as she approaches. Not long after, a termite lands on the blanket. Fortia watches it crawl around, and for a moment, it attempts to bite the blanket, but to no avail. Soon, others join, and they all crawl around the outside of the blanket. Occasionally, one of them bites it, but with no success. Strangely enough, none of them approach the level of the grass and attempt to slip themselves under the blanket's edge. They must have a natural proclivity for avoiding grass and various other aspects of this forest.

"I think this will work, Arty," she says, feeling more confident about the idea.

Arty is not feeling so sure as he cowers on her shoulder, not even feeling brave enough to growl at the threat of these bugs all around. Fortia pushes forward and follows the movements of the vial as she goes. Occasionally, a larger termite lands on the blanket. Its shadow is somewhat alarming for them, and the noise of these bugs all around is particularly distracting.

"I know, boy…" She tries to make the best of it. "Hopefully, it won't be much of a hike to get there." She keeps moving, and that alone is probably the most comforting thing.

~ ~ ~

The journey in this manner is perhaps longer than Fortia would like. She steps over roots and moves around shrubs as she goes. The blanket occasionally gets caught on a branch overhead, and there is a brief struggle to release it. The endless threat of termites is ever imminent and were it not for the unique combination of both bravery and willful thinking, Fortia might have preferred to just head back to Pignoli.

As she moves further and further into the forest, she notices that the small fluid-filled vial is behaving differently. Where earlier it would slowly turn to tell her which direction she should go in, now it is turning much more rapidly.

"We must be getting closer to whatever this thing reacts to, Arty." She watches as it swings slightly left now, and she cautiously redirects her movements to follow. Almost without end, the termites around her crawl over the blanket. They are relentless, it seems.

The sun is getting closer and closer to the horizon, and Fortia notices that it is becoming more and more difficult to see anything through this blanket. The lower the sun gets, the more fearful she becomes about this process. Turning back now is not an option, but she begins to hate the idea of walking through this forest of bugs in the dark. Arty appears to have made peace with it all at this point, and he has resigned himself to lying on her shoulder with a worried look.

Some distance ahead, she can see something large through the blanket. It is difficult to make out the form of it in the reducing light of evening. With what limited amount she can see, it appears to be a large tree stump, and the vial is guiding her directly toward it. She can't quite make it out from this distance, though.

As they approach it, though, she is happy to see that the bugs are shedding off her. They seem less and less interested in her as this large object grows nearer.

Soon enough, she can reach out and touch it, and it feels like a stone of some kind. She can still hear termites flying nearby, but as far as she can tell, there are none actually on the blanket attempting to get at her. Consulting the vial in her hand, it becomes clear that this device has reached the limits of its usefulness. It has begun to spin wildly in place, offering no additional guidance, it would seem.

"Arty, you may not like this…" She pets the pup a moment, and he whines at her. His eyes fill with fear as she pulls the blanket over her head, and it flaps onto her arm.

In front of her is a tall cylindrical tower-like structure made of whitish-gray blocks that appear to have been quarried from larger opaque gemstones. They have all been roughly hewn to the shape of large blocks and stacked in a cyclopean manner to form this structure. The noise of the termites is still obvious, though, and as she turns around, many of them remain hovering about ten feet away from this cylindrical structure.

"Strange creatures…" She shakes her head in confusion. "They don't like grass or dirt and don't like rocks. They don't seem interested in eating the tree trunks either." Arty grumbles a response. "They must eat dead leaves and branches…" It's the only reasonable assumption, she thinks, but Arty huffs in return, not at all happy that they tried to eat him.

Obscured by the trees here, she can see something of a beautiful sunset forming. Were they not continuously threatened by big termites only ten feet away it might be a nice place to set up camp. Arty appears too worried about all this to really take an interest in the sunset, and the presence of this tower-like structure has piqued Fortia's interest. Spending the night resting here barely even enters her mind.

Fortia takes Arty off her shoulder and rests him at the foot of the stone structure. She folds up the blanket, and after removing her rucksack, she stores it inside. Placing Arty on top of everything inside the rucksack, she loosely binds the flap over him. He can still peek his head out to observe this unique place around them. Carefully, she straps the rucksack back on her shoulders.

The structure in front of her is large enough to be a foundation for a tower, but it clearly is not meant for that. The rounded walls that form it come to a clean termination roughly thirty feet up, with no signs that there was once something built above it. Fortia walks around it and searches for an opening. Finally, she spots something.

Roughly twenty feet up the backside of it is a square opening. Large enough for someone to crawl through but high enough off the ground that climbing to it could be difficult. There is no ladder built into this cylinder, but on closer inspection, Fortia can see that the blocks in the wall have just enough space between their edges to form a handhold.

Knowing that she will need to climb this, she removes her canteen and takes a refreshing sip of water. She suspends it again on her belt line and bends down to gather some dirt. Dry hands are crucial when climbing anything such as this, and the journey on foot underneath a blanket has left her warm.

"Hold on tight, boy." She confidently places her right foot into a gap in the wall, just one knee length off the ground.

Skillfully, she reaches and grabs the edge of a block above her, then pulls herself up. Seeking another spot for her left leg to make purchase on the wall, she finds one and progresses upward nicely.

The edges of these blocks are rather generous, but it is clear that if someone was not strong enough or agile enough to free climb, the entire process of getting into this opening would be marred by the lack of a rope or ladder. Being skilled at this, though, Fortia is making good progress, and she does not feel much risk of falling.

She makes short work of this wall, and without too much effort, she can now reach the edge of the opening. It is a generous enough gap that she won't even need to remove her rucksack. Wiggling her way inside the structure, it is obvious that there is another drop-down just ahead. The structure is indeed cylindrical with no roof above her, and minimal light from the sunset enters overhead. Fortia can see at least part way down into this space, and it is relatively deep inside. A good fifty-foot drop, perhaps, though the bottom is not easily visible.

Fortia takes a moment to catch her breath. She looks around the interior of this structure, but soon enough, she realizes that there is no ladder on the inside either.

"You aren't gonna like this, Arty." She shimmies her hips forward, then turns her body and legs so that they dangle over the inside ledge. Having a strong grip, she slowly lowers herself until she can feel a good rim of stone for her foot.

Lowering herself down even more, she is relieved to find that the blocks on the inside have more of a slope to their alignment. The interior of this cylinder is deep, but the wall is built with increasing depth, which gives the space here a cone-like shape. As she descends, she is approaching a narrowed space at the bottom.

Her eyes acclimate to the darkness here, but the glistening of this gemlike rock holds the sun very well. While a torch or lantern would certainly help, the light is sufficient.

By now, though, Fortia has definitely descended enough of this space that she is below ground level. Soon, though, she becomes frustrated. This cone-like space is narrowing to a rather small circular opening at the bottom. As she approaches it closer and closer, she can see that there is no light inside. There is an eerie hint of a mist rising from below, but she cannot see anything that is underneath this space.

Finally stepping onto the lowest point near this opening, she bends forward and tries to get her head closer to it. Hoping for a clue regarding what is below, she listens for any noises and scans the inside for something to catch a glimpse of. It sounds somewhat like running water underneath this opening, but it is a distant noise. Nothing is visible in that darkness…

The idea of jumping into this dark pit is not appealing to her. Looking around the interior of this structure, she sees a small fragment of gemmy rock, about knee high. It is slightly less secured to the wall than the rest of the blocks around it. On attempting to move it, it is loose, but still wedged into the wall. Using both hands she steadies herself on the small area she has to stand on. With a swift kick, she dislodges the stone some. Another kick, and it moves easier. She gets a good grip on it and slides the stone out of place.

Turning to the dark opening below her, she drops the stone. It falls for a few seconds of silence until a splash is audible.

"That doesn't sound too bad, Arty…" Regardless, it is not easy to feel happy about dropping herself into a dark pit. She kneels and slowly lowers herself into the narrow opening. Feeling around with her foot, there is unfortunately no ledge immediately available here. Slowly she lowers her weight into the hole and continues to search for any spot where she can get a grip with her foot. Nothing…She sighs, now accepting the reality.

"Hold your breath, Arty!" She releases herself.

For a second, she falls through a stone shaft. Quickly, she feels the air rush around her as she drops into a wider open space. She splashes into the water, but it's not very deep, and her left ankle cracks. Shrieking at the pain, her weakened leg quickly gives out, and she falls to a knee. It seems that there is nothing immediately threatening to her here, but she is now partly submerged in murky cold water.

Arty whimpers. His head is fully hidden within the rucksack, even as Fortia remains kneeling and still. Much of her torso is above water, and while she tolerates the pain of her ankle well, it is difficult not to cringe during every attempt to move. She needs a moment to recover.

It is almost pitch black inside this space. Save for a bit of light coming from the opening overhead. She can see almost nothing but the portion of water that she is standing in. This is just enough light to reveal something lying in the water next to her. It is an iron ladder.

Fortia rolls her eyes. At least she knows it is there when she has to get out.

She can still hear the sound of running water, though, and as she kneels there, it becomes obvious that the water itself is slowly moving in the direction she is facing. Gathering strength, she pulls her leg forward and rests weight on it. Grinning at the pain, she bears it well and gets back to her feet.

Limping through the pool of water around her, she edges herself forward. The hint of light from the cylinder overhead grows more and more distant as she progresses, and now there is only the growing sound of running water to guide her.

Fortia can hear Arty whimpering behind her, and she can't help but feel anxious herself. It is pitch black, and she is underground in a cavern with almost nothing to guide her but the noise of water. As she makes more progress moving forward, she still cannot see, but with her left hand, she can feel a solid stone surface next to her. Leaning on the wall with each step, she uses it as a crutch to help her move. A thought in the dark develops.

Using her hand to reach over the opposite shoulder, she feels the top of a long sleeve on her rucksack. She slides her fingers under the flap covering this and removes a single piece of the antler. Gripping one end of it tightly, she makes a swift motion and strikes it on the wall. A spark briefly lights up the darkness. Again, she strikes the antler until a bright flash fills the area. The tip of the antler catches fire, and a strong, consistent light emanates from it. The light is almost overwhelming, but she can see again, and a sigh of relief is hard to restrain. Like a large slow-burning matchstick, it lights up the space well.

She is in a manmade tunnel, roughly twenty feet wide and twenty feet high. The walls and ceiling of it are composed of the same gemmy rock that the tower above was, and it seems to stretch behind her for a considerable distance. Ahead of her, she can see that the tunnel leads to a larger open space. Pushing herself to continue forward, the rock wall beside her provides a modicum of continued support, but the pain of every footfall is clearly a deterrent. The noise of the water ahead slowly becomes more and more aggressive. A waterfall may be close by.

Soon, she approaches the edge of a large opening. The water is indeed slipping over the edge, but it is not a raging waterfall. This is clearly a structure built for some larger purpose, and the water is sliding down a spillway at a reasonable rate. A steep stone front is ahead of her and stretches downward for at least a hundred feet below. The light of the antler is abundant and Fortia can see the spillway terminating into a settlement pool below. As she holds her flame up high, her eyes widen with amazement. The grand space before her is on full display.

The opening she stands in is two-thirds of the way up in a huge cavern. The floor of the cavern is loaded with gemlike stones that reflect the light of her small torch well. There is an enormous array of huge geodes here. They fill the floor of the cavern almost entirely, save for the pool of water that this spillway dumps into and numerous areas of gravel scattered throughout. These geodes have likely been forming in this place for millennia. Many of them are a variety of colors and geometric shapes, but most of them are the same blunted white color that the tunnel and cylinder structure above are made of.

For Fortia, this is a spectacular place. Her eyes are alight, and while illuminated by only her one torch, the sight of this rivals nearly everything her eyes have taken in on this journey. The ceiling of this place is closer to her than the ground, and while there are a handful of large geodes that formed above, much of the ceiling of this cavern is composed of thick roots. They are the roots of many trees above, woven within and over one another. They extend down the side walls of this cavern and mix into protruding rocks and geodes in the cavern walls. The mist that was subtly venting out of the opening above the tunnel is now more prominent at the top of the cavern. It appears to be collecting here, but it is not so thick that it obscures the view much.

At the far end of this cavern, she can scarcely make out the form of three natural openings, which lead to branching tunnels. The water that is pooling at the base of the cavern trickles slowly across a crick, and this continues into the center opening. The other openings are very hard to see from this distance, but regardless, it appears that Fortia will need to get across this deposit of geodes.

Having taken in this enormous space, she looks around for a way to safely descend from such an elevated height. While the builders of this tunnel were remiss in giving people easily accessible ladders to climb in with, they were at least reasonable enough to add a rudimentary staircase here. It is not very wide and has no railing, but it appears to have been crafted well out of the natural rock surface. Even after untold amounts of age, the risers of this staircase do not show much wear.

Struggling with one injured leg, Fortia begins to descend this narrow and precarious staircase. She leans her weight toward the wall as best she can, though it is not hard to imagine that with the wrong movement of her weight, she could easily slip over the edge. As she goes,

Arty peaks his head out of the rucksack, now feeling curious enough to take a look around.

Having reached the bottom of the staircase, she begins the arduous process of traversing this enormous field of geodes. Most of these geodes are much larger than her and could easily be the size of a comfortable bed or dining table. Given the burden of an injured ankle and all that she is carrying at the same time, climbing up the sides of them is not easy for her. The grainy fibers of her wooden legs ache, and the crystalline surfaces all around her are very slippery.

Holding the antler for light limits her to mostly one hand at a time, which slows her down even more. The best footholds come from wedging her feet in the crevice between two geodes and stepping forward from there. It is slow moving, but soon, she finds herself making good progress across the cavern floor.

There doesn't seem to be any life down here. No obvious insects are lurking about, though they may have been scared away by her light. Regardless of the moisture and darkness, there are no clusters of fungi growing here either. It is simply one geode after another. Even the crick of water nearby appears to play host to nothing but gravel and silty sand underneath. There are no fish or other living creatures to examine or take interest in.

As she traverses this place, Fortia notices smaller crystals are scattered about. Some have such unique shapes and colors that they are difficult to ignore. In one such case, Fortia picks up a small gemlike stone and takes an interest in it. It appears to be a near-perfect cube, red-orange in color, and it seems to have originated from a nearby cluster of others just like it. Intrigued by it, she places it in her pocket and continues to make progress across the cavern.

Climbing over one final large geode, she slides herself down to a gravel space at the far end of the cavern. The three natural tunnels she saw from the top of the stairs are just adjacent to her, but she is very fatigued. It is difficult to build enthusiasm for another leg of the voyage right now.

"I need a break, Arty…" She catches her breath and sits on a large flat geode that is nearby the central opening. Wedging the bottom of the antler into a crevice in the geode helps to free up her hands.

The crick nearby runs into the dark space within the center tunnel. Fortia looks at the three tunnels from her place of rest, but she has no good ideas for which one to follow. The map never detailed anything about these tunnels, and she is assuming that only her father would know which direction to travel in at this point.

"Arty, your guess is as good as mine…"

He nudges her, a sign he wants to step down. She removes him from the rucksack and rests him on the ground by the crick. He scurries over and sniffs the water. It seems okay, so he takes a quick drink from this.

"Good to know." She is thankful for a source of potable water here.

She takes out the vial and stone bowl, then positions these for use. The vial begins turning, but soon enough, it is simply spinning in place again.

"That's not much help." She places it back into the rucksack and removes the folded map. Laying it flat on the geode near her, she is surprised to see the map has changed.

Where before the map showed the layout of the various kingdoms, with roads leading from each of those into the "Kingdom of Roots," now more markings have appeared on it. As though drawn on with an invisible ink, there is a shorter drawing emanating from the words "Kingdom of Roots," which consists of three lines. At the end of the line on the left is the word "Aurufex."

"It must be the mist here, Arty." The little pup is resting on the gravel surface at her feet. He whines a bit, and Fortia realizes it has been some time since they ate anything.

She reaches into the rucksack and removes a rationed amount of nuts and jerky. Splitting the meat in two, she takes a few bites as Arty quickly chews up his portion. He sniffs around for more, and seeing this, Fortia smirks. She gives him the rest of her meat and instead eats a handful of nuts.

Sitting together for a moment of quiet in this strange place, she pets her pup a few times. Perhaps mostly for her own comfort, though, as this cave does not exactly make someone feel at home. While she has a source of light, a path of retreat, and the comfort of a friend, she would have never imagined herself in a place like this just days ago. The map suggested that the cave on the left was the next step in the journey, but for Fortia this is not much guidance. Were it not for this long-lasting light source she has, it might be very easy to feel trapped down here.

Fortia folds the map up, conceals it back in the rucksack, latches the flap on it, and straps it onto her back. She raises the light from the antler and reluctantly begins her approach to the leftmost opening in the cavern walls. Arty follows, occasionally needing to jump onto and over smaller geodes as he goes.

She steps into the left tunnel, and the floor is slippery. Being mostly composed of smooth, cleaved stones with an upward slope, she struggles to gain friction with each step. There is a large rock blocking much of the entry, and the height of this space is really only tall enough for a small person to stand upright in. Having space to slip around the rock on the left side of the opening, it is just a matter of wedging herself into the small gap she has and moving around it. Following this is another rock on the opposite side. Similarly, she pushes herself past this. Yet again, she is confronted by another similar rock on the opposite side of the cavern. It is very tight in here, and if she were any larger, she simply would not be able to fit.

Just as she clears this third small gap, her progress is immediately halted. To her surprise, she is greeted with a very short stone staircase, the risers of which are no more than two inches high each. At the top of this stair is a shallow landing with a small manmade stone archway at the rear of it. The stairs are obviously constructed for a much smaller creature, and even as short as Fortia is, she could step up them in a single step if she really tried.

The archway is no more than three feet tall at the keystone, and it is very attractive in its details. It would seem that someone with great skill assembled this opening. Fortia can obviously tell she is going the right direction, but she is still very confused. What sort of person could walk under such a small archway? If this is the right direction, why not make this opening much larger for an adult-sized person?

As she considers this quaint little entry event, Arty sniffs around on top of the landing. He is interested in this place as well but not sure what to make of it. She bends forward over the stairs, not quite sure if she will even fit through the archway with her rucksack on. Gazing into the space beyond, it is entirely dark inside, but she can tell that there is an open space there. Not really knowing what else to do, she assumes she is at the entry to an occupied space.

"Hello?" She waits for a response, but nothing.

Curious, she extends her arm inside the archway and shines the light into the space beyond. There appear to be numerous objects inside, but it is hard to see what resides there with the flame from the antler blocking her.

"Me quaeritis?" a small voice says from behind her.

Fortia swings around in shock. She quickly looks for the voice but cannot see anything. Glancing to Arty though, his tail is wagging playfully. His gaze is fixed on the direction of her feet. Looking downward now, she soon realizes where the voice had come from.

Not far from her feet is a crablike creature wearing a greenish-blue leather robe. It is roughly two feet tall and holds a net full of small wiggling bugs. It has a head and a torso, as well as two chunky legs and four arms. Each arm has three finger-like pinchers extending from it. The torso is composed of a platelike crustacean shell which overlaps in various areas that would allow it to articulate its core. Its face appears to be crustacean in nature, though it is similar to what Fortia would recognize as a face. Its eyes are very wide, and its mouth is obscured underneath a very pronounced nose.

Still waiting for a response, it uses one of the pincher arms to reach into the net. It retrieves a small living bug and quickly eats it. Crunching on it for a moment. Ascending the stairs briefly, it removes a second bug from the net and offers it to Fortia.

She is too stunned to really respond yet, and perhaps if she was not, it might be hard for her to accept this particular offering. Instead, it offers the bug to Arty, who gleefully grabs it from the tiny pinchers and chomps away at it.

Arty appears very comfortable around this creature, who now looks at Fortia again, this time with some degree of curiosity as it surveys her form.

Fortia is still stuck on acknowledging this new reality where creatures like this even exist in the first place. It takes her a moment to recover from the surprise.

"Quod animal est hoc?" it says to her, referencing Arty.

Fortia begins to snap out of it, but she is still very lost in the mystery here.

"Umm…" she stammers, "I'm sorry. I don't understand."

"Non-important," it casually says. Steadying the net of bugs on its back, it quickly moves into the small archway. Fortia watches as it enters. She feels like the creature may expect her to follow, though she is still unsure of it all.

"Adventum?" it says from the adjacent room.

Fortia takes her rucksack off, bends forward onto her knees, and crawls inside the archway. Arty follows her. Then she turns around to pull the rucksack in behind her.

There is not much space available for Fortia and Arty. She can barely fit herself in here while kneeling down and standing up is not even an option. For the creature, though, it is a rather generous room, and the light of the antler fills the space well.

Fortia can now see that a variety of surfaces have been carved out of the stone walls all around her. Small platforms that act as countertops and shelves are laid out around the perimeter. There is a small chair carved into the rock, with armrests even for the comfort of four upper extremities.

At the opposite side of the room, there are the makings of a rudimentary forge. A deep hearth is here which fills nearly the entire adjacent wall of the space and is made of the same gemlike stone as the tunnel Fortia entered from. A rectangular chunk of steel that resembles an anvil is positioned to the left, and a small iron crane is built into the sides of the firebox. A pit at the base is difficult to see clearly without inching closer to the hearth, but there is definitely space to work and build a blazing fire there.

On the wall to the right of all this is an array of iron tools that hang from pegs. Between this and the forge pit is a small pool of water. It appears to be draining and refilling continuously from the crick in the tunnel nearby.

The creature hangs the net of bugs on a metal peg that protrudes from the wall near its chair. It then moves over to its chair, and much like an elderly person with bad joints, it sits down, nestles itself into a comfortable position. It reaches next to the chair on the floor and lifts up a small blanket, which it uses to cover its lower extremities. Having made itself comfortable now, it soon turns its attention to Fortia.

"Quomodo auxilium I?" it says with a kind smile.

Fortia is not sure how to respond. She glances at Arty, and he appears very comfortable here, already lying down not far from the archway.

"I am Fortia. Daughter of Constans."

"Ah, Constans!" Its eyes lit up. "Optimum venator."

Fortia smiles, not sure what else to do, really.

"Ego sum, Aurufex." It gestures to itself, a nice little introduction.

"Aurufex…" Fortia repeats it, now recalling the name on the map. She reaches into the pocket of her rucksack and removes an acorn. She shows the nut to the creature.

"Can you make us a Golden Nugget?" she asks, almost with a pleading in her eyes.

"Nux aurea. Forsit." The creature sits a while, though, comfortable and warm.

"Nux aurea…" She feels like she understood, though she is not entirely certain.

"Habetis oblatio?" It seems to not be convinced that it will get the response it wants.

Fortia smiles an uncertain smile at this otherwise gentle-looking creature. She has an idea, though…She opens her rucksack and removes the items from the chest. Placing them on the floor one at a time for Aurufex to see.

Aurufex watches, and when Fortia removes the small gold bars, it stands up. It moves over to the forge area and grabs the edges of a small melting pot. It is relatively large for this creature, but with some effort, it drags the pot over to Fortia and leaves it in front of her. It waits for her to take the next step, but Fortia responds with a confused look.

Aurufex walks over to the gold bars. With its four pincher hands it pretends to make an attempt at lifting the gold bars. It stops, looks to Fortia, and shakes its head with a sad frown.

Fortia smiles. She picks them up and quietly offers them to Aurufex. It nods in response, so she places the bars in the bucket. With that, Aurufex grabs the edge of the bucket and starts dragging it over to the forge area. Struggling, it manages to relocate the bucket near the forge.

Moments later, it returns to Fortia and gestures toward the burning antler in her hand.

"Cum pace tua."

Fortia hands him the antler. Even as light as it is, Aurufex can barely carry it with all four arms. It successfully moves to the forge area and dips the burning end of the antler into the base of the firebox. After a moment, a fire within begins to flare up, and Fortia notices that the smoke from this area is naturally channeled to the left of the forge and out a small rectangular opening there. Clearly, there is a well-designed system in place here to damper the smoke. Aurufex blows on it some, stoking it a bit with its breath until the fire lights.

It carries the antler back to Fortia, hands it to her, and then walks back to the forge area.

"Serva ignem," it says and returns to her with a small wooden bowl of water.

Fortia seems to understand. She dips the burning end of the antler into the water and extinguishes it. The forge is now providing more than enough light for this tiny room.

"Requiem," Aurufex says and briefly gestures to the floor she is kneeling on. "Hoc maxime noctis."

Fortia raises an eyebrow, not really understanding any of that. As far as she can tell, though, Aurufex knows what it is doing. Placing some of the items back into the rucksack, she leaves the blanket out. She settles herself on the floor, and Arty soon joins her. The blanket is plenty large enough for these two weary travelers.

The forge crackles not far away. Aurufex is hard at work. It heats up the fire with a small bellows and occasionally adds more wood. The fire is going good now. Soon, it drags the casting pot closer to the forge and arranges the crane so that it can lift the pot over the fire.

Fortia watches the hearth burn. She lies comfortably with Arty, who already seems fast asleep. The fire flickers, and regardless of this rather pleasing experience here with Aurufex, she cannot help but still feel uncomfortable around fire. The unpleasant thought of her home burning flashes into her mind, but she shakes it off. Represses it. She inches closer to Arty, and perhaps her greatest comfort is knowing that he is there with her.

She grows tired the longer she lays down. While this strange little creature is hard at work, she cannot help but feel like she is safe enough to close her eyes a bit. She drifts off, taking hold of some well-earned rest.

~ ~ ~

Fortia's eyes flutter open. There are high-pitched noises of rapid hammering bouncing off the interior of this small space, and the hearth is blazing still. Staying in her comfortable spot, she gazes over to Aurufex, who remains hard at work. The creature has a hammer in each of its four pincher hands. In an amazingly rapid sequence, it is able to strike each hammer one at a time in a quick, repetitive succession of four blows. This is followed by another four blows, then another four, over and over in a rhythmic manner.

While Aurufex appears to be working very rapidly, each strike of those four tiny hammers would only minimally help to shape a metal object. This creature obviously has to work much harder to get any kind of good result from those hammers.

The repetitive four-part rhythm continues for some time, and Fortia closes her eyes again, feeling tired enough still to sleep some more.

~ ~ ~

Fortia wakes again, and the fire of the hearth is ongoing. The hammering continues for a time but suddenly stops. She glances over to Aurufex and watches as it lifts a metal spoon full of powder. It sprinkles the powder on top of the object within the belly of the forge. Aurufex places a few more sticks from a nearby pile onto the fire, and now looking fatigued, it moves toward the chair to sit and rest. It reaches for the net of wiggling bugs and plucks another snack out of it. Chewing with the satisfaction that good food can offer, it nestles itself into the chair.

Still lying down, Fortia lifts the flap on the side pocket of her rucksack. Tearing off a piece of jerky, she separates it in two and eats a portion of it herself.

Gesturing to Aurufex, she offers some jerky. It takes an interest and stands from the chair. Taking the piece of meat from her with a gracious smile, it bows to her briefly in thanks. While small to Fortia, it is a good piece of meat for this creature.

"Gratias tibi." Aurufex tastes the jerky, and a bright smile appears on its face. Fortia smiles in response, glad to know that it is enjoying what she has shared. As the creature eats this treat, it begins to hum a gentle tune.

Fortia chews on her food, still enjoying this moment where Aurufex seems so pleased. Moments later, she recognizes something…She realizes that the tune Aurufex is humming is the same tune her mother often hums while cooking in the kitchen. As awkward as this whole interaction has been for her, she cannot help but feel comforted by this.

The creature casually walks over to a stack of wood and places more sticks on the fire before returning to its chair.

"Nux paene cocta." It continues to enjoy the meat.

Fortia has a complacent smile on her face as she watches the little creature nibble away at the jerky. Soon Aurufex has finished eating, and getting comfortable with a blanket again, it closes its eyes. It nestles into a moment of relaxation, and they both rest for a while longer. It is as good a place as any to be at peace, and Fortia closes her eyes again. Perhaps no longer tired enough to sleep, she lets herself simply relax and be quiet.

Soon enough, though, the fire of the hearth is growing dim. Aurufex, even with its eyes shut, is alert to these types of things. The creature soon stands and moves over to the hearth. It grips the crane on the side of the hearth and pulls on a lever numerous times. A small chain lifts whatever is inside the pit of the hearth.

The fire continues to die down, and the object grows closer and closer to the top of the pit. A radiant light is coming off of it and this becomes more and more obvious as the object surfaces from the firebox.

At the noise of the pulley chains, Fortia becomes alert and sits up. She can see the strong, radiant light emerging from the pit, and she rises to her knees now. Arty wakes finally and yawns as he stretches out from the night of relaxation.

Soon, Aurufex has the nugget fully out of the pit, and the room is full of a powerful golden light. The creature maneuvers the crane arm forward out of the hearth. Reversing the pulley next, it lowers the glowing nut down to the stone floor, letting it finally rest there in front of the hearth.

The fire of the hearth has died down, and the glowing nugget is doing all of the work of lighting the room. Aurufex proudly gestures with all four pinchers to the nugget, and Fortia finally gets a chance to examine it more closely. She shuffles herself forward on the rigid stone floor and makes a movement to pick it up. The creature quickly steps in front of her and urgently waves its arms to stop her.

Moving over to her rucksack, Aurufex pulls the flap open. It crawls inside the sack and rummages around some. Soon, it emerges with the glove. The creature drags it over to Fortia, lays it on the floor between her and the nugget.

Lifting the edge on the bottom vent of its leather robe, Aurufex runs the fabric of the robe along the Golden Nugget. Fortia can see that the robe begins to burn some. Next Aurufex pulls the glove over and rubs a fourchette from this onto the Golden Nugget. It does not burn.

Fortia immediately understands. She picks up the glove and fits her hand into it. Soon she holds the Golden Nugget and can examine it more closely.

The nugget is larger than the two gold bars would seem to have been, suggesting to her that it is at least partly hollow inside. It is perfectly spherical save for a delicate pattern of overlapping squares on the surface. Aurufex has expertly hammered an exceptional pattern into the nugget, which gives it a nearly holographic appearance. This, combined with the impressive light that emanates from it, is enough to capture the gaze of anyone who has laid eyes on it.

Fortia is amazed and rests in awe of this glowing orb. She does not know when or how it happened, but this unique little creature seems to have imbued a magical power in this item. Seeing this now and holding it in her hand, she knows for sure that what Tonitro crushed during his coronation was definitely not the same thing.

Chapter 12

FORTIA AND ARTY step over the stairs as they exit from Aurufex's home. The creature has followed her out to see her off, and she cautiously grips the glowing Golden Nugget in her gloved hand as she goes. She and Arty are about to walk away, though Fortia turns and hands the creature another piece of jerky.

It smiles and seems excited by the opportunity to eat this meat again. It bows to her, a subtle thanks for this gift. Fortia smiles and bows in return. Soon, they wave goodbye to one another, and she embarks on her journey home.

As she did when traversing the field of geodes before, Fortia has Arty in her rucksack, and she cautiously maneuvers herself over each enormous crystal. Her ankle is already feeling somewhat better, but it is still not making it easy on her. The light of the Golden Nugget, though, is very abundant in this otherwise dark space, and it provides more than enough illumination to assist with sure footing.

Cautiously she ascends the stairs into the tunnel up above the cavern. She steps into the water above the spillway, and soon, she can see the opening overhead in the distance. Carefully gripping the nugget, she is able to use her opposite hand to slowly tilt the iron ladder up into an appropriate position for use. It is a struggle, though…With only one hand it is difficult to get the leverage she needs to angle it upward, but she eventually figures out the geometry of it.

Once she steps up into the cylinder, she can see it is still very early in the morning outside. The sun has not yet breached the horizon to shed any light from above.

Knowing it will be impossible to scale this wall with the Golden Nugget in her hand, she finds a suitable rock ledge to place it on and then bends forward to pull the ladder up into the cylinder. She positions the top of the ladder by the square opening in the cylinder above, and the length of it is close enough that she can make the climb with one hand.

Having climbed up to the opening in the wall, she is rather annoyed to hear the buzzing of termites not far away. It is still too dark to see them, though, and as she lifts the Golden Nugget up through the opening, she immediately notices a change. Curiously, the buzzing noise of insects grows distant as the light of the nugget shines through this opening.

She maneuvers herself through the opening to the opposite side of the wall and cautiously lowers herself as best she can with one arm. She drops herself down from there, and the pain in her ankle is punishing but not overwhelming.

There remains no sound or sight of the termites even after she is exposed to the forest. The unique brightness and magical qualities of the Golden Nugget must be a deterrent to these insects, and Fortia is rather glad to discover this. Walking through this forest again with a blanket over her head while holding the Golden Nugget in one hand and the small vial in the other would be a feat of coordination that she could easily fail at.

Fortia consults the vial for guidance as she begins the process of walking back to her horse. Now moving away from the direction that the vial instructs her to go, she cannot help but imagine her father on this same journey. How many times has he done this? Would he know the route through this forest by heart already? She picks up her pace, now with a renewed eagerness. It would be a joy to tell him about her journey and all she has achieved.

As time passes, walking through the Unbroken Woods, the sunrise begins its journey into daylight. Fortia sees the tall grass of the Grasslands nearby. She recognizes the small tree where her horse would be, but the horse is not there. Frustrated by this, she moves over to the tree and scans the area for any sign of what happened.

There is no suggestion of a tree branch having been broken or the horse escaping by force. Its hoof prints are all around, so the animal must have spent some time lingering there, but not far away, there appears to be a pattern in the grass of two horses walking off. Frustrated, she consults Arty, as his strong sense of smell may come in handy here.

"Do you smell anything, boy?" She moves him out of the rucksack and onto the ground nearby. He sniffs around for the scent of the horse and then slowly starts to follow the vague trail of hoof prints into the Grasslands. Fortia follows him into the tall grass, careful not to lose sight of him. With her free hand, she removes her dagger and grips it tight, ready to face whatever danger may be ahead.

As they step through the tall grass all around them, Fortia follows right on Arty's heels. He is not moving terribly fast, but it does seem like he is determined to follow the trail of a scent. Moving further and further into the Grasslands, he eventually stops and looks intently at something in front of him. Growling at the space ahead, he is not eager to continue.

"What is it, boy?" She cautiously walks forward into the grass until she comes to a clearing. Moments later, she sees it.

Their horse lays dead on the ground ahead of them. Strangely enough, the grass itself appears to be smothering the animal, having wrapped itself tight around the mass of this once loyal creature. It is almost as though the grass is attempting to crush the horse from the surface inward, pulling it into the sappy soil underneath.

It's a frightful scene for Fortia, and she is overcome with fear and sorrow for this animal. Knowing that the horse is already dead, though, she can do nothing to help it. She turns away from it and regains her calm after a few deep breaths.

"Let's go, Arty. We need to get back to the road." Propping him up on her shoulder, she consults the vial again. Quickly making progress through the Grasslands, she is eager to get out of this place in one piece. It is clear now that anyone who isn't making steady progress here may never make it home at all.

Soon enough she has reached the main road, and it is something of a relief for her. Where before the Grasslands were a mysterious and misleading place, almost somewhat enchanting at times, seeing her horse being consumed by it has made her consider the fate of the operatives who ambushed them yesterday. She has experienced an awful reality. The Grasslands are a sentient living thing that feeds on whatever gets trapped inside them, and as far as she is concerned, she need not visit this place ever again.

Placing Arty on the gravel of the road, they stop here for a rest. Regardless of sleeping last night, she is tired, and she yawns at the otherwise energetic sunlight all around her.

Struggling with only one hand, she eats some nuts from her pocket then shares a few of them with Arty. A sip of water from her canteen is a welcome refreshment in the growing sunlight of the morning. She becomes frustrated, though, as she struggles to place the cork back into her canteen with one hand. The idea of holding this glowing nugget for days and days to come feels unrealistic. Not only will she likely end up dropping it and possibly losing it at some point, but the light of this object does not lend itself well to subterfuge. She takes a moment to consider her options, and a thought swiftly crosses her mind.

Gripping the rolled cuff of the glove with her free hand, it is clear that the glove is rather flexible. Whatever is inside of it fits very nicely. Still gripping the nugget tight, she pulls the cuff up and over the nugget, then wraps the nugget fully inside of the glove. This seems like a perfect solution, and for a moment Fortia realizes that this was perhaps one of the expected uses of this glove by its creator.

She takes off her rucksack and removes most of the items from inside. After placing the nugget at the middle of the sack, she re-packs the other items. After a moment of consideration, it becomes clear that everything in her rucksack is not going to catch on fire. Strapping it back on, she and Arty resume their long journey.

She is comforted by the knowledge that she is moving north now, the direction of home and the direction of freedom for her parents. Everything she has done thus far has been in service of that goal. The importance of the nugget to everyone else is secondary in her mind. Her family is all she has truly cared about, and even though they are still locked away from her, she is happy to be on a path back to them.

After some time walking, the sunlight has surpassed the height of morning. The road ahead is bathed well with light, and the beauty of the tree line opposite this road becomes more prominent. Having something to enjoy looking at definitely helps move the peril into the background, but Fortia has a nagging thought that refuses to leave her.

"That guy in black must have killed our horse…" Arty huffs out his unhappiness at this idea. "We need to be on the lookout, boy. Hopefully, he won't bother us again, but he probably would assume that we have the nugget by now."

Arty seems alert and ready for danger, and Fortia is strengthened by his resolve. She picks up the pace. Her ankle still slows her down, but it does not impact her enthusiasm.

~ ~ ~

Nightfall approaches in the forest. It has been a long day of travel on foot for Fortia and Arty, and if she doesn't get some rest, it will be more difficult to make good time tomorrow. They have situated themselves in the space between the lateral roots of a large tree, not far from the main road but far enough away that they won't need to worry about being noticed as they relax.

Together, they enjoy some cold jerky and nuts for dinner. It's the best food they can expect at this point, though the desire for a good meal is not at all far from their minds. She has the map open and consults it to see how far away from the city of Pignoli they are.

"I think if we are up before sunrise, we should be able to get there before noon tomorrow." She seems confident of their location and stores the map away in the rucksack. Again, using the blanket for warmth, she and Arty nestle themselves together in the sanctuary of these lateral roots.

For a brief period of time, it seems as though the night will be uneventful, but soon enough, Fortia hears hoofbeats approaching on the road. She hushes Arty with a finger, then slips herself out of the blanket. Moving with stealth, she stays in the shadows as she approaches the road.

North of her on the road, Malleus is on horseback with a torch in his hand. He moves southward at a good pace, but he is clearly making an effort to search the tree line as he goes. Fortia freezes, well concealed behind a line of shrubs. She waits for him to pass by and gain some distance before she moves back to Arty.

Wrapping the blanket over them both, she pets her companion for comfort, thinking hard about the challenge this man poses to her.

"I don't know if we can fight him, boy." It is a concerning thought. "We may need to avoid the road instead." Arty huffs at this. He knows it will slow them down. Feeling safe in their concealed spot, though, they both settle in for the night.

~ ~ ~

In the light of morning, Fortia and Arty move through the woods at the best pace they can muster. The terrain is rough, so Arty is again riding at the top of the rucksack. She is walking parallel to the road but keeping a good distance of twenty or thirty feet away from the road's edge.

It is difficult traveling this way. Occasionally, she needs to climb over a felled tree or redirect herself around large thatches of shrubbery. Worse yet, nearly any time Fortia hears someone on the road, she has to duck for cover.

Not far ahead, she is pleased to see the peak of a rooftop. A small house in the Open Forest, somewhat reminiscent of her own home. A scattering of farm animals wander about in the sideyard, and a large backyard space is penned off for a generous number of chickens. This quaint home must be a chicken farmer's residence, and it is humbly appointed as one would expect for such an occupation.

"We must be getting close, Arty." She moves nearer to the side fence of this small farm property. Not wanting to draw attention to herself by trespassing, she is forced to detour onto the main road briefly. Stepping just a moment into the road, she checks both directions for any sign of Malleus. Not seeing anyone, she hurries as best she can past the front fence line.

Her ankle is mostly healed now and is barely holding her back. She moves at a swift pace, though she cannot help but notice a few comforting details of the adjacent house. The chimney of the home puffs up smoke as a good fire gives comfort to the occupants within. The subtle comforts of a home are an experience that she yearns to return to, but the distance between her and that place is still unmeasured.

Two horses are eating from a grain trough in the front yard, and the recollection of her own horse having been killed and left in the Grasslands hits her again. Even these depressing thoughts cannot fully impede her sense of progress right now. There's no time for these self-indulgences. She shakes this off and moves past it all as fast as she can. Drawing any attention to herself right now could have awful consequences for the residents of this home.

It seems that this quick detour went well, and she approaches the end of the fence line without any concerns of being spotted. She maneuvers back into the coverage of the tree line. Her pace picks up now as she feels she must be close to the Closed Forest of Pignoli.

Suddenly, hoofbeats move in quickly from behind her. Fortia scurries further into the forest and works to stay as quiet as she can while still moving toward cover. She is fortunate to find a young and relatively wide tree not far away. It makes for a good hiding place.

The hoofbeats approach at a gallop and stop at the edge of the adjacent farm. From behind the tree, Fortia can barely see the road, but she can tell it is Malleus in the distance. He jumps off his horse and slowly begins to walk in her general direction. With a menacing gaze, he scans the area for any signs of movement. He is convinced he saw her…

"I saw your footprints on the road late last night, child." An awful smile develops from his shattered and jagged teeth. He continues moving closer to her hiding spot. "I will not rest until I find you."

To Fortia, Malleus sounds like a man obsessed. She cannot help but tremble inside, but she must maintain her calm as best she can. It is crucial to stay quiet for as long as possible.

"Just come out now and give me the nugget. I'll let you live." He creeps in closer, though he seems to gradually veer off in a different direction, away from her true location.

Fortia watches this from behind the tree. Regardless of his menacing tone, he does not actually know where she is. She checks her surroundings, though, an effort to find another hiding spot that she could maybe sneak over to.

Malleus is roughly twenty feet away from her now, and continuing his search, he is almost parallel with the tree she is concealed behind. She must move, or he will certainly spot her.

Fortia quietly shifts herself around the tree trunk. It is as silent a maneuver as could be expected, but a soft scraping noise is made. She freezes.

Malleus hears it. He halts himself and slowly turns in her direction. His awful, burned face scans the area, determined to find any source of the noise. Even if it was just a squirrel, it would be a dereliction of duty not to find it. He has a thought, though, and his devious smile widens even further.

"Your mother will be executed soon." He pauses, waiting for the movement.

On hearing this, a look of rage begins to grow on Fortia's face. The adrenaline starts pumping through her sap, and she feels like she wants to fight. She knows he is too strong for her to face alone. Speed is her best advantage. A few slow breaths help her to temper down the anger, and she again considers what other options she has.

Malleus continues his slow and menacing path in her direction. He is still a good fifteen feet away from her, but Fortia knows she has to move. Now more eager to escape, she frantically searches for a quick path of retreat. There is no way to move again without immediately being seen. She considers running to the farmhouse nearby and pleading for help, but that would only endanger the people there. Her anxiety is suddenly quelled, though. She has another idea…

Malleus continues to creep forward. As he does, he draws his knife from his belt line. The tree Fortia is behind is only ten feet away now, but his position is slightly further from the road than Fortia's hiding spot.

Fortia dashes from behind the tree, sprinting toward the road as fast as she can muster. Malleus is shocked for a moment, but he begins the chase without much delay. She has a good lead and is very fast on her feet as she sprints directly toward his horse. Malleus soon realizes that she intends to steal his horse. He charges after her but stumbles as his injured leg nearly makes him fall into the brush.

"Hold on, Arty!" She jumps forward. Launching herself over a shrubbery on the edge of the road, her foot perfectly catches the stirrup on his saddle. She swings herself onto the horse. With a swift kick, the horse leaps forward and accelerates into a gallop.

Malleus enters the road and screams out with rage. With a sneer of anger, he watches as his horse speeds away.

She glances behind her to see this furious man who immediately turns and makes a direct line of approach to the horses in the farmer's yard. With a look of concern, she leans into the saddle and holds the reins as tight as she can. She kicks and kicks, and the animal picks up even more speed, pushing itself into a rapid gallop. Fortia has a very good lead but she glances behind again.

Malleus is riding bareback on the farmer's horse, and he rapidly gets the animal up to speed. Her fear is warranted, but she has to focus on staying stable. This saddle is much too big for her, and the horse is a war horse, a much larger beast than her own horse was. If she doesn't stay focused, she could easily get bounced off it. Regardless, she kicks and kicks.

Malleus has matched her speed, though. He is pushing this farm horse to move as fast as it has ever gone, and they are quickly gaining on her.

Fortia's horse huffs and grunts with deep and intense breaths. It sprints forward, moving with the charging gallop it has practiced many times before.

Ahead of her she can see a grouping of Pignoli soldiers who are casually riding on horseback. Likely just a group out on patrol, but not far ahead of them are the petrified city walls.

Fortia's horse blazes past the soldiers. They are stunned by the animal, and soon, they pick up the pace a bit. Malleus and his horse quickly rage past them.

"Halt! Both of you!" The soldiers give chase. They push their animals to get up to speed as this could easily be a threat to their kingdom.

Glancing behind her, Malleus is still gaining ground, but Fortia is relieved to see the main gate just ahead. She pulls hard on the leads and drags the horse to a stop. It halts so quickly that she struggles to even stay in the saddle.

"Open the gate! I am Fortia, daughter of Constans!"

"What's this racket!?" a guard on the parapet yells down.

Out of nowhere, Malleus screams out and rams her with his horse. In the same movement, he jumps off and tackles her in the air.

Both of them fall toward the gate, and they strike hard on the ground. Malleus loses his grip on her, though, and the momentum rolls them both forward. The impact of the fall knocks the breath out of Fortia, and the latch on her rucksack tears open.

Everything in the rucksack comes barreling out. Arty tumbles out and rolls some distance away from her. The glove bounces away, and the nugget comes out of its safe covering. It rolls to a stop on the dirt only a short distance from Malleus.

Even in the afternoon light, the Golden Nugget gives off an immense glow. Everyone in the vicinity of this front gate cannot help but look at it in wonder. The guards at the ground level, the guards up on the parapet, they all stop in amazement and gaze at this small but distinctly incredible object.

Fortia and Arty are both stunned by the fall. She tries to get her bearings and struggles to grow alert to what happened. A look of panic grows on her face as she realizes the nugget is just near Malleus.

Malleus shakes off the impact from the fall, and he cannot help but struggle as he attempts to rise from his knees. Seeing the nugget, though, he instinctively lunges at it.

"Stop him!" Fortia screams at the guards.

Malleus scurries on his hands and knees toward the nugget. With both hands, he grabs it, and kneeling there, he is immediately mesmerized. The beauty and glowing brilliance of it is overpowering—

"AAAAAAH!" Malleus shrieks out as he suddenly realizes that the nugget is burning into his bark. Smoke rapidly emanates from his hands, and they burst on fire. He can barely understand what happened, and he instinctively drops it. It rolls to the ground nearby one of the guards, who cannot help but be terrified of it now.

Malleus shrieks out as the blazing hot fire spreads up his arms. He bellows out with fear and terror. His leather armor catches fire, and he drops to the ground, rolling to save his own life. Smashing his arms into the dirt all around, he desperately tries to put out the fire.

The guards run to him. Using water from their canteens, they douse him to extinguish the flames. Even for Fortia, knowing the unique qualities of this object, she is surprised to see this outcome. All he did was hold it in his hands for a few moments…

While the guards deal with Malleus, she walks over to the glove on the ground, slips it onto her hand, and casually picks up the Golden Nugget.

The other guards up on the parapet and nearby at the ground level are stunned. They have never seen anything like this, and they watch as this child handles the nugget with ease. She holds the glowing orb in the palm of her hand as she casually turns to address them.

"I must speak with King Potilius."

Chapter 13

FORTIA IS SITTING at King Potilius's well-appointed dining table, having just eaten part of a plate of nut cakes. She appears jittery. Too anxious to eat all her food, it seems.

Arty rests in comfort on her lap, still recovering from the trauma of the fight by the gate. The rucksack is on the table near them, and the glove is again folded over the nugget. A hint of glowing light from the nugget is visible from its cuff, but if someone were not aware of its contents, they might just think of it as a rather dirty old glove right now.

While she should be relaxing, Fortia seems to be in a rush to go somewhere. Soon enough, Matthius and Tiler enter the room. They are very happy to see her alive and well, and she smiles brightly at them both. Soon, though, she realizes that Matthius is walking with a limp. Resting Arty on the floor, she moves rapidly over to embrace them with a hug.

"How did you ever pull this off, Fortia…?" Matthius holds her tight, somewhat in disbelief that she was able to recover this object on her own.

They move to the table and sit. Arty literally jumps at the opportunity to rest in her lap again. Fortia still has a lot on her mind, though.

"Is Harris recovering?" She is eager to hear good news. Matthius smiles at her in response, himself rather happy to be sharing it.

"She is resting now. The injury to her head kept her unconscious for some time, and only yesterday did she start to come back to us."

Fortia is glad to hear that, but there is still too much on her mind to sit still. Seeing this, Tiler becomes worried and hopes to find out what the issue is.

"Fortia, what happened after we turned back?"

She is about to respond, but King Potilius enters along with Salamena.

"Fortia!" Potilius waddles to her as fast as his old body can arrange. "My goodness, the days have gone by so slowly."

Salamena shares a smile with them. "Ever since Matthius and Tiler came back without you, the king has barely slept."

She is flattered, and they all stand to greet Potilius. Arty has had it with all this up and down, though. He nestles himself on the floor near Fortia's chair instead.

Potilius sits down, and Salamena marches off toward the kitchen. Fortia is again sitting at his left side, and she still appears very unsettled. Potilius is too astute to overlook this.

"What troubles you, Fortia?"

She settles herself and gathers her thoughts. "Right before I escaped with his horse, Malleus told me my mother was to be executed."

A look of sadness passes over Potilius's face. He was hoping that she had not learned about this just yet.

"We're not sure when, but that is what my sources have said as well."

"We need to go NOW!" Fortia jumps up from her seat, startling Arty as she does.

"Fortia, I promise you, on my crown, I have a plan in place to prevent this."

She feels slightly better hearing that, but it is hard to completely ignore her anxiety and frustration. Not wanting to just sit there, she starts pacing back and forth beside the table. Salamena re-enters with a teapot and four teacups. She serves everyone as Matthius looks to Fortia.

"Come Fortia, have some tea with us. We will tell you about the plan…"

After a frustrated moment, she heeds his advice. She sits but suddenly remembers something important.

"How did you ever bite that nugget?" she abruptly says to Potilius. "I watched Malleus's hands catch fire after holding it for just a few seconds. How did you ever survive?"

Potilius is shocked and impressed by this question.

"You are so much smarter than I was at your age, Fortia." He seems to be genuinely amazed by this question but makes an attempt to explain.

"May I see your knife?" He offers his hand, and she removes it from her belt.

"You likely know by now, but this is Oaken Steel, made in the forges of the Kingdom of Oak just before war tore that city into two." He shows her the knife as he continues.

"No living thing can crush the Golden Nugget." As he says this, he reaches into his pocket and removes a handful of nuts. He flicks one to Arty, who happily catches it in his mouth.

"Even holding it in their mouth for more than a moment, a king or queen would never recover. They would be scarred for their entire life."

"Then how could you crush it?" She is perplexed by all this. "How could anyone?"

"The Ordo Nux Aurea does not just protect access to the nugget, Fortia. It protects the line of ascension to a throne." Potilius holds one of the nuts up for her to see and touches the tip of the dagger to the meaty surface of it.

"Only an Oaken Steel blade can pierce the skin of the Golden Nugget, and only if the Order has determined that there is a rightful heir to the throne will the Tracker pierce the nugget before a coronation. That tiny rupture in the nugget weakens it, disrupts the power of the nugget itself, and thus makes it possible for a royal to crush it."

With that, he pierces the small nut in his fingers, pops it in his mouth, and chews it up with a smile. Fortia chuckles. It makes sense now, but soon, she realizes something else. Her eyes light up as she speaks.

"Even if Malleus had gotten the nugget, Tonitro would still not be able to crush it."

Potilius smiles, very glad to see her intuition at work.

"Please, tell me the plan?" She is eager to get moving.

~ ~ ~

Outside the front façade of the prison of Macadamia, the morning light shines on numerous citizens who are busy going about their day. Sedo is still in the pillory, a torturous position to be in for days and days. A guard approaches her from the front gate and unlatches the device. Another guard joins him, and they both lift her, one arm draping over each of their shoulders, they drag her back into the prison. She is very weak from days in that awful device, and she can barely lift her head.

They deliver her to the sitting room Constans was taken to previously. Cautiously, they prop her weak body up in one of the large chairs there, and a guard positions the console table so that it is now in front of her. Were she not so exhausted, Sedo might find all this curious, but for now she struggles to even open her eyes. The other guard returns with a serving tray and places it on the table in front of her.

It is full of fresh foods. Nut cakes, sweet oil, fruits, plump nuts, tea, and many other delights she would have prepared at home for her family.

Both of the guards exit and leave her there alone for some time. Eventually she sees the food in front of her, but she is barely strong enough to reach for it. Slowly, she grabs a piece of fruit and gets it into her mouth. She is enamored with the taste…It gives her new energy, and soon, she is working to sit upright and enjoy what she has.

Moments later, Queen Julianna enters. She quietly sits in the chair opposite Sedo. Seeing her queen, Sedo makes an attempt to stand, but Julianna gestures for her to relax.

"That is surprising." Julianna is curious. "That you would stand for me."

"You are my queen, still." Sedo talks over bites of her food and sips of tea.

Julianna considers this, but she is here for a specific reason. A moment of silence passes, and Sedo cannot help but notice that Julianna looks very unsettled.

"Is there something troubling you, my queen?"

Julianna realizes her emotions have betrayed her. She sits upright and gathers her senses.

"Sedo, I regret to inform you that tomorrow evening you will be executed."

Hearing this does not seem to impact Sedo much, though she does briefly pause her meal to consider it. It is a thought she perhaps has already made peace with.

She continues eating but takes a moment to ask a question.

"Why did you come here to tell me this? Surely, one of the guards could have delivered this message to me."

Julianna takes a deep breath before responding. "I know you are not truly a traitor, Sedo, but things being as they are now, I cannot change the decisions my son has already made."

Sedo nods; she seems to understand that idea.

"It took some convincing," Julianna continues, "but I have arranged for you to stay in this room until your execution. I had hoped to have you moved here last night, but my son insisted you be kept on display until this morning. For the coming days, you will have clean clothing, food, tea, and a comfortable bed."

"Thank you, my queen." Sedo humbly bows her head.

"Being who he is, Tonitro was resistant." Julianna frowns at this. "He would only concede to these conditions if I delivered the news of your execution to you, myself."

"My queen, it is hard for me to imagine the difficulties you have been confronted with since your husband's death."

Julianna's smile seems to indicate a humble appreciation for that sentiment.

"Would you have some tea with me?" Sedo offers, almost optimistically.

"Thank you, but unfortunately, I must attend to other duties." Julianna is about to stand—

"If I may," Sedo interrupts, "may I have one request regarding my execution?"

"Of course," Julianna says, almost out of a sense of duty.

"Please do not let my daughter see me die. She needs to remember me as I was."

A troubled look passes over Julianna's face. Sedo can see that she is almost trembling now, but she successfully contains her emotions once again.

"I will do all that I can to prevent that." Julianna seems sincere. "We do not know where your daughter is right now, so I do not know if I can fully deliver on that request."

Sedo appears content at hearing this. At least she knows that Fortia is not in this prison. She continues eating, still famished from days of no food. Julianna stands, moves across the room to exit, but Sedo again speaks.

"I suspect that Tonitro has had no luck finding the Golden Nugget?"

Julianna freezes, somewhat confused, but she maintains her royal composure.

"Sedo, how is it that you have the insight to ask that question?"

"Everyone in the Order is aware that the nugget was fake, my queen," Sedo says matter-of-factly. There is not even a hint of bragging in her tone. "I do not know anything more about it, but I know that they have everything they need to recover the true nugget themselves."

On hearing this, Julianna seems to smile. The anxiety in her almost seems to wash away. Sedo cannot help but notice that Julianna looks almost complacent now. For a moment, a sense of calm lands so heavy on her that she must steady herself on the back of the chair.

"I don't suppose it hurts to tell you," Julianna is almost smiling now, "but it is true. Tonitro was expecting to hear from his men by now, but I suspect that they will not return."

Sedo sips her tea and continues speaking. "I would imagine that Tonitro has many spies, perhaps even one in the Order. Surely, he must know the truth about the nugget."

At hearing this, Julianna frowns in confusion. A moment passes before Sedo acknowledges this, and she quickly realizes something…Her face grows very sincere. Laying her teacup on the table and not blinking an eye, she looks squarely at Julianna.

"If you care for your son as I care for my daughter, then please heed this advice. Do everything you can to keep him from biting the real nugget. It will either kill him, or it will scar him for life."

Julianna looks Sedo over for a moment, unsure whether she can believe that statement. Regardless of all that has been done to Sedo, she cannot help but feel like there is honesty being shared here.

"I do not know if I can prevent that." Julianna bows her head with a deep concern for her son. "Tonitro has never truly been a good recipient of either my or my husband's council."

Sedo frowns at the thought, and soon, Julianna offers her a humble smile.

"I promise you, Sedo, you will not suffer any more than you already have."

With that she quickly exits, leaving Sedo to the relative comforts of this place.

~ ~ ~

The bridge at Gruff's home is a busy place this morning. A handful of troops from Pignoli are crossing on horseback, and a rugged carriage waits by the front of the home. While it is likely a relatively comfortable vehicle, it is something of a lightweight version of what a king would usually travel in. It does not have the lavish appearance of the official transport that Potilius might otherwise be using.

Gruff and Potilius are in front of the home, engaged in conversation with Salamena, Fortia, and Angelus. He and Gruff shake hands as they prepare to exit.

"I wish we could stay longer, Gruff. We left well before sunrise, and we will need to ride all day and night to make this work." Everyone begins to mount their horses and continue the journey. Gruff helps Potilius step into his carriage.

"With your permission, my king, Angelus would like to join your mission. He has prepared a parcel for travel, and he is skilled with a bow. He can help you."

Potilius steps into his carriage and settles himself on a seat near the window. It becomes clear now that

Malleus is in the cabin of the carriage, chained to the wall.

"We would be honored to have his assistance."

Angelus smiles bright at hearing this and looks to Fortia. She is already up on her horse, and she tries not to smile too quickly as he runs off to grab his equipment.

"Besides," Gruff whispers to Potilius, "he won't stop talking about Fortia." He winks, and Potilius releases a boisterous laugh.

"Then he has good taste, my friend!"

Soon, Fortia and Arty are sauntering across the bridge on their horse. Angelus gallops to catch up, puts his horse next to hers in the caravan formation. Knowing that they will be traveling together for a while is reason enough for a mutual smile of appreciation.

~ ~ ~

Riding through the night is difficult. With only the light of torches and the moon to guide the riders, the pace of the caravan moving north on the forest road is slower than Fortia would like. Arty is deep asleep on the back of her horse, and Angelus has maintained his position riding next to her.

"What a truly incredible story." Angelus smiles with amazement. "Aurufex must be some kind of immortal creature."

"If he is as old as those fossils you showed me, then he must be immortal indeed." They both think on this for a moment, and a sense of awe is shared.

"Here…" Fortia reaches for her pocket. "I brought something back for you." She hands him the small square crystal she took from the field of geodes. Angelus gazes at this in wonder.

"Thank you, Fortia." He seems to be getting emotional, clearly something of a romantic.

"King Potilius says it will bring you good fortune and prosperity."

"I have not stopped thinking about you since the Dry Woods, Fortia." He has a humble smile. "Gruff was growing tired of hearing me talk about you. He told me to make you a gift, so I created this for you."

Reaching into his pocket, he hands her a braided leather necklace. It is made with a simple but attractive woven pattern. After admiring it for a moment Fortia relaxes the reins of the horse. She ties the ends of the cords together at the back of her neck, and wearing it now, she smiles at him. Again, she finds herself speechless amidst the flattery of this young man. He reaches out, offering his hand to her. She cannot help but feel comforted by his warmth and kindness. Taking his hand feels like the best way to acknowledge that.

Tiler and Matthius are just behind them in formation. They see this gentle moment unfold ahead of them, and it is certainly easy to appreciate. Tiler smirks, now having a brief realization.

"Well, if nothing else good comes of all this, at least we can take credit for that." They both chuckle for a moment.

"I never asked you." Matthius becomes curious. "It's been years since David died…Have you ever considered finding another partner?"

"Perhaps someday." Tiler is somewhat sullen at the thought. Without thinking, he rubs an old ring situated on his left ring finger. It is almost worn out from this behavior.

"Our military has kept me too busy," Matthius continues, "but perhaps that will change. It is hard to imagine how…"

"If things go to plan, my friend, you will be too busy to even have an ale with us."

They both chuckle at the thought.

The nighttime ride continues through the moonlight, and inside King Potilius's carriage, he eats a small plate of food for dinner. Across from him is Malleus, who is chained to the wall by his neck, legs, and arms. He has enough freedom of movement to feed himself, so he lifts his burned hands up to his mouth and eats a handful of raw nuts.

"I'm sorry that we can't make you more comfortable, Malleus," Potilius says between bites of food. "You have proven yourself as too devious."

Malleus says nothing but gives a brief sneer in response. He chews on the handful of nuts, not even looking in the king's direction.

"I have known many men like you in the past," Potilius says. "Things have always ended badly for them."

Malleus chuckles. He continues eating with disregard.

"Once things play out in Macadamia, you may want to consider what the consequences will be for you."

"Will you kill me, good king?" Malleus sneers, already disregarding the response.

"That will not be for me to decide. We must leave that to your future king."

Malleus widens his toothy grin. "I have killed kings," he says, with almost a sense of pride in his smile now. "They die like any other man."

Potilius smirks. He is glad to hear this spoken aloud as it feels like something of a confession for the murder of Serenus. However, he is beginning to wish he had brought another carriage so he doesn't have to be around Malleus for so long.

Finishing his food, Potilius yawns for a moment and lays his head back in an attempt to get comfortable and sleep. He closes his eyes, but Malleus glares directly at him.

"If I get out of these chains, I will kill you." The thought seems enticing to him.

Potilius leans forward, looks him squarely in the eyes, and offers to him not even a single moment of fear.

"I have lived long enough and traveled far enough to know my future well." Potilius closes his eyes and rests his head again, leaving Malleus to confront that thought.

Chapter 14

THE SUN IS RISING, and the caravan seems to have made very good time. Fortia yawns, now feeling fatigued from the trip, but she is still alert enough to be scanning the forest. The exceptional colors of the Open Forest in autumn are in full bloom this morning. She and Angelus are keen to observe their surroundings.

"I recognize this place." A smile grows on her face. "We are not far from our farm."

Looking in the distance, she sees the small clearing where the tree limb collapsed under her weight. The memory of it returns to her…While it was barely more than a week ago, it could almost be a different lifetime for her.

The travel continues, and soon enough, the wreckage of Fortia's home becomes visible. Heavy timbers do not burn easily, and most of the timbers that compose the front portions of the first level are still standing. The roof and the second floor have collapsed, and these have crushed the back half of the home completely. All the farm animals have escaped by now, making this place feel even more desolate.

Fortia and Arty gaze at their lost home as the caravan passes by. An air of sadness is obvious from everyone who recognizes this place. Angelus, still riding beside her, reaches out to her, and she takes his hand. Nothing can be said to truly relieve the ache of such tragedy.

As they move closer to the side of the property, Fortia can see beyond the remaining parts of the front façade. While the upper part of the chimney has been pulled down under the weight of the collapsed roof, the large and well-built hearth of her home is still standing. Aside from some scorching to the stones, it is entirely intact.

Seeing this grand hearth in good condition brings a smile of pride to Fortia's face.

~ ~ ~

As the caravan approaches the Cowan's Eaves, Tiler rides ahead to see who may be there. As he enters the front drive, he sees another discretely equipped carriage with a handful of horses and soldiers lingering nearby. They wear the uniform red and white armor that identifies the Kingdom of Pecan.

Seeing Tiler at the entry of the drive, one of these soldiers swiftly walks over to the carriage and knocks on the door. He opens it, and soon enough, King Colomena dismounts the carriage. He has a noticeably dark bark and a bold, proud posture. Also wearing red and white, it appears he has not spared the embellishments of jewelry and furs for this trip.

On seeing this, Tiler turns his horse back onto the road and signals the caravan. Slowly, everyone funnels into the front drive. The carriage stops, and with the help of a nearby soldier, King Potilius steps out. He thanks the soldier but immediately turns and walks over to King Colomena who has remained waiting by his carriage.

"Thank you for meeting us, Colomena."

"Spare me the pleasantries, Potilius. I rode all night for this." Colomena glares suspiciously, and while Potilius is just preparing to respond, he interrupts.

"I trust you are taking care of my daughter," Colomena says as he glances over to Salamena. She is still on horseback, not far away.

Potilius looks at him with absolute sincerity. "If I did not have two sons already, she would be my heir."

Salamena dismounts her horse and approaches them both.

"Father, I am very pleased to see you again." She reaches for Colomena's hand, and he offers it to her. She kisses his ring. Colomena is pleased by this greeting, though he is still looking somewhat cautious about this whole scenario.

"Tell me how this will work, Potilius, and please, spare me the old adages you tend to apply. If my daughter had not taken up residence with you years ago,

I likely would have burned your kingdom to the ground by now."

Potilius gives a tolerant smile in response to this. He gestures toward the tavern.

"Please join me in the tavern. I will explain everything."

Fortia and Angelus are still on horseback, not very far away from them. Having overheard most of this, Fortia turns to Angelus with a confused expression.

"She is King Colomena's daughter?"

"Yes. Amazing, isn't it? My uncle told me about it when I first met her. He tells the story like it was the most incredible thing he ever saw."

Fortia listens intently and watches the two kings walk toward the front entry of the Inn.

"There have always been skirmishes between the two kingdoms, but the last true war between Pecan and Pignoli was ten years ago," Angelus continues as he dismounts and starts to unpack his horse.

"Neither army was gaining any ground for months, but countless men and women were dying each day. Potilius had offered a truce, but Colomena refused."

Angelus helps Fortia off her horse, and she seems eager to hear the story.

"One day, amidst a particularly heated battle in the Marshlands, Salamena walked out onto the battlefield with no armor and no weapons. Gruff said it was like she was glowing. Everyone around her suddenly stopped fighting and just watched her walking. She went right over to King Potilius and knelt before him."

Fortia glances across at Salamena as she follows the two kings into the tavern. Before this, she thought of Salamena as a lavish and skilled caretaker. Fortia cannot help but regard her in a very different light now.

"She must be incredibly brave…" A look of amazement crosses over Fortia's face.

"Her actions forced Colomena to understand that not everyone in his family supported the war. Thankfully, he was humble enough to accept that reality."

Fortia helps Arty to the ground, and she begins to unpack her horse. Matthius approaches them with his saddle supported at his hip.

"When you are ready, join us around back. We will start preparing soon."

Matthius moves along. The entire caravan is working to unpack after a long journey has been rushed into a short period of time. The energy of the day seems to be rapidly building, and perhaps there is a good reason to feel optimistic.

~ ~ ~

Much of the day has passed in the Closed Forest of Macadamia, and the stone stage of the prison has a few dozen people standing in front of it. Their attention is focused on something, and they do not appear to be very happy about it.

The pillory has been removed and replaced with a single upright timber which is driven into an opening in the surface. A piece of parchment is nailed on it with a message written for everyone to observe.

"Execution Tonight"

The small crowd around it appears frustrated by this, and some discussion between them is obvious. Within the group is an older man, dressed humbly and supported by a cane. A sad frown has settled onto his face as he turns to his son.

"There hasn't been an execution in Macadamia for more than fifty years…"

The young man is confused. "But she's a traitor, Father."

"There have been many traitors before, son." His frown transitions into an aching look of frustration.

A peasant woman carrying a bundle of nuts nearby responds to them.

"She killed King Serenus, I heard. Shot him with an arrow in front of the queen."

The crowd here seems to understand this, maybe even agree, but the old man is not at all convinced.

"Give her to the Open Forest then, in exile…" Many of the people around him seem to appreciate this opinion. Another peasant woman nearby is returning from the market with her children. They all carry baskets of goods. She seems to disagree with the older man, though.

"My father gave his life in the Open Forest. A traitor has not earned that honor."

Some people nod in agreement, but the old man just turns, walks away with disappointment.

"Son, we cannot become like those butchers in the south. The Macadamia I know is a symbol…" His son follows, now unsure how to feel about it all.

Soon, a prison guard with a speaking trumpet on horseback approaches. Moments later, he raises it to his mouth. "EXECUTION TONIGHT," he commands into it as he guides the horse further out into the city. "EXECUTION TONIGHT." Continuing deep into the fabric of the city, he repeats this announcement for everyone to hear.

Not terribly far from here is the main gate of the city. From the inside, the safety that this gate provides is obvious. Its enormous doors are composed of huge timbers, roughly three feet wide each, and bound to one another by thick bolted iron bands at narrow intervals. It is an imposing gate that would take any battering ram many days to push through.

A smaller carriage door is only a short distance from this. A steady flow of people on horseback and in small carriages pass through this from the Open Forest. The thick walls of the city form a tunnel just beyond it, and while there is no restriction on entry today, there is the watchful eye of armed guards who are busy profiling everyone who enters.

Approaching here are Angelus and Fortia, both of them on the back of one horse that Angelus is steering. They are dressed rather well like citizens with some coin to spend. They stop at one of the guards, and Angelus confidently addresses him.

"Guard, which direction to the storage depot? We need oils for the inn."

The guard points him down the adjacent road and waves him off. They ride on, though Angelus tosses him a coin first before they exit.

More peasants, merchants, and guards enter and exit on foot. Soon enough the carriage that Potilius was in comes rolling through the tunnel. Matthius and Tyler are steering it from the driver's seat, but they are dressed as prison guards. The carriage now has iron bars fitted on it, having been transformed to look like a prison cart. Through a window, it is obvious that Malleus is still chained up within the cabin, though a hood is over his head. They ride through, not even slowing down as they turn onto the adjacent road.

A large crowd has gathered at the prison stage by now, and this only continues to grow as time passes. A mixture of soldiers and citizens blend into the viewing areas. The front door of the prison has been opened, and two guards wearing black masks stand at that entrance, waiting for things to proceed.

The stage appears to be set for the event to begin, and the sun has dropped low enough that the trees of the Closed Forest are offering an array of shadows and dim light within the city. A few other guards nearby begin lighting torches as the darkness of night will soon gather around them.

Adjacent to the prison is a small civic building built from a similar pinkish stone material as the royal residence. On the second floor of this structure, just next to the stage, is a porch space with two thrones waiting for the king and queen.

The crowd has become a bit unsettled, and a few of the people here are bordering on passionate. Others are simply engaged in a discussion about the path of their kingdom. Most of them have never seen this type of event in their lifetime, and being uncertain of what they are about to witness, they are filled with a silent fear. Many people are just watching this event play out, and this is not at all an unrealistic perspective.

With so much power in the hands of a king or a queen, it requires a great act of willpower for one citizen to feel like they have any influence at all. It is sometimes difficult to stand up and say out loud that what is moral is still of benefit.

The attention of the crowd shifts to the right of the square. On a branching road, Tonitro, Julianna, and a small entourage of royal guards make their approach on horseback. Soldiers nearby them work to clear a path in the crowd, which grows increasingly larger still. Soon, the entourage stops near a doorway situated under the porch of the civic building.

Tonitro and his mother dismount with two guards and enter there. As the timber door opens, a stone staircase leading to the second level is obvious. After a moment, they emerge from a doorway at the rear of the porch, and they take their seats facing the stage. With the king and queen here, the event can now proceed. The guards at the front gate of the prison look up to them, awaiting an expected signal. The unsettled crowd quickly gains their composure, expecting that the king will speak at any moment.

At the opposite end of the stage, the carriage with Matthius, Tiler, and Malleus passes by the crowd at a good speed. It moves quickly toward the side alley where the captain's processing room is.

Tonitro seems to barely notice this carriage. Just another prison arrival from his perspective. Instead, he stands and steps forward to the stone rail of the porch. Everyone in the crowd gazes up to him, eager to hear the explanation of what will unfold here.

"People of Macadamia, while my father's policy for much of his reign was to suspend the execution of prisoners, no matter how grievous the crime, the age we are living in now demands a more rigid approach to justice."

As Julianna hears him say this, she has a clear look of frustration and disappointment on her face. The crowd is largely silent though, but many people still appear suspicious at hearing Tonitro's justification for this policy change.

"While this prisoner is a woman, she is no regular citizen. Once a member of the disbanded Shield Maidens of our Operative Forces, she is a person of great skill and cunning. She alone killed two of our finest soldiers prior to her imprisonment."

The crowd murmurs at this. They don't know that this is something of a lie, and they start to react more in unison with this rousing and confident speech.

In the adjacent alley, though, the carriage pulls up to the entry of the prison stables. The two guards posted in this area approach it rapidly and signal for it to stop.

"Wait there!" one of them orders as the carriage grows near the entry. Matthius ignores him and steers the carriage into the prison stables. He stops the horses just short of running into the two guards.

"What cart is this?" a guard says, appearing confused. "I don't recognize you."

"We are from the prison at the Northern Inlet," Matthius says confidently. He gestures toward the door of the carriage. "We have a prisoner transfer."

Tiler steps down from the driver's seat and quickly moves over to the carriage door. He grabs the handle of the door and pulls it open. The second guard angrily stops him just as the door begins to swing open.

"No! No! We're not expecting a transfer from—"

Tiler lifts his hand and suddenly strikes the guard on the head with the butt of his knife. The guard falls limp to the ground. The other guard sees this and reacts fast, rushing to restrain Tiler. Matthius jumps from the seat and pounces on him. They struggle, wrestling on the gravel floor of the stables until Tiler steps next to them and puts his knife at the guard's neck. The guard stops but he sneers out of anger for being caught like this.

Just then, the door to the captain's office casually opens.

"Why is this cart here?!" The captain is about to step out, but he freezes. Seeing the commotion here, he quickly steps backward. He's about the slam the door shut, but—

A knife strikes his hand. He falls backward into the room and shrieks at the pain.

Harris appears in the carriage door. She is also wearing black armor, and she appeared very much like Malleus. With one swift motion, she pulls another knife and throws it through the doorway. It strikes the captain's arm as he again reaches for the door.

Harris jumps out of the carriage, and with just a few quick steps she is through the door and into the processing room. She pounces on the captain and, using the black hood in her opposite hand, she quickly pulls it over his head. Just as he begins screaming, she covers his mouth with her hand and muffles his cries.

At the front of the prison, Tonitro is still standing at the stone rail on the porch and continues to lecture the crowd. He appears to still be in command of their attention even after speaking for so much time.

"What some of you will see today may feel unsettling, but I reassure you, this act we commit, together, as a kingdom, is no different than any other death in a time of war."

The crowd murmurs in agreement at this. It seems that many of them, who were reluctant, are now coming around to agree with this path for the kingdom.

Tonitro signals down to the guards standing by the front doorway. They both enter the prison as he continues to speak.

"These four men," he gestures into the crowd, "will be our executioners today."

At this, four guards emerge from within the crowd carrying loaded crossbows. Each of them has a black mask over their faces. They march up to the front of the stage area and form a line. Standing at attention, they await orders.

"They are the finest marksmen in our kingdom, and each of them will fire one arrow into the prisoner, stopping her heart immediately."

The crowd murmurs softly, almost fearful from hearing this plan.

"This will be terrifying to witness, but I reassure you, it is far more merciful than a death on the battlefield."

The two guards wearing masks emerge from the prison, and they are dragging Sedo by the shoulders. She has a black hood over her head now. While she has the clothing of a prisoner, she appears very clean. It seems that until now she was well cared for, as promised by Julianna. Her arms are tied behind her back, and her ankles are bound. She attempts to scream through the hood, but only a muffled tone is heard. There must be a gag underneath.

They drag her over to the post that is standing upright on the stage. Using ropes positioned on the floor nearby, they bind her at the chest, neck, and legs. She begins to flail as she tries to break free. She continues to protest through the gag and hood, but it is impossible to understand her.

At seeing this, the crowd becomes unsettled. Everything Tonitro said up until now sounded rather noble, but now seeing a person about to die, they are having second thoughts.

Sedo keeps trying to yell something repeatedly, though it is very hard to hear anything clearly through the gag and the hood. One of the guards rests their hand on the hood and looks up to Tonitro. Awaits orders to pull the mask off.

The firing squad at the front of the stage loads their crossbows, each of them raises their bow and aims toward the prisoner on stage. Tonitro motions with his arms to settle the crowd, calming everyone before things proceed.

"Archers, when the guard pulls the hood off the prisoner, you will fire. Aim for her heart. This must be quick and merciful."

The guard holding the hood watches Tonitro, still waiting for the signal. At this point Sedo has stopped screaming and appears to be sobbing within the hood.

Tonitro gives a sudden nod of his head, and the guard quickly yanks off the hood.

It is Malleus. Gagged and crying with his eyes pinched shut, he expects his death at any moment and struggles to even look at the approaching threat.

Tonitro's eyes burst open with surprise. Julianna jumps from her seat with a similar look of shock.

The archers all turn their crossbows and fire upward to the porch level. Two of the arrows strike the royal guards behind Tonitro. One arrow hitting each of them in the shoulder. The other arrows bounce off the wall behind them. Tonitro is still too stunned and amazed to even move, but the quick woosh of arrows makes him flinch. He snaps out of it and quickly yells into the crowd.

"SEIZE THEM!" he screams to the soldiers as he points at the archers.

The crowd panics. They quickly move away from the stage, and the soldiers draw their weapons as they push inward. They are moments away from attacking the archers when one of the guards on stage pulls his mask off.

"Soldiers! Wait! It is me! Your captain, Matthius!"

The soldiers are stunned at seeing Matthius suddenly. The crowd has cleared space, though, and many other soldiers are moving to the front of the stage now.

"Please! My friends! Frigus. Daniel. Cannileus." He points to three of them, calling them out by name. The men realize it is truly Matthius. "Please, hear me out, brothers!"

"I demand that you seize them!" Tonitro yells again from the porch. While the soldiers hear this, they return their gaze to Matthius, wanting to hear from their trusted leader.

Seeing this, Tonitro becomes enraged. It is probably the first time that he has ever been ignored by someone in his entire life. With a fury in his movements, he marches through the door at the back of the porch.

"This man!" Matthius gestures toward Malleus. "He killed our great King Serenus!"

The soldiers appear frustrated and angry at hearing this, but Matthius continues.

"He has admitted it to us!" Matthius is becoming impassioned. He needs to hold the attention of these men as best he can right now. "And worse yet, he did this at the order of Tonitro! The true traitor of Macadamia!"

Tonitro marches toward the stage. He is so full of anger and frustration that he doesn't even give the soldiers time to move but instead shoves his way through them.

"What are you waiting for!?" Tonitro barks at them. He steps onto the stage quickly and points at Matthius. "I am your king! I demand that you arrest this man!"

"And what of this murderer's confession!?" Matthius responds, gesturing to Malleus.

"What of it!?" Tonitro shrugs it off. "You are no longer captain of this army, and your word cannot be trusted!"

Matthius cannot back down now, though. There is too much at stake.

"Of his own free will, he admitted to killing your father!"

Tonitro turns to his army, though, and with a practiced expression of sincerity, he engages them.

"On my honor as your king. If it is proven that this man killed my father, he WILL face a traitor's punishment!"

Malleus's eyes burst open in panic. He mumbles rapidly through the gag. The second guard on stage pulls off his mask. It is Tiler, and he quickly removes Malleus's gag.

"It was Tonitro!" Malleus yells. "He ordered me to kill Serenus! I had no choice!"

The soldiers all angrily gaze at Tonitro, who is now completely stunned. Unsure what to do next, he tries to speak but instead stumbles on his words.

The soldiers all turn their attention to the right as Queen Julianna steps up to the top of the stage. She approaches Tonitro, disappointed and struggling to hold back her biting anger. Tonitro's brow furrows with confusion as he sees his mother approach. Tears of anger and disappointment fill her eyes, but the regal posture that she maintains is still prominent in her. Now within arm's reach of her son, she briskly slaps him across the face.

He is stunned…Amazed…His otherwise humble mother has never once struck him, and he has no idea how to respond. A similar hush falls over the entire crowd here.

Moments later, Julianna turns to the soldiers, removes her own crown, and quietly places it on the stage. She is humble enough to know the truth when she hears it, and having failed as a queen and a mother, she clearly cannot expect this kingdom to respect her family line.

There is a silent awe everywhere. Never in the history of any kingdom has something like this happened before. Matthius and Tiler can barely believe what they just witnessed.

Even after this incredible act of humility, a powerful fury is building on Tonitro's face. He tries to restrain it, tries to keep his composure and retain what is left of his status as a royal, but he fails.

"I am the heir to the throne of Macadamia!" he screams at her, then turns to the crowd of soldiers. "I am your king! I broke the Golden Nugget!"

"NO!" a voice from the crowd interrupts.

Everyone turns to see Constans. His clothing is tattered and dirty. He is weak and barely able to stand as Sedo and Fortia help to support him. He looks at Tonitro with determination.

"You came to me in the prison days ago, Tonitro. You admitted to having destroyed a fake nugget during your coronation."

"Traitor! Liar!" Tonitro furiously replies. "You have no proof of that!"

Constans lifts his palm upward, and resting there is the shard of the fake nugget that Fortia found. He holds it out for everyone to see, and numerous people nearby try to inspect it.

"It's true!" Fortia announces. "Immediately after the coronation, I found this piece of the nut that Tonitro broke."

Soldiers and citizens alike boo and shout at Tonitro. There is an obvious anger and frustration growing among them. Tonitro is again dumbfounded. He struggles to respond.

A trumpet blares from a distance, then quickly blares out again. Everyone turns toward the announcing noise behind them. At the distant edge of the square, a shimmering light interrupts the darkness of the evening. The power of its brightness obscures everything behind it. The soldiers are amazed to see this awe-inspiring object.

Potilius, Colomena, and Salamena approach with a few of their guards and a trumpeter. In his gloved hand, Colomena carries the Golden Nugget. The crowd instinctively opens space for this incredible display of powerful light that is approaching them.

The two kings regally step up to the stage. On seeing this, Tonitro struggles to gather his senses. There is so much changing so fast it is hard to even know how to respond. He straightens his back and tries to regain some dignity.

"King Potilius…" Tonitro stammers, still shaken and disoriented. "King Colomena…What are you doing here?"

"Tonitro," Colomena says, "we present to you the true Golden Nugget."

Within the darkness of night, everyone here is amazed by this unique glowing object. Even Tonitro has trouble pulling his gaze from it.

"Decades ago," Colomena continues, "I broke a nugget just like this one. I swear on my crown that it is a genuine Golden Nugget."

"As do I," Potilius states. "It was more than a century ago for me, but I still remember it like it was yesterday. This is a true Golden Nugget."

Tonitro is almost mesmerized by this object, but he soon looks up from it to meet their eyes. He still does not understand why these two leaders are here to present this item.

"We two kings," Potilius continues, "pledge our loyalty to you, Tonitro, if and only if you can crush this nugget as your father once did."

Tonitro's eyes widen at the thought. He can barely believe what Potilius just said, but soon, his face fills up with a smile of lust and greed. Knowing of no reason to fear this challenge, he begins to step forward. Suddenly, Julianna grabs him by the shoulder.

"No, son!" Her urgent tone is almost begging him. "Do not do it…" Her eyes plead with him, but Tonitro looks bewildered and confused. It makes no sense to him. Why not? Power over three kingdoms is just within reach. Julianna has his attention, though, and she begs him again.

"Please, son…The nugget is more powerful than anything in all of Oakenmeer. While you are your father's son, your actions have betrayed your crown. If you bite the nugget, it very well may kill you."

Tonitro hears her say this, but he soon beholds her words with disgust. He is not deterred. His frustration grows into anger. His anger fumes into rage. His lust for power blinds him from taking her advice in this defining moment.

"I WILL NOT GIVE UP MY FATHER'S KINGDOM!" Tonitro turns quickly. With both hands, he grabs the nugget. Colomena retreats backward from this, and Julianna quickly turns away in horror. She just can't look…

His hands sizzle and burn as he holds this magical orb. He is a man-obsessed, though. The pain grows, but his lust for power blocks every reflex to drop this object. He shoves the nugget into his mouth, and smoke immediately billows out as he clenches his teeth. With all his might, he sneers at the pain. Snarls at it. Like a madman fighting a battle within himself. He clenches harder and harder. Refusing to give in.

The crowd can barely process this moment. Even still, many of them cannot look away. Tonitro is just so blindly committed. His determination to be the stronger man fills him with an almost animal-like ignorance. It is a sickness that can never be cured.

Suddenly, Tonitro shrieks. Overcome with searing pain, he bellows out, and his entire mouth catches fire. The flames spread quickly. Within seconds, the entire left side of his face is burning. Filled with terror, he again shrieks and leans forward to spit out the nugget.

His crown quickly falls off his head and strikes the stone stage with a hollow clang. Fully intact, the nugget slips out of his mouth and strikes the stones with a metallic thud. Still steaming, it rolls, settling not far from the crown of Macadamia.

Tonitro screams and wails. He swats at the fire on his face, now desperate to salvage what is left of his life. One of the Archers removes his mask. It is Angelus. He grabs the canteen on his hip and quickly douses Tonitro with water.

Falling to his knees, Tonitro hides his face. He can think of nothing else but the overwhelming pain. Julianna rushes to him and offers him comfort, but she herself is full of tears from the horrors of that difficult moment.

The crowd is stunned, struggling to recover from it all. So much has been revealed all at once. Secrets of kings and knights, magical powers that can barely be comprehended. All of this has been put on display for mere men and women to observe and accept as reality. It is almost too much for the average person to take in all at once.

Colomena frowns as he watches Tonitro cower and wail in pain. He turns to Potilius, hands him the glove, and nods.

"You were correct, Potilius." A difficult admission for Colomena. "Perhaps all these years, you have been correct…"

"About what, good king?" Potilius asks, but Colomena is again looking toward Tonitro.

"Even today, I might still have done what he did." Colomena seems to again realize the shame that is inherent in his own lust for land and power.

Acknowledging this, he steps off stage, and his guards follow him.

Potilius smiles, glad to be the steward of this moment where a lasting peace with Pecan can perhaps take hold. Wearing the glove, he reaches down and picks up the incredible shining nugget. He folds the glove over top of the nugget and carries it to Constans. Handing it to him, he shares a smile with his old friend before walking away.

Fortia and Sedo stand at Constans's side, still helping to support him as he holds the nugget. He turns to Fortia and slowly offers her the glove. She takes it from him, helping him to handle this burden right now. Constans soon turns his attention to Matthius.

"Matthius," the crowd listens closely, "by the ancient constitution, when no other heir is apparent, until a suitable successor of royal sap is identified, you, the captain of the army, must temporarily lead us."

Matthius understands that this was always part of the plan Potilius had created, but it is not at all what he wants. He is reluctant, but he is also deeply committed to his kingdom.

Salamena bends down and picks up the two crowns. She carries them over to Matthius and offers them to him. He takes them from her, and gazing at their bejeweled designs, he frowns at their golden form. Matthius knows all too well that they represent both a burden and a privilege to whoever carries them.

Salamena offers him a smile, a quiet salutation before she turns to walk off stage. Matthius stops her, though, laying a gentle hand on her arm.

"You have many years of experience working with King Potilius." Matthius is sincere, but there is something hopeful in his eyes. "Please, Macadamia will need your advice and wisdom, Salamena."

Giving a humble smile, she turns in the direction of Potilius, yet she struggles to find him in the distance of the crowd. He has stopped at the edge of the square and is gazing back in her direction. Their eyes meet for a moment, and there is a regal pride on his face. With one subtle gesture, Potilius bows his head to her.

Salamena is confused for a moment…She suddenly realizes that this is always part of his plan. Her eyes smiling bright, she struggles to hold back a tear of joy and gratitude.

Turning to Matthius, she takes his hand. Together, they face the crowd surrounding them. Many hundreds of citizens and soldiers alike now give a collective cheer. While the future of the largest kingdom in all of Oakenmeer is still very uncertain, the greatest outcome of these events seems to have made manifest.

Chapter 15

AMIDST THE SWAYING of tree limbs and rustling leaves the sun is setting on another day in the Open Forest. Squirrels move with their regular agenda, and the fence line of Fortia's family property is their occasional place of rest. There has been some obvious progress on reconstructing the home, though there is still much work to be done.

Within the sideyard, there are many stacks of large timbers organized and waiting for use. An array of stones and bricks are stacked neatly, and the narrow boards of interior walls are placed in an adjacent pile. The noise of hammering is everywhere, accompanied by the rhythmic banging of a sledge as it reverberates from the structure now in progress.

The decimations of the fire have been cleared out, and only the sturdiest of the old original boards and timbers have been salvaged. A considerable amount of progress has been made in rebuilding the first floor. The work of a few weeks seems to have been completed, and the framework appears to be prepared for raising the joists of the second level.

Constans, Sedo, and Tiler finish shoring up the framework of the rear wall. A few diagonal boards are nailed into the floorboards which intersect at an angle to meet the newly erected wall. It is now ready to be left upright for the night without fear of collapsing from the wind.

Fortia is hard at work carrying a pair of heavy firebricks over to the hearth. A change has taken place in her, though…For the young people of Oakenmeer, the autumn weather brings out variation to their foliage. The green leafy colors of her hair have turned to a brilliant yellowish orange. As she matures into adulthood, the foliage of her youth will eventually fully shed away. Only the promise of spring can reveal for certain if she has reached that time in her life.

Two at a time she piles the bricks up in the living room space, so they are ready when needed. Arty climbs onto the pile of bricks she has created. With the usual whimsy of a dog, he yawns and stretches himself into a lazy position on their cool surface. He flops his body down and relaxes. Fortia chuckles and gives him a swift pet on his head.

Constans and Tiler enter the living room area with a variety of tools in hand.

"Tiler has dinner for us back at the inn, Fortia." Constans smiles at her and the pile of bricks she has built here. A quiet appreciation of the considerable work she has done. "We should have time to eat before the meeting."

Fortia smiles bright and appears very excited at the idea of this. Sedo approaches with a hammer and a sack of nails.

"Feeling ready for tonight, darling?"

"Yes." She raises her chin with confidence. "I have been practicing each night."

Constans wraps his arm around her, smiles at the idea of her participating in what they have planned. The group moves toward the sideyard to mount their horses.

~ ~ ~

The sunset has nearly fallen behind the walls of the Closed Forest, and the usual movements of citizens and soldiers around the king's residence are slower today.

In the dining hall, Matthius and Salamena are eating a dinner of nut stew and seeded bread at the same small table that Julianna would often sit at. They are enjoying their food with a comfortable silence, and were a caretaker present here, they may very well notice that Salamena's right foot and Matthius's left foot are positioned very nearby one another.

Matthius spoons some stew into his mouth, and as he does, he glances with uncertainty at the large dining table nearby them. Salamena notices this and smiles. He cannot help but want to acknowledge her beauty at that moment. Quickly, though, a look of humility crosses over his face.

"I'm sorry, Salamena." Matthius shares a humble smile for her. "I don't know if I will ever feel at home while sitting at that table."

"I am rather fond of you for that." She gives him a quiet look of admiration.

Matthius humbly bows his head, too reserved to relish in that compliment. With a brief and subtle motion, Salamena slides her right foot over some, now touching Matthius's foot.

Realizing this, his eyes light up and soon they are gazing at one another.

From the entry nearby, a Caretaker approaches quickly and stops by the table.

"Captain, apologies for the interruption, but the Historian has returned with his report."

Matthius wipes his mouth with a napkin and settles his silverware before speaking.

"Thank you. Please, show him in."

The caretaker bows, though he briefly notes the position of their feet. A smile crosses his face, just long enough for Matthius and Salamena to recognize it. Salamena winks at Matthius, then slowly moves her foot away from his.

The caretaker exits, and shortly after, the Historian enters. He is a rather tall and lanky fellow, young for his position and appearing rather studious in his duties. At first glance he has the look of someone who has spent considerable time educating himself. Approaching their table, he begins to unfurl a roll of parchment, then places this open document on the table nearby them both. Humbly, he gives a quick bow in their direction.

"Captain. Princess. Thank you for this opportunity to speak with you both."

"Of course, Narato." Matthius is already interested in the document. "Please tell us what you uncovered during your study?"

"At your request, for these past few weeks, I have explored the lineage of each royal family throughout the five Surviving Kingdoms. I am pleased to report that, while they are all considerably displaced in their lineage, there are four potential heirs to the throne of the Kingdom of Macadamia."

He references the parchment now, which contains numerous very detailed family trees. First, he points to the lineage of the Kingdom of Cashew.

"Queen Cassius of Cashew has no brothers and two sons. The oldest of them, Prince Brutus, was killed on a merchant ship when it was attacked by pirates. The second of them, Prince Natet, will be turning ten years of age later this year. Unfortunately, by the old laws, he is not of age to take the throne and cannot be considered."

Matthius nods his head, a silent agreement with this statement.

"Next," Narato continues, "is Prince Ira, the younger brother of King Furorem of Colocynth. At this time, though, the location of Prince Ira has remained a mystery for twenty years now. King Furorem was the last person to see him alive, that event being only a few days before his coronation."

Salamena and Matthius both appear surprised by how nefarious that story sounds.

"There is, of course, the first son of King Potilius of Pignoli, Prince Uvenis, by all accounts, a very reasonable choice for a future leader. However, he has already committed himself to the throne of Pignoli at his father's death."

"And the fourth possibility?" Matthius asks, looking up from the document and giving a soft smile to Salamena.

"Last but certainly not least," Narato gestures a brief reference to her, "Princess Salamena of Pecan. The oldest daughter and oldest offspring of King Colomena of Pecan."

Salamena works to restrain a smile on hearing this, though Narato continues with his detailed explanation.

"We should keep in mind that Princess Salamena is older than both Prince Natet and Prince Uvenis and, therefore, by the old laws, they would not be the preferred heirs. Notably, though, should Prince Ira somehow resurface after twenty years of absence, it is possible that he could legally make a claim for the throne as he would be three months older than Princess Salamena. It goes without saying, though, that he is believed to be deceased."

Matthius smiles at Salamena, who is now struggling to hold back her happiness. She forces the smile on her face back into place and silently wipes away a small tear of joy.

"Please keep this parchment as your record," Narato continues, and he takes a moment to point at the bottom of the document. "My recommendations to you, as your Historian, are noted at the base of the document, just there."

"Thank you, Narato." Matthius stands and offers him his hand, which Narato humbly shakes. Matthius waits for him to exit. Once Narato is out of sight, Matthius lifts the parchment and begins to read aloud the recommendations at the bottom.

"I, Narato of Macadamia, First Scholar of the University in Heights, on this the twenty-second day of the Questing Month, in the first year of New Leadership, do hereby verify that Princess Salamena of Pecan is the most-worthy heir to the throne of Macadamia."

As Salamena hears Matthius read this aloud, she slowly stands from the table and adjusts her dress, wanting to look proper for this moment.

She turns to face him, takes the parchment from his hands, and with the regal and upright gestures of a noble person, she reviews it for a moment. Laying it on the table moments later, she returns her gaze to Matthius.

Confidently, she reaches out to him, offers her hand to him. He quietly takes it, and she lifts it up to her face, presses the palm of his hand to her cheek. She closes her eyes, savoring the feeling of his touch. It has largely been denied to her for weeks now, and knowing that she will be queen, she will have no more of that.

With smiling eyes, Matthius appears to be overtaken by her appreciation of him. She pulls him closer and embraces him in a passionate kiss.

He instinctively wraps his arms around her, for he cannot help but want this moment to last as long as it possibly can. Eventually, Salamena breaks her lips free. Still holding him close, she slowly rests her head on his shoulder and enjoys a moment of embrace.

"I guess I will need to find myself a king…"

He chuckles with her, and they both know that something grand is about to begin.

~ ~ ~

In the basement level of the Cowan's Eaves, the Ordo Nux Aurea has gathered for a meeting. Unlike the last time this Order held a meeting, the candlelight in this room is abundant today. The various chairs here are filled by the members of the Order, save for just a few who remain absent still.

A lot has happened since their last meeting and there is much conversation occurring throughout the room. Harris stands beside the chair of Lady Callidus, who relaxes her elderly trunk in her seat. She recounts something of a story.

"Tonitro and Julianna knew only what Matthius and I had discussed. As far as they were concerned, I was telling them every secret of our Order." She smiles, almost a devious look on her face, and Harris chuckles at the idea of this subtle deception.

"Lady Callidus, I will venture someday to be as cunning and clever as you are. No wonder you have succeeded in amassing such wealth."

Callidus laughs, and with a finger, she gestures to Harris.

"Do you want to know the secret to becoming wealthy, Harris?"

Harris leans forward, and Callidus whispers something into her ear. Slowly, a smile builds on Harris's face until, finally, she begins to laugh aloud.

From the antechamber, Matthius marches into the room. He has energy in his movements tonight, and not even his wounded leg can slow him down. As he approaches his chair at the head of the circle, Tiler comes over to him with a curious smirk on his face.

"You're rather lively today." Tiler holds back a laugh.

"Yes." Matthius grins back. "Yes, I very much am."

Tiler chuckles but soon takes his seat. The members of the Order who are present all take their seats. Two chairs remain empty, though.

"Come to order," Matthius says, and any remaining chatter becomes silent. "Let us begin with a moment of silence for the loss of our fallen brother."

Everyone present stands, and a silent moment begins to take hold. Matthius gazes across to Laderas's seat. His cheerful mood begins to dissipate some, though not for very long. Soon, he begins to recall the greatness of what his friend had achieved and the sacrifice he made to save Fortia.

"Soft and safe to thee, be thy resting place." Matthius smiles. "Bright and glorious be thy rising from it." With that, everyone sits, save for Matthius.

"Brothers and Sisters of the Order, as you are all aware, we have gathered here today to create a new position within our group."

With these words Constans and Fortia together enter the room from the antechamber. Fortia is now wearing a lightweight suit of deep red leather armor. It is very similar in appearance to the armor Laderas once wore. In her hand, she carries the Oaken Steel dagger which she carried all throughout her journey. She straightens her back and takes a deep breath, summoning her confidence. Together, they walk up to the podium at the center of the room, and on their arrival, Constans leaves Fortia there and takes his seat.

For a moment, Fortia appears to retract from being the focus of everyone here. She does not like being the center of attention like this, and the memory of what she experienced when she was last here is still prominent. She summons the strength to straighten her back and do what she came to do.

"Fortia, daughter of Constans and Sedo of Macadamia," Matthius addresses her boldly. "While you are too young to take the chair as a lady in our order, it is the decision of our membership that you be bestowed the title of Discipulus. When you have come of age, you will have the right to take the seat of Laderas, which will remain empty until that time."

Fortia gazes at Laderas's chair. Knowing that he died to protect her, she recognizes the burden that taking the seat would represent. She cannot help but feel like the emptiness there is, a weight she already carries on her shoulders.

"Are you prepared to give your oath?" Matthius confidently asks.

"Yes," Fortia dutifully responds. She lifts the dagger in her right hand, and with it, she pierces the bark on the meat of her left hand, just adjacent to the thumb. She draws some sap. Bending her left elbow, she exposes her hand to everyone, making it clear what she has done. A line of sap begins to form on her forearm as she speaks her oath.

"For the protection of the secrets herein, I offer my sap."

Moving the knife to her other hand, she pierces the bark of her right hand now, again revealing to everyone the sap that drains from it.

"For the protection of my brethren here, I offer my sap."

Everyone there watches for a moment as Fortia's sap continues to seep out of her palms and down her arms. It is quiet for a time, but soon enough, Matthius approaches her. He removes from his pocket the ointment he had used previously to close up the wound on his leg. Applying it to her hands, there is a brief burn, but the sap clots up quickly.

Moments later, he shows her his own hands. Two marks are also present in the same area of his hands, though they have formed scars here long ago. Next, Constans proudly approaches her, and he shows her the same two scars on his hands. One by one, each of the members of the order stands and shows their hands to Fortia.

Even though many years have separated them, they have all shared the same oath. They have all shared this same experience, and they will forever be bonded to one another in this way.

End

Author's Biography

Born in Philadelphia, Pennsylvania, Johnny has lived in seven different states and four different countries. Educated as an Architect, a Physician, and a martial artist, he has written numerous screenplays and short stories, with Oakenmeer being his first novel. He lives in the Twin Cities area of Minnesota with his wife, baby Pepino, and one overly energetic dog.

Find him online at Facebook as Johnny O'Shea, and on Reddit as Oakenmeer.